TEXAS TRIGGERS

Eugene Cunningham

Chivers Press • G.K. Hall & Co.
Bath, England   Thorndike, Maine USA

This Large Print edition is published by Chivers Press, England, and by G.K. Hall & Co., USA.

Published in 1998 in the U.K. by arrangement with Golden West Literary Agency.

Published in 1997 in the U.S. by arrangement with Golden West Literary Agency.

U.K. Softcover   ISBN 0–7540–3390–2 (Camden Large Print)
U.K. Hardcover ISBN 0–7540–3032–6 (Chivers Large Print)
U.S. Softcover   ISBN 0–7838–8204–1 (Nightingale Collection Edition).

The text of this Large Print edition is unabridged.
Other aspects of the book may vary from the original edition.

Set in 16 pt. New Times Roman.

Printed in Great Britain on acid-free paper.

British Library Cataloguing in Publication Data available

Library of Congress Cataloging-in-Publication Data

Cunningham, Eugene, 1896–1957.
    Texas triggers : a western novel / Eugene Cunningham.
        p.   cm.
    ISBN 0–7838–8204–1 (lg. print : sc : alk. paper)
    1. Large type books.   I. Title.
[PS3505.U428T49   1997]
813′.54—dc21   97–13094

Library at Home Service
Community Services
Hounslow Library, CentreSpace
24 Treaty Centre, High Street
Hounslow TW3 1ES

Working in partnership with ⧠ Hounslow

0	1	2	3	4	5	6	7	8	9
THompson				784		36	80	3308	739
	341	522		6684		9970	767		
		7942			780		3177		
					3325				

P10-L-2061

To Eve

CHAPTER ONE

'DON'T SHOOT A DEAD MAN!'

Mesquite, Lance Craig thought, looked very much the same. There were the two rows of squat 'dobe houses on the town's main street. There were the men drifting along dirt or plank sidewalks and the cow-horses dozing at the hitch-racks.

'Yes, much the same,' he told himself, after closer inspection. 'I wonder if the old C Bar has moved a little...'

So he whistled *Whisky Johnny* softly while he regarded the front of Manuel Nabor's long 'dobe saloon. The Two Flags was very white, very still. Then—rather as if his whistling had been a signal—a gun exploded inside the place.

A man fell backward through Nabor's swing-doors. He made a gagging sound and died. At least, Lance decided that the man was dead, and he had seen men die in China, the Philippines, Central America, Mexico, and half a dozen other places.

Lance stiffened until he sat very straight in the brand-new swellfork saddle bought from Sam Myres in Sweetwater, on his way to the border, here. In a saddle pocket was the walnut-handled .44 Colt that, while new like his roping hull, had been very thoroughly

1

tested on trailside targets. He wondered about getting it out, but decided against the move.

There were more shots in the Two Flags. The roman-nosed gray under Lance fidgeted slightly. A second man came through the swing-doors. But this one held his pistol and all of battle that Lance could see about him was the blood dripping from his left arm. He came at the run toward Lance. His head he kept down—a red head that somehow had bulldog fury about the set of it. In spite of his fast retreat from Nabor's, he looked almost as if he came charging an enemy.

The shadow of Gray Eagle jerked his head up. He lifted the Colt and the muzzle covered Lance.

'Momentito!' Lance cried. 'One small moment, my friend! I'm a stranger in Mesquite. Don't buy me into your war—not until I know what your war's all about!'

'Craig!' the redhead snarled. 'You're Lance Craig. So—'

He looked behind him and dropped flat into the dust of the street. Lance glanced from him to the saloon. A lank, dark six-footer stood, now, just outside Nabor's. He wore crossed shell-belts, and in each hand was a gun. These moved vaguely, threatening several points of the compass.

'Hold 'em!' Lance yelled. 'Don't point those cutters at me—not unless you're certain your clothes'll stand the climate. I'm Lance Craig.

2

Out of the C Bar Craigs.'

'Oh!' the tall man said jerkily. 'Oh! Lance Craig.'

Lance stared at him. This tall and undecided man was a stranger. But, then, he had been out of Mesquite County—out of the United States, usually—for more than seven years. Seven years meant changes, even in Texas, even in Mesquite.

Then he saw the twinkle of a badge on the gray shirt, all but under the buttonless and sagging vest. An officer...

He looked down at the redhead, who lay moveless, now, with outflung arms and head pointed toward the saloon. Lance saw the Colt under the redhead's laxed fingers. He saw, also, the spreading patch of blood on the cowboy's shirt, almost at the spine, almost at the waistband.

'Hit twice,' he thought. 'Didn't see that, before.'

The tall man came walking stiffly toward them. His twin Colts covered the still figure of the cowboy. Lance's eyes shuttled from one to the other, up and down and back again.

'He dead?' the officer grunted. 'Oh! I'm Ull Varner, Sheriff. Reckon you don't know me—yet.'

Lance stared. When he had left Mesquite old Harmony Pond had been sheriff. There *had* been change in his absence!

'No, I don't know you,' he admitted.

3

He could have added, after his searching glance at the long, narrow face, with its tiny, close-set dark eyes, that he had no desire to know Sheriff Varner. But he had learned a great deal in seven wandering years. He tightened his mouth.

'You know him?' Varner demanded suddenly. He seemed calmer, now; easier of mind. 'Nah, I reckon you wouldn't.'

Lance shook his head and the sheriff looked left and right, then shrugged.

'Tough cowboy name' Fagan,' he said drawlingly. 'One on Nabor's sidewalk is another like him. Acker. Hard cases, the both of 'em. Started a fight in the Two Flags. I—we—I got both of 'em, looks like.'

'Ah! But did you?' Fagan snarled abruptly. '*Maybe!*'

His fingers closed on the pistol-butt. He lifted it and moved like a snake on the ground. With the Colt's explosion Ull Varner staggered. But his guns had been trained on Fagan—cocked. By accident or design he let the hammers drop. Fagan had come to his knees. He fell under the impact of two bullets from the sheriff's Colts. This time there was no doubting his condition—he was dead!

'The son!' Varner yelled. 'The dirty son! *He hit me!*'

'Cut it!' Lance commanded. 'Don't shoot a dead man! Even if he did burn you. Keep those cutters down, fellow!'

'You listen,' the sheriff cried with sudden fury. 'You keep that trap of yours shut around here. Don't you think because you own the half of what's left of the C Bar, you can strut it around Mesquite. *Them* was C Bar hands! Fagan and Acker both! And now look at 'em!'

Lance leaned backward. His hand was not in line with Varner's eyes. So the new .44 came out of a saddle pocket and Lance held it against the saddle-fork. The muzzle was very steadily trained upon Ull Varner's middle. He was grinning, but there was nothing pleasant about that lip-stretching.

Varner saw the pistol after seconds. His hands moved slightly. But he did not raise his own guns. The muzzles of them quivered somewhere between his waist and his knees.

'C Bar men,' Lance said softly. 'And I'm looking at 'em. I see 'em. And looking at 'em does seem to change things, somehow. For I didn't know, when the fireworks started, that they rode for the C Bar. It does seem to me that things in Mesquite these days are just a li'l' bit past me—sort of over my head. You! just for instance. When I pulled out of Mesquite a real man was under that star, not a big, shaky bean-pole. Old Harmony Pond was sheriff and he was a real sheriff! He—'

Varner made a snarling noise, but Lance went on grimly:

'We averaged about a killing in ten years. Because John Craig and Orval Kane didn't

5

hold with wild shooting. It might interest you to know that I left here because of an argument with the *Jefe*—my father—over a killing I had to do. It might interest you because—Put up those cutters or use 'em!'

The sheriff stared into the grim, brown face of the younger man. Again his Colts wavered for the fraction of a second—but sagged.

'Now, you listen!' he said shakily. 'Don't you try to come it tough in Mesquite! Some has, since I been wearing the badge your old Harmony Pond wasn't man enough to keep wearing. And they went to Boot Hill—fast!'

Men were coming out of the Two Flags, out of stores and saloons elsewhere along the street. But none seemed sufficiently interested in the sheriff's conversation with a stranger to cross to the sprawling Fagan.

Varner turned, now, to wave them forward. He reholstered his pistols, and Lance slid his own smoothly into the waistband of his overalls and tucked his shirt over it. Some of the men coming he had known for all his life; others were strangers.

'Quite a bunch of newcomers,' he thought. 'But there's Wilbur Logan of the Spear L, Elbert Gore of the 99, Nathan Wingo of the Flying W, Levi Dunn, the old 99 wagon boss, and Manny Todd, who's topped the rough string for the Spear L since John Paul Jones was an ordinary seaman. And—if my poor, old sea-scarred eyes don't deceive me!—there's

Oscar Nall…'

He stared at the tall and handsome man behind gray Elbert Gore. He had not seen Oscar since their schooldays. For Nall had been taken to San Antonio by a rich uncle, when Oscar's father and mother died here in Mesquite.

'We were both about fifteen—no, sixteen—then,' Lance recalled. 'Oscar was going to be a millionaire before he quit. He told us so. He was strutting it around town as soon as he heard about the rich uncle coming after him. He began to look down on us country mice, right then. And now—here he is, back in Mesquite. I wonder why…'

Logan, Gore, and Wingo, like Levi Dunn and Manny Todd, stared curiously at the wide-shouldered, yellow-haired, blue-eyed stranger on the roman-nosed gray, before looking down at Fagan. Then old Gore leaned suddenly a little and squinted up at Lance.

'Why—why, Lance Craig!' he said incredulously. 'Why—why we certainly never figured to see *you* ag'in, son! Why, we heerd you was drowned 'way out in them South Seas! Where you been? When'd you come in?'

Manny Todd—Lance had ridden many a mile with Manny, and driven many a head of horses with the scarred and grizzled little buster—pushed up to Lance's stirrup and banged him on the leg.

'Why, y' damn' li'l' sidewinder, y'!' he cried.

7

'It's a sight for sore eyes to see y', boy! It—'

'What the hell's this, anyhow—Old Home Week?' Ull Varner inquired acidly, and Wilbur Logan punched Manny hard, from where he stood beside Oscar Nall.

'What I say!' Logan growled. 'What you aim to do, Ull?'

'Carry Fagan over to Zoe Quisenberry's store. We'll put Acker in Quisenberry's, too. 'Course, we got to have a inquest, to make her all legal. Anybody see Isidor Yelton recent?'

Men stooped to pick up the redhead. Lance slouched in his saddle and watched grimly. So this fighting cowboy had been a C Bar man— and that other, Acker, as well … Why, he asked himself, had Fagan and Acker come into Mesquite and gone on the prod? Why did this narrow-faced and shifty-eyed new sheriff seem to bear a grudge against the C Bar? Or had he held enmity only against the two dead men, as individuals?

Then memory came, of a remark Ull Varner had made: 'You own half of what's left of the C Bar—'

'Now, what did he mean by that?' Lance asked himself. 'I don't actually own any part of the outfit. In fact, the *Jefe* told me that he was going to cut me out, in his new will. It still belongs to him and Cousin Orval. And when they're gone it's likely to belong to Cousin Lucy. "What's left…"'

'Well?' Oscar Nall said, and brought Lance

8

back to the immediate present. 'So you finally came back.'

Oscar had a roundish, a very smooth, a dark face. His steady eyes were so murky that they looked, always, like jetty marbles. Lance remembered that steadiness of Oscar's stare. Oscar had always been the one 'to lie faster than a horse running,' in Lance's expression, but without a flicker of eyelids to indicate that he spoke anything but gospel. Now, he looked Lance up and down inscrutably.

'I finally came home,' Lance replied evenly. 'Just about in time, it does seem, to ramrod into things I don't know about. What happened, there in Manuel Nabor's? Why did that slinky sheriff powder two C Bar men? Or did he and his bunch—I gathered that he wasn't the only man shooting at Fagan and Acker, from what he said—and one look at him made me pretty certain there *must* have been others—unload at the two on general principles, and not because they were C Bars?'

Oscar shrugged without change of expression.

'It might have been because Fagan and Acker needed killing,' he said tonelessly. 'In fact, I think it was.'

'In my day'—Lance kept his voice as level and expressionless as Oscar's—'the C Bar did something when one of its hands got killed. If the killing looked like shady business.'

'The C Bar ... Your day ... You have been

9

away, Lance. Seven years, I seem to recall.'

'Seven years, about. But if you're trying to tell me that a little matter of seven years had greatly changed "Big John" Craig—Cousin Orval was never much on the fight—'

'*Four* years have changed John Craig ... *Two* years have changed Orval Kane ... To do something about this affair of today—or anything else—both of them would have to tip over their tombstones. Your father's been dead nearly four years; Orval Kane—he was your father's fourth or fifth cousin, wasn't he?—was killed on the river-trail about two years ago. The C Bar is on the way many a Texas outfit has taken: The bank holds a mortgage that covers the C Bar like a blanket.'

Lance stared at him incredulously. His father dead, his father's partner, distant cousin, dead—It seemed impossible!

'And—and Lucy?' he asked thickly. 'Don't tell me that Lucy's dead, too.'

'Oh, she's still here. In fact, after her father was killed, she tried to keep the place going. But it had been running downhill in Orval Kane's hands—your father was the cowman of the two, as you know. Well—Lucy simply couldn't make a go of it. The bank loaned her additional money—Orval Kane had mortgaged it pretty heavily—and she lost that, too.'

He lifted a thick shoulder and let it sag; got a slim, green-mottled cigar from a pigskin case.

10

Lance watched him clip the end of the cigar with a gold cutter, then light it. But his stare at Oscar was mechanical.

'This is certainly a home-coming!' he thought. 'The *Jefe* and Cousin Orval both dead ... Lucy Kane mismanaging the C Bar ... The old outfit on the way to going under...'

Aloud, he asked how his father had died.

'The same way Orval Kane died. Almost at the same spot. Killed on the river-trail by a bandit named Jake Hopper. Or that's the guess. Well, I have things to do.'

Abruptly, Oscar turned away, before Lance could ask about this Jake Hopper. But he halted briefly with Lance's grim drawl.

'I've been a long time away,' Lance said. 'Too long! For I should have known about the *Jefe* and Orval Kane. And I didn't know. I haven't had a word from Mesquite in all the years. But I'm back—and there's one thing you can put your money on: I'm back here to stay!'

He shut his mouth hard. He had been about to add that the first thing he intended to do, being back, was to learn why two C Bar punchers had been killed by Sheriff Varner in the Two Flags. But there was no reason to tell Oscar Nall. Facing Oscar's uninterested stare, he realized that he disliked this tall, sleek, well-dressed young man as much today as when they had been boys.

'That's fine,' Oscar said carelessly. 'If you can manage it, that will be just fine. Anyway,

11

you can hang around Mesquite until the bank forecloses on the C Bar.'

He turned again and walked slantingly across the street. Lance lowered after him, then touched Gray Eagle with a rowel and rode straight over to Zoe Quisenberry's hardware and furniture store. Here he let the reins drop and swung down, to duck under the hitch-rack.

There was a growing crowd about the place, moving inside. Lance went in with the other men, attracting no attention. Everyone was staring toward the bodies upon Quisenberry's counter; watching Sheriff Varner and the ratty little Isidor Yelton, who had been justice of the peace in Mesquite time out of mind. Apparently, Yelton was well along with his inquest. He put a question to Ull Varner. The sheriff shrugged.

'Why, they was on the prod when they lit,' he said earnestly. 'There in Nabor's place they kept on a-making remarks about me, while I was standing close to 'em at the bar. I seen what they was after. I knew well enough they was egging me on, a-looking for trouble. But I held in. Then I caught Acker with his hand on a gun. I went after my cutters, then. Fagan, he was pulling his gun. I shot Acker *jist* as he was a-throwing down on me. He backed outside, shooting at me. I cut down on Fagan after he'd shot at me. Acker, he flopped right on the sidewalk. But Fagan run out and across the street, then flopped. When I went up to look at

12

him, he shot at me and I was too fast for him. I settled him right then and right there. That's all there is *to* it!'

'Uh-huh!' Isidor Yelton grunted, bobbing greasy bald head. 'Uh-huh. Well, it's my verdict the deceased come to their end at the hands of the lawful sher'f of this county and come to it'—he drew a long breath and his light voice took on impressiveness—' *le-git-i-mate!* Reckon that winds up the cathop.'

'Does it?' Lance thought furiously. 'Oh, *does* it? We'll see what we'll see—and what you'll see—about that!'

CHAPTER TWO

'I WANT TO SEE A GIRL'

Lance turned quickly and pushed outside. One glance at that official set-up in Quisenberry's store told him that nothing was to be gained by staying longer. Whatever had really been behind the killing of Fagan and Acker, Justice Isidor Yelton had no desire to air it; uncover it, even. The place to learn about Mesquite County and its politics and personages of today was—

'Just anywhere but among that bunch of Mesquite's *politicos*,' Lance summed it up savagely. 'So—I think I had better talk to old

York Insall, if *he* is still alive.'

York Insall's freight corral was around the corner from Manuel Nabor's saloon. Of all the residents of the county seat, Lance best knew this gaunt, taciturn and most competent freight-contractor.

So he mounted Gray Eagle and sent him at the trot to the great gateway in Insall's 'dobe wall, and pulled in. York Insall thrust his eggbald head out of the office door and stared. Then, just as if Lance had been away a week, instead of seven years, he nodded.

'Howdy, Son,' he drawled. 'How you been?'

'*Por dios!* I'm glad to see you,' Lance told him earnestly. 'Why aren't *you* down at Quisenberry's?'

'Nothing to me,' the old freighter shrugged. 'I seen too many dead men in my time—some of my killing. And it wouldn't amount to much, to hear Ull Varner tell his tale and Isidor Yelton bobble his head and yap like the damn' trained poodle he is, helping Varner out. Varner egged Fagan and Acker into pulling— when he was ready for 'em to try; when he had his bunch ready to wipe 'em out.'

'But why? Why?' Lance demanded furiously. He got down from the gray and went—tall and lean and wolfishly quick in step—to glare at the lined face of his father's old friend. 'What's happened in Mesquite County, that my father and Cousin Orval were

14

killed? Oscar Nall told me the *Jefe* was killed; that—'

'He was murdered on the river by Jake Hopper. Or that was what Ull Varner claimed. Same for Orval Kane. You seen Lucy, yet?'

'I've seen nobody!' Lance snarled. 'I got here just in time to see Varner's little murder party at Manuel Nabor's. What little I know I got from Varner. And from Oscar Nall.'

'Oscar Nall,' York said slowly. 'Yeh, you said you seen him ... Well, Lance, did it come to you, *when* you seen Oscar, that you were just—about—looking—at—Mesquite? Yes, sir! It is plumb like that nowadays. Since Oscar come back he has certainly stepped up. The money he got out of Santone, from that uncle of his'n, he invested fine. He about owns the bank. And he owns the C Bar.'

'There wasn't a nickel of debt on the whole hundred sections when I left!' Lance protested. 'What happened?'

'The usual,' York told him dryly. 'It was Big John Craig that had cow-sense. After he got killed, Orval tried to run the place. But he never made a go of it. *He* had to borrow. Then he was murdered. Lucy's been trying her hand. And it's a mightily poor, puny hand. So—*you* pay off ten thousand, or the bank takes the C Bar. That is, Oscar Nall takes the C Bar.'

Lance stared at him fixedly. Then he drew a long breath and fumbled in a pocket for Duke's and brown papers.

'I've had quite a few jolts today,' he told

15

York. 'But now that I've had 'em I think I can come up from the ground and sort of get my ideas separated. And—do something about it all. The *Jefe* didn't care much for my notions. You knew that. So did everybody else. For when he didn't like a thing you could hear him a mile against the breeze. We didn't get along. Then I had to kill Foxy Drew and hightail it. But the *Jefe* was murdered—by Jake Hopper. That brings us up to—'

He lighted his cigarette and drew in smoke.

'Yeh? Brings us up to what?' York asked drawlingly, his narrow old eyes probing the grim, brown face of the younger man.

'To Jake Hopper! Who's Jake Hopper? Where does he hang out? Why did he kill 'em?'

'He used to be a tol'able bank-robber, train-robber. Then, when the Rangers made it too hot for him in Texas, he moved across to Tenedor. He's boss over there, nowadays. He just comes to our side the line to clean out the ranches. Sometimes, he hits a bank or a train over here. John Craig sent him word to lay off the C Bar. And so, when John was found dead on the river-trail, Ull Varner says it was Jake Hopper done the murder. Ull had come into the country and, by Oscar Nall's help, he got made sheriff.'

'And Cousin Orval?' Lance prompted him, his tone very quiet. 'Did *he* send Jake Hopper a warning, too? It wouldn't be like him. He never was much on the fight, but he was a stayer once

16

he got started in a row.'

'No. The C Bar got raided oftener than any other outfit. About the time Orval'd be fixed to sell something and make money, the cattle or the horses would take wings. We sort of figured that he run into Jake accidental and got rubbed out before he really knowed what hit him.'

'Jake Hopper ... Tenedor...' Lance said softly. 'Where would Lucy be, these days? I have got to see her, of course. Between us we own what's left of the C Bar. And she's been running it. I have got to see her.'

He did not add that he *wanted* very much to see the slim and dark and lovely daughter of his distant cousin; that she was not the least of the attractions which had drawn him home after wandering years. York seemed not to observe Lance's hesitation.

'Yeh! Oh, yeh! She's been running it, all right,' he grunted. 'Right into the ground, she's been running it. With Oscar Nall's good help. Oscar gives her a lot of good advice, but it somehow don't never turn out right. So—more money from the bank! Oscar tells her she can have all she wants. He—Well, maybe he thinks she's cheap at ten thousand—considering he'll have the C Bar, too.'

'Like that!' Lance said, even more softly. 'Well, where is she? Out on the C Bar?'

'No, right here in town. She come in yesterday. I reckon it was to talk to her that Acker and Fagan rode in. Acker was foreman,

17

you see. He had passed remarks about Ull Varner; said Ull could do something about the rustling, if he was minded to. He even said that maybe Ull was making something out of the stealing. That was his death warrant... Lucy'd be up at Judge Oakes' with Nancy Oakes. Well—'

'See you some more. And thanks a lot,' Lance told him absently. 'Thanks just the *hell* of a lot, York.'

But when he mounted and York Insall followed to the gate to watch him, Gray Eagle was not turned up the street toward the big white-plastered 'dobe house of Judge Oakes. Instead, Lance went with a hand in his overalls pocket, jingling gold. Coming abreast the door of Zoe Quisenberry's store he looked sidelong and made the gold ring more loudly.

'They were C Bar hands. They were murdered here because Ull Varner was afraid of their talk,' Lance said to himself with conviction. 'It would be no more than decent to take care of their funerals. But—I've got less than a hundred dollars left. There's going to be plenty happening around Mesquite County— and maybe over in Tenedor. Things! And things that will cost money. Shells and gun-hire. If I guess right, from looking at Acker and Fagan, they'd a lot rather have my last dollars spent for rubbing out the ones who downed 'em than for coffins and tombstones. Anyway, that's the way I'll play her. Yes, sir! I'll play her that way clear across the board; play her to the last white chip!'

He rode through thickening dusk and pulled in at the hitch-rack before Manuel Nabor's door. There was nothing, now, about the flat, white front of the Two Flags, to recall that flaming moment when Acker had stumbled outside to fall and die; when Fagan had burst through the swing-doors with blood dripping down his arm and Sheriff Varner like an emboldened coyote snapping at his heels.

Only the mutter of voices inside carried to Lance, the sounds of men gathered at the long bar, or about the gaming tables on the other side of Nabor's big room. In the air, now, was the smell of smoke, but it was not the acrid vapor of powder. It was the pungent odor of mesquite roots, coming from dozens of supper fires about the county seat.

So Lance swung down and knotted Gray Eagle's reins in a cautious slipknot about the cottonwood crossbar. Then—having turned a little so that any on the sidewalk could not see—he got the Colt adjusted in his waistband more comfortably and conveniently, under blue chambray shirt.

The bar-room was dusky, but it seemed to Lance that every man in the place turned to look at him. They stared until he crossed with clink-clump of spur rowels and boot heels to the bar and there found the grizzled Carlos, who had tended bar for Nabor so many years that nobody recalled when he had not been behind the long pine counter.

'*Que quiere?*' Carlos asked Lance tonelessly. 'What do you wish? In the old days, I remember, it was always whisky.'

'It is still whisky,' Lance assured him with a grin.

He filled his glass and without seeming to look studied the men on his right and left. As his eyes grew used to the gloom he could make out faces. And it seemed to him that he had never seen so many hard cases in any single spot. But he was not a nervous soul. Even at seventeen, when last he stood here at Nabor's bar he had not troubled much about the way men looked at him. And seven years up and down the world, in the toughest parts of the Seven Seas, had done nothing to soften him. He moved a little and felt the butt of his Colt cuddle his belly. He grinned faintly.

Ull Varner he did not see. Levi Dunn, the old 99 wagon boss, stood with Manny Todd, the bronc' buster. They were several places down from him and, if they had seen him come in, there was nothing about their attitudes to show it. Lance recalled how Manny Todd's friendliness had been checked by his boss's snarl. He grinned unpleasantly and hummed to himself:

'Jack o' diamonds, jack o' diamonds, I know you of old.

You robbed my pore pockets of silver and
   gold...
They say I drink whisky, well, my money's
   my own,
And them that don't like me can leave me
   alone...'

A small towheaded man came up the bar and
stopped behind Lance, who felt, rather than
saw, him.

'You!' the towhead said grimly. 'What you
doing, wearing a gun in town?'

There was something about that flat voice
which Lance found deadly. He did not make
the mistake of turning quickly. Instead, he
lifted his whisky, drank it, and set down the
empty glass. He gave no indication of having
heard. So a hand jerked at his sleeve. Then he
pivoted deliberately.

'Speaking to me?' he asked.

He saw the glint of the badge on this
towhead's vest. But it was the boy's eyes which
he really watched; the coldest, palest of gray
eyes that shone, just now, unnaturally bright.
Not even the drawn pistol aimed at him by the
deputy drew Lance's stare down from those
killer-eyes.

'Speaking to you! Ram them paws up to
your ears. Keep 'em there. We'll looky how
much cannon you're packing. And don't make
no funny move. Me, I'm Homer Ripps!'

'It smells!' Lance told himself. 'In Manuel

Nabor's, where you could outfit a young army, just by taking the hoglegs off the customers, it does smell. So—'

He twisted his body, slapped down at Ripps's pistol and whipped up a knee, all in what seemed one flashing motion. Ripps staggered and groaned. But from the bar behind Lance someone struck a numbing blow with a pistol that grazed his head and crashed upon his shoulder. He stepped out from the bar. There was a flurry of movement and the man who had hit him fell against him, then slid to the floor. A stocky, shabby figure stood by this fallen one, grinning one-sidedly at his victim. He, too, held a pistol.

'He won't bother you none, not again,' the stocky one told Lance. 'But the other 'n' might!'

Homer Ripps had twisted on the floor. The gun he had drawn before challenging Lance was still in his hand. Lance considered quickly, then stamped viciously upon Ripps's gunhand. The deputy groaned and released his gun.

The man knocked out by the stocky stranger was also motionless. Up and down the bar there was the hush that comes of indrawn, tight-held breath. Lance looked to right and left, then nodded to the dark, square-shouldered one.

'Thanks,' he said briefly. 'Drink?'

For perhaps twenty seconds the dark man studied him. Then his thin, hard mouth twitched. He nodded and rammed his pistol back under his shirt. They stood all but on the floored ones and drank.

When the empty glasses were set again upon the bar the dark stranger looked at Lance with—it was not friendliness, Lance decided; rather, it was confidence. The kind of confidence that a man shows another whom he has tested.

'If you'll kindly ram your feet against his neck, I'll buy one,' the stocky man said, with jerk of dark head toward Homer Ripps.

Lance looked at the bar-room crowd once more. He saw old Levi Dunn staring; saw Manny Todd and a dozen others whose names he did not know. And it amused him for a moment to show them all what he thought about them.

He raked the pistol out of Homer Ripps's reach.

'I'll be glad to drink with you,' he said.

As the dark man poured the drinks, Ripps made a snarling noise, on the floor. Without looking at him, Lance said:

'Stay quiet! Stay quiet until I tell you to move.'

He lifted his glass and looked at the dark man.

'My name is—'

'Lance Craig. C Bar Craigs,' the other drawled. 'Yeh, I know. I go by Tom Ziler. If you're done with the liquor, we'll be leaving.'

Lance grinned unpleasantly. At this moment Homer Ripps jerked and thrust out a dirty hand toward the Colt which Lance snapped away from him. Lance kicked him deliberately and watched Ripps go limp.

'Ready?' Ziler asked in a conversational tone. 'If you are, I think we might's well drag it.'

Nobody at Manuel Nabor's seemed interested in stopping them. But as they walked toward the door both kept their heads slightly turned, so that out of the corners of their eyes, they could see the first hostile gesture. At the swing-doors Tom Ziler turned and looked down the bar-room.

'Go ahead,' he grunted to Lance. 'My horse is down at the end. Cover me while I gather him.'

Lance went in a single smooth step outside. There he turned and for the first time drew the Colt from his waistband. Tom Ziler passed him and vanished into the thickening dusk. Lance waited. Toward him, running down the sidewalk came the tall figure of Sheriff Ull Varner.

Varner did not seem to see him. He came on, running awkwardly, holding a Colt in each hand. Then Lance stepped out from the heads of horses at the hitch-rack and his pistol covered the sheriff.

'Trouble?' he asked in an anxious voice. 'Looking for something? Or somebody?'

24

'I—' the sheriff said gaspingly. 'A cowboy says there was trouble at Nabor's.'

'No trouble,' Lance assured him. 'A would-be hard case—Ripps, I think he said was his name—*asked* for trouble, but he just got himself bumped on the head. He's in there, now. On the floor. But there's been no trouble.'

'Who—uh—bumped Homer on the head?' Varner asked slowly. The Colts sagged in his hands. 'Who hit him?'

'I did. I don't like his looks. So next time I won't hit him on the head. Next time—you'd better tell him this, Varner, if you value him—I'll kill him. Now, I'm leaving.'

Varner stood staring fixedly. But the pistols did not rise; did not even begin to rise. He swallowed with a sticky noise and looked at Lance.

'I—I—' he began.

'Hell, man! You've said that twice,' Lance told him. 'Go on in and read him a lecture on that famous old subject. You know! About a man biting off more than he can chew!'

He stepped backward to the hitch-rack and felt behind him. Gray Eagle's reins came free in a jerk. Tom Ziler spoke from somewhere behind the roman-nosed horse.

'Fine!' Lance told him. 'I'm ready, too.'

He backed farther and ducked under the crossbar, straightened, all without for an instant losing the magic of the drop he held on the sheriff. He was beside the gray, a foot groping for the stirrup, going into the saddle. Still the Colt was trained upon the sheriff.

'Better tell him!' Lance called. 'Tell him what I said.'

Then he spun the ugly gray and he and Tom Ziler thundered down the sandy track that was Mesquite's main street. They vanished into the darkness of the mesquite flat beyond the edge of town. Behind them was no sound of pursuit, so Lance laughed and pulled in. Tom Ziler rounded about and came up to his stirrup. He made a questioning sound.

'I want to see a girl,' Lance told him. 'She's at the far end of town. We—I can ride around Mesquite and come in at the other side. And I sure do thank you for dropping that friend of the deputy's. It might have been inconvenient, trying to handle two of 'em at once.'

'We can ride around, all right,' Tom Ziler said evenly. 'No trouble a-tall.'

'But, where were you heading for?' Lance asked him. 'You can't go mixing into affairs like—like mine are, today.'

'I'm heading for the C Bar,' Tom answered carelessly.

'What for? From all I hear the C Bar's a busted outfit.'

'I do'no',' Tom admitted. 'But after the shooting in the street I did hear this and that. I knew that if you stuck your head into Nabor's—as everybody expected you to do— you'd be knocked over by the sheriff's pet

26

killer, Homer Ripps. Seemed to me that everybody in the place knew about it except you. I stuck around, just to see how you'd take it. And I liked the way you took it. So, if you're aiming to head for the C Bar, I think I'll ride with you.'

CHAPTER THREE

'YOUR TIME WILL COME'

Lance stared through the darkness toward the stocky man. Tom Ziler hummed *Buffalo Gals* most placidly.

'Not much reason for anybody riding to the C Bar,' Lance said slowly. 'It's a busted outfit. About all a C Bar man is due to get from this on out is one of those grand chances you used to read about in the *Third Reader*. You know: A chance to die nobly for your country, or something. A chance to push up the daisies from the roots, anyway. And why *you* would be hunting that—'

'Me, they had to loop and drag me, to haul me out of the *Second Reader*,' Tom Ziler drawled. 'So I wouldn't know about things like that in the *Third Reader*.'

Lance pushed Gray Eagle closer and put out his hand. Tom Ziler's hard fingers gripped his. Then Lance nodded.

27

'You're certainly just the kind of man I'd like to have siding me. And if I don't cash in my checks, the way my father and cousin did, maybe I can make it up to you.'

'I know about them, too. You see, I've been around Mesquite a week. That's how I know about this girl, this forty-'leventh cousin, you aim to see. Well? Ready?'

Stirrup-to-stirrup they galloped, rounding the lines of houses which made the county seat. Lance made a snarling sound and Tom Ziler grunted questioningly.

'Just thinking,' Lance told him. 'It's queer. Damn' queer. Seven years, I've been away from here. I've seen the elephant and I've heard the owl, up and down. China. South Seas, Alaska, Latin America, Europe, India, lots of other places. I headed for this one little spot on the Texas map, all ready to settle down. And I run into this! Bull right into something I can't make out.'

'Want the answer to the ciphering—in two li'l' bitsy words? If you think you can take it, I'll hand her over free-grattus-for nothing: Oscar Nall. He runs the county. He says who'll be sher'f. He says who can have money. He says all over what'll be done. Yes, sir! Busy as a bird dog, a spotted bird dog, Oscar is. I don't say you can figure Oscar Nall out. But you want to keep an eye on him, for when you figure him you'll have everything else settled.'

'What? You don't mean you think that

Oscar Nall could say—'

'Can happen! He could say that he wanted the C Bar. But that John Craig was too good a cowman, too much of a man, to let the likes of Oscar Nall put his hooks on the spread. He could say, after John Craig was killed *so* convenient by Jake Hopper, that Orval Kane kind of stuck up in the way. Until Orval Kane got killed by Jake Hopper, too. And it'd be *easy* for him to tell Ull Varner and Homer Ripps that you coming home, when nobody figured on you doing that, sort of dumped the chuckwagon.'

'Oscar Nall...' Tom Ziler said softly, very thoughtfully. 'And—I have had the oddest feeling about it all, ever since I saw the changes in Mesquite. Oscar Nall...'

'Talk to your Lucy Kane, then,' Tom Ziler counseled him briskly. 'See what she has got to say. Me, watching her walk along the street only yesterday with Oscar, I might be anti-godlin and slaunchways about it all. So—well, you talk to her and listen to what she says. But, special, I would listen to how she says it, if I was you.'

They went on silently until the horses came to that long, white wall that enclosed Judge Oakes's big house. Here Lance swung down and Tom settled easily in his saddle.

'You go right ahead,' he told Lance. 'Me, I ain't what you would call a neighborly body. I'll stay out here till you find out what you want to know, or what you think you want to know. If any of Ull Varner's gang comes along, you will know it. Yeh, by my six-shooter going off.' Lance scrambled up the 'dobe wall and dropped from it into a rose garden. He waded out of the soft dirt and crossed a lawn. There were lights shining in the low, rambling house. He went the familiar path to the kitchen and was accompanied by a harsh, unmusical voice chanting:

'En mi campo yo tengo la rosa,
Y esta rosa se llama—'

He laughed suddenly and shook his head.
' "In my field I have a rose and this rose is called—" Why, that will be old Maria, Maria-of-the-Five-Husbands!'

He stopped just outside the door and called softly:

'Maria! Oh, Maria! Are there *tacos* of chicken for the dinner, tonight?'

'Who is there?' the old Mexican woman answered instantly and her vast bulk darkened the doorway. 'The voice, it is one known to me, but—'

'It should be known well to you! It is the *muchacho* who found for you that third husband.'

'*Zapatazos!*' Maria swore incredulously. 'Lancito! Lancito! Now, this is the work of *el buen dios!* But never did *I* believe that you could go beneath the water as some *tontos* here would say that you had gone! Enter! Enter, Lancito! Come under the light so that I may see you. The girls are in my *patrona's* room. The judge is at the courthouse. Come in and—have you eaten?'

When he stood inside the kitchen she flung both thick arms around him, smiling widely, swaying him back and forth as if he had been a child. She let him go only to stand with gray head on one side and eyes narrowed shrewdly.

'*Ay de mi!* It was a boy who went away, but it is a man who comes back. A man—and one who has caused women in the world, in this place and that, much of trouble—and pleasure! A man who has seen much and, I think, done somewhat . . . But—you have the hunger? The thirst? There is dinner, of course. And Scotch whisky of the judge. And—'

Light, quick footfalls came toward the inner door of the kitchen. Lance turned and it seemed to him that his pulses hammered strangely with sound of Lucy Kane's step. He knew it for her step; knew it as if he had heard it only an hour before.

She stood framed in the doorway, tall, slender, auburn hair drawn back from her forehead in a way Lance remembered from their childhood. Her level, steady eyes were hazel, the exact shade varying with her mood. He remembered that about her, too. It seemed to him, now, that he had forgotten nothing. He

31

went impulsively toward her.

'I should have been back long before this,' he said quickly. 'But—one thing and then another came up—to go east I would have to ship west and north—it goes like that when you're moving up and down on a shoestring, or flush one day and broke the next—and when you're chased up and down because the side you fought for in a revolution got beat—I didn't hear a thing about Mesquite—about the Jefe—about Cousin Orval—only when I rode in today—'

'I heard that you were back, just awhile ago,' she answered, moving a little so that Nancy Oakes stood beside her. 'I'm glad you know about everything, now. Glad you're back. But if you had managed to come back a few years ago—It's no use talking about that, now. You—what do you intend to do, now that you are back?'

Nancy said nothing, only looked at him as if he were a stranger. She was as blonde as Lance himself; in her contrasting color as lovely as Lucy Kane. Now, as always, Lucy dominated her; she was like a mirror for Lucy's mood.

'I'm going to stay,' Lance said quietly. 'Naturally.'

She was very different, he thought. Seven years had worked changes in her beyond the mere passage of time. There was something hard and set about her face and mouth and eyes—particularly about her eyes. There was no such change in Nancy Oakes. She had been a pretty youngster. Now, she was a pretty girl. That was all. Yet she and Lucy were of the same age; she was twenty-two. Then he told himself that the tragedies on the C Bar had naturally changed her. For she had worshiped her father; she had been almost as fond of Big John Craig—the *Jefe* of the C Bar and of Lance himself.

'It must have just about wrecked her life!' he said inwardly. 'And seeing the old outfit go to rack and ruin, on top of the murders—'

He moved with sudden sympathy closer to her. But there was no softening in her mouth, her eyes. She seemed not to see his raised hands. And at her elbow Nancy Oakes was like her shadow, regarding him as if he were facing judgment.

'I'd give just anything, if I could wipe out all that has happened since I left,' he told Lucy earnestly. 'If I had heard—known—nothing would have stopped me; I would have come back. But I had no reason to think of anything like the mess Mesquite County seems to have got itself into. I—it's no use talking about it, as you said. The important thing is, I am back. Back to do just whatever I can do, for the C Bar, for you, for—us.'

She nodded, with that same set hardness of expression. Lance lifted a wide shoulder and let it sag. He got tobacco and papers from his shirt pocket and began to make a cigarette almost

33

blindly, staring fixedly at his thick, deft fingers. He was seeing, again, Fagan in the dust of the street; Acker on the sidewalk before the Two Flags; Ull Varner and—Oscar Nall.

'I'm going to do my best to clean up some of the mess. They say the *Jefe* was murdered by Jake Hopper; that this same Hopper bushwhacked your father. And nothing done about it! *I* intend to do something. About those murders and the two of today. I want to know several things. Why an imitation bad man like Ull Varner is sheriff of Mesquite; how the slimy teacher's pet of the old days, Oscar Nall, comes to be putting the like of Varner behind Harmony Pond's star; what's behind Varner and his gang dry gulching C Bar men. If it's Oscar's doings, Oscar had better hunt himself a storm cellar. For something's going to land around his ears! He—'

'Stop!' Lucy commanded sharply. There were vivid spots of color on the pale ivory of her cheeks, now. 'You don't know what you're talking about. You are practically a stranger in Mesquite. You've probably been talking to that ancient idiot, York Insall. He's not a stranger, but he knows as little about— everything, as you do. It's utterly silly for you to drop out of nowhere and begin talking about murders; about Oscar—'

'Don't mind him, dear,' Oscar Nall said quietly from the darkness behind Nancy Oakes. 'As you say, he's practically a stranger.

34

When he comes to know conditions, as you know them—But even if he still dislikes me, that doesn't count. For you know what I've done.'

Lance stared from the sleek, handsome Nall to Lucy. It seemed to him that she leaned against Oscar with sound of his voice. But that was only a trick of the light, he saw—and of his irritation.

'Now that you are back,' Lucy said slowly, 'you'll want to know about the ranch, of course. It's half yours. That's the reading of the will. We didn't know where to find you, or we would have told you four years ago. If you'll sit down quietly with me, I'll try to tell you just how everything stands. If'—her voice became colder, more metallic—'you can forget all the silly gossip York Insall and some other old donkeys may have repeated to you and listen to me. If anyone knows about the C Bar, I know.'

She came farther into the kitchen. Nancy and Oscar, also, moved into the room. And now Lance saw another man, in the dusk of the hallway behind Oscar. He stared, eyes narrowing, a thumb coming up mechanically to hook in the waistband of his overalls over his hidden Colt.

'Who's that?' he demanded sharply.

'Frank Larkman,' Oscar told him, without turning. 'I don't think you've met Frank. He's Sheriff Varner's nephew. Come on in, Frank, Mr Craig is a trifle nervous, tonight. And he's likely to start shooting the floor and the ceiling if he's not humored.'

Larkman came in without speaking. He was big and almost too good-looking—Lance thought—for a man, with his wavy reddish hair and clear, pale face and large blue eyes. He regarded Lance steadily, but as if he thought of something else. Lance looked up and down the well-dressed length of him and conceded the attractiveness of Larkman's gray suit. Then he dismissed the sheriff's nephew from consideration. For Oscar had slipped a hand through Lucy's arm in a sort of proprietary way and the gesture infuriated Lance.

'Of course I want to sit down with you and go over the whole record,' he said, careful to keep his tone level. 'But we had better do that out at the house. There's more company here than I like, for one thing. For another—I didn't expect to have a long session with you, tonight. I just wanted to see you; to tell you that I've heard enough—gossip or not—about the *Jefe's* murder and your father's—to make me give a promise to myself. Unless I'm stopped, as they were stopped, I'm going to get the man or men who killed them; try to change whatever it is that's put the C Bar in the bank vault—'

Oscar laughed softly, contemptuously. Lance looked at him quickly and knew that his face had reddened angrily. He made a movement of gun-hand and Oscar lifted his free hand to shake a finger warningly.

'None of that!' he cried sharply. 'You know very well—or you should know—that I never carry a pistol and that I don't hold with this silly shooting and fighting you cowboys are so fond of. We hire officers for that, nowadays. And when killers like Acker and Fagan start a row—'

'I was going to let both of them go,' Lucy told Lance abruptly. Her voice, with mention of them, was strangely husky, different. 'They were always making trouble. They intended to kill Wilbur Logan and some of the Spear L hands.'

'I'll talk to you on the C Bar,' Lance said grimly. 'I started to say that there's a good reason for my leaving town. I spread one of Ull Varner's would-be gladiators over the Two Flags floor. He was looking for trouble. Out of that whole crowd, he picked *me* to accuse of packing a gun!'

'And you—didn't have a gun?' Oscar drawled.

'Why, as it happened, I did! But Homer Ripps made it so special—twenty other men in Nabor's were bulging around the belt or under the arm. Well, one thing is certain: The next time Homer wants to ask me something, he'll bring a posse with him! I'll see you at the ranch, Lucy.'

He looked hard at her and waited. But she only nodded and turned. He watched them all

37

disappear into the darkness of the hallway. He shook his head, big hands clenching, unclenching. Maria-of-the-Five-Husbands, who had stood quietly at her table as if she understood no word of English, grunted soothingly.

'Not here,' she said softly. 'Not now. Wait! Your time will come, you young wolf. *He* will not match teeth with you.'

''*Sta bueno!* I won't do anything tonight. He could always talk the bird from the bush. But you are right: My time will come and then—'

He closed a fist slowly, significantly—as if Oscar's smooth, soft neck were within his fingers—and shrugged.

'Now,' he went on quietly, staring blankly at the white wall beyond Maria, 'I go to do something that none other in Mesquite seems to have thought to do, or care to do, in all the years since the *Jefe* was murdered.'

'You will cross the Bravo,' Maria said placidly, nodding. 'You will ride to Tenedor to find the man Hopper who, the sheriff has said, killed your father and hers. That will be a road of danger, *Lancito mio*. But not for nothing were you named "*lanza*." Very like a lance are you, today. But remember this, when you come to Tenedor: It is not Hopper for whom you should be most on guard. *Nunca! Jamás!* It is a small one called Ramon Razo. He is a devil of devils! I should know, for he was my first husband.'

Lance nodded and smiled vaguely at the earnest face. He said good night, and shook his hand when she offered him food and whisky. He went out and crossed the yard again, to scramble up the wall. On the top he heard Tom Ziler's placid voice:

'Reckon we better hightail. I took a looky down the street and there's too many men straddling their horses to suit me. If it ain't Ull Varner's bunch I'm bad mistook. You know the trails up and down, I take it? Listen!'

Lance dropped lightly from the wall and scooped up Gray Eagle's reins. He heard the soft hoofbeats of many horses as he swung into the saddle. They came from right and left.

'Trail?' he said between his teeth. 'Yeh, I know the trail—the one I'm going to ride. I know it as well as I know the lines in my hand. It's the trail to the river; to—'

'Yeh, to Tenedor,' Tom Ziler grunted. 'Let's go!'

They moved off at the quiet walk. Hoofbeats sounded louder ahead of them. In the darkness they could see horsemen bunched. Someone called to them.

'Reckon they went the other way,' Tom Ziler answered in a careless tone. 'That noble nitwit, Ull Varner—'

'Huh? You calling me a nitwit?' a high, outraged voice snarled. 'Who're you, anyhow?'

For answer, Lance yelled shrilly and drove

his rowels into the ugly gray's sides. Gray Eagle grunted savagely and lunged forward. He cannoned into a horse—Lance had guided him toward sound of the sheriff's voice—and Lance swung sharply down with his Colt. He felt the barrel crunch on a skull and sensed his victim going sideways from the saddle.

'Come on!' he called to Tom Ziler. 'Ne' mind picking *these* daisies.'

The darkness behind them was spangled with the orange flashes of shots as they pounded away. Close to them slugs whined like wasps. But Lance led the way, roweling Gray Eagle, bending low, heading for the tangled *bosque* that fringed the river.

CHAPTER FOUR

'AM I DEAD?'

Some in the sheriff's party were both daring and well mounted. Close behind them, Lance and Tom could hear the thud of their horses' feet.

Lance sent Gray Eagle ahead faster than he had yet gone. There was a place just beyond the last house of Mesquite where the *bosque* was threaded by trails of stock. It had always been so and he guessed that there, at least, change had not come in his years away. Once in that

40

tangle of willow and tornillo and cottonwood, he thought they would be safe.

'Rake your goat!' he yelled over his shoulder at Tom. 'We're almost to cover. Rake him like hell!'

They pounded like quarter-horses past that final house of the county seat and made the dark wall of brush and low trees. A stock-trail opened like a tunnel into the *bosque*. The shooting behind them was heavier, now; faster; a frantic fusillade. Tom suddenly made a gasping sound and his horse stumbled. Lance jerked Gray Eagle to a sliding stop, lifting in the saddle, turning. Tom's horse rammed into them and the saddle was empty. The yells of the posse were nearer.

Lance stopped the other horse and caught the trailing reins. He dropped off, holding both animals with left hand. His Colt was in his right. He fired down the trail in the general direction of Varner's men, then moved on, leading the horses. He found Tom sprawling across the trail and bent to shake him. Tom was limp, apparently unconscious.

Lance stood for an instant, scowling. Then he reloaded his pistol swiftly, surely. The pursuit was sweeping toward them. He squatted and got Tom's Colt. Aiming low, he emptied it as fast as he could thumb back the hammer and let it drop. Then he shoved it, with his own, into his waistband. Pursuit had stopped short with his volley. Men yelled at

41

one another.

He picked up the limp figure with grunt and strain, to put it across Tom's saddle. Still the Varner men called to each other. Varner's high-pitched voice he thought he recognized, and he mentally complimented the sheriff upon possession of an iron skull.

'What you waiting for?' the snarling yell carried down the tunnel of the trail. 'Scatter out! Git that son! You aim to let him jist walk off? Go ahead!'

He heard the crashing of horses in the brush; more yells from man to man. He turned the horses and began to go at the walk toward the river. But the posse was coming too close, once more. He let Gray Eagle and the other horse walk on and stepped back to fire his own pistol. Gunfire answered him instantly, but he had the advantage of being on the ground. He heard bullets whine overhead, or beat leaves and branches with the sound of raindrops. Once, something picked at his sleeve; again, he flinched automatically as a slug rapped his hat crown. But his shooting halted the posse.

He mounted and led Tom's horse along the trail. To left and right he could hear the possemen's horses thrashing in the *bosque*. He considered grimly.

'They'll line the bank,' he thought. 'They'll cover the ford. So we won't try to cross here.'

He went on quietly until he reached a cross-trail that opened on his left. He turned into it, pointing away from the river. Behind him, growing fainter with distance, sounded the noise of the posse going toward the ford. Occasional shots came muffled from the *bosque*. Lance laughed.

'Turn a bunch of excited fools loose in the dark,' he said aloud, 'and it'll be a plain, shining marvel if they don't shoot each other. That goes for Texas, the same as it went in Guatemala and Venezuela and Honduras. Probably, I'll get credit for every bullet hole that gang packs to town.'

He went on steadily, if slowly, across open mesquite and greasewood flats, going generally toward the C Bar. Tom groaned at last, and before Lance could turn he had slid from the saddle to the sand. Lance swung down, calling him.

'I—reckon I got one smack in the head,' Tom snarled. 'Must've been nothing but a crease, though. For as near as I can figure out, with this headache I'm entertaining, I ain't dead. Or what do you think about it? Am I dead? If I am, we have both got to be.'

Lance squatted beside him and flicked a match to flame on his thumbnail. He held it close to Tom's head, looked and laughed. Tom got to his feet and seemed to find his horse in the darkness by instinct. There was the sound of leather creaking.

'Well,' Lance reported deliberately, 'I doubt if you'll ever look the same. But you're not in

43

Boot Hill—yet. And I don't think you're ready for sixteen gamblers and the Dead March tootled on a flute. But you certainly did scare the living hell out of me when you grunted and tried to dig a hole in the trail with your skull. Varner's coyotes were pretty close behind and burning the air, about then, with as wild a bunch of lead as I ever saw. Wonder there's a star left! Mostly, they seemed to be shooting in that direction—'

'But you stopped—and you held 'em off—and you picked me up and got me across a saddle,' Tom cut in slowly, with an odd drawling note. 'How'd you manage to stop 'em and keep 'em off while you h'isted me up and toted me off?'

'Nothing to it!' Lance told him lightly. 'That bunch of bar-room gladiators Varner had with him—Hell! It was just like yelling *Boo!* from behind a tombstone at a boy whistling by. All they wanted was an excuse for stopping.'

'Yeh. Yeh, just like that,' Tom grunted. 'I—bet!'

'Listen!' Lance said wearily. 'The chief difference I see, between you and any other jack, is the size of your ears! You bought into my private war, there in Nabor's joint. For no reason at all. Chances are, you kept me from cashing in right then and right there, and making Varner's C Bar tally three for the day, instead of two. And it may seem queer and quaint to you, but I had my face set against

44

cashing in. There are things I want to do; things I mean to settle! And when we rode out of Mesquite, you siding me, it was on C Bar business. Well! In my day, the C Bar took care of its hands and C Bar men hung together. That was my day seven years ago; it's my day again. When you did your frog play back there, I stopped and smoked up the posse and picked you up—naturally! And I don't want to hear any more about it. What's that you're strangling? Don't tell me it's water!'

'It ain't—though I have drank some of that, too. It's Two Flags red-eye. I slipped five pints into my *alforjas* yesterday. Won 'em off old Carlos the bartender, matching dimes. Here!'

Lance drank, then moved to his own saddle. Out of a pocket he got a new shirt, a white shirt intended for dress occasions. Now, he tore it into wide strips and turned back to make a bandage for Tom's bleeding head. As he wound the strips around the stocky cowboy's skull, he thought a good deal about his patient.

'And I do wonder what your real name is, my friend,' he said to himself. 'Tramp-cowboy you *may* be—and nothing else. But there's something about you that makes me guess otherwise. Mesquite—the Border—always has seen some pretty quiet, salty people. Ah, well!—'

He stood back, accepting the bottle again.

'Now,' he commanded, 'you climb into that kak of yours and don't talk so damn' much—or say something when you do talk! When we hit the house, we'll wash you up right. Probably, I won't know you when you're scrubbed. And if any of the sheriffs or marshals on your back-trail run into you, they won't know you, either. Which makes you luckier than *this* dashing young cowboy. I'd better be sprouting me some long pink whiskers, the way Ull Varner's making a set at me!'

They rode on through the darkness, to the accompaniment of soft hoofbeats on shifting sand, the rustling creak of saddle leather, the occasional blowing of the horses as they mounted a rise or slid into an arroyo.

Lance whistled absently, as he looked alternately up at the stars in the black sky and ahead to where the C Bar range lay invisible in the darkness. He had walked and ridden many trails in seven years. Some of them had led to danger, and through danger, and this one, it came to him, was no different from those jungle or mountain roads to battle. Mechanically, he sang *Sally Brown*, as he had sung it on ship and shore, hundreds of times. Tom asked how far it was to the C Bar house.

'Bunch of rocks straight ahead,' Lance told him. 'Four miles north of that is John Creek line camp. The house is ten miles beyond that. This is the long way we're taking.

'Sally Brown, would you marry a sailor?
Way—hay, Sally Brown!

46

Sally Brown, would you marry a sailor?
I spent my money on Sally Brown!
For seven long years I courted Sally.
Way—hay, Sally Brown!
When I asked would she wed me, maybe—
I spent my money on Sally Brown!
For answer she showed me a lubber baby.
Way-hay, Sally Brown!'

Somehow, Lance was more cheerful than he had been since hearing of his father's death and the troubles of the C Bar. He was as grimly determined to pay off that account. But a man needed a friend more than he needed anything else in the world. And something told him that this stocky competent at his stirrup was the stuff his kind of friend was made of. Tom Ziler—or whatever his name might be—had chosen to throw in with the C Bar, with him. And together they would cross to Tenedor and hunt this murdering Jake Hopper whom nobody else seemed anxious to face. The C Bar score, the Craig score, would be settled. Then, he told himself almost contentedly, he would show Lucy Kane how raids on Craig-Kane herds would stop. She would alter her opinions—

'She'll see things as they really are,' he said abruptly, aloud. 'She's got plenty of brains under that red hair of hers. She'll come to see Oscar Nall for the clever sneak he is—always was. I'll show her the real Oscar. I know him as well as anybody could. When I clean up some of the dirt that's been heaved over se-vei-ral things in this county, she'll see. She can't help seeing!'

'Oh!' Tom grunted. 'Oh! Like that, huh? What lovely weather we're a-having, Mister Craig. Such a bee-you-tiful night. Makes a man feel awful young. Makes some men feel about ten year old—and innocent like you wouldn't believe. She's crazy about him, you nitwit! They *pasear* down the street together and she hangs onto his arm and she looks up at him google-eyed—I watched her!'

'But that'll change,' Lance persisted. 'Yeh, that'll all change. After she sees what I'll show her, she'll never look at Oscar again—not even at his funeral.'

'Now, what'd I do with them other bottles?' Tom grunted. '*That* just wore off all the good of the first one. Ah! Here we are. There's sense to this!'

He made gurgling noises, then shoved the flask out.

'Here! My pa used to say liquor made a pore man feel like a millionaire. But if that was all it could do, I wouldn't gi' it to you. For you got plenty of that kind of notion right now. Maybe it'll just sober you up.'

'All right,' Lance said serenely. 'You'll believe it when you see it. Well, yon's our bunch of rocks.'

48

They passed the landmark and rode on, Lance following the familiar trail without thinking of where Gray Eagle set his trim hoofs. Presently, they came to the little stone cabin set on a ledge above the deep, narrow cañon of little John Creek. Lance hailed the place and, when nobody answered, he got down with a grunt for Tom.

'When I pulled out of the county, this was a two-man camp. Now, it looks like a ghost camp. Shows how things have gone to pot on the C Bar.'

He scratched a match and went inside. Automatically, he turned, inside the door, to the rough shelf where always a candle stood, thrust into the neck of a whisky bottle. He set the flame of his match to the wick, lifted the bottle, and held it overhead.

'*Amor de dios!*' he breathed. 'Look at that!'

'That' was a grizzled cowboy sprawled face up, eyes wide and glassy, in a corner. One glance at the blood-soaked shirt, the unnatural twist of the head, told that the man was dead. Lance crossed to hold the light over him.

'Stranger to me,' he said grimly. 'But a C Bar man, at a guess. And the place has been stripped—not that there could have been much here.'

Tom came in and stared thoughtfully at the dead man, then looked vaguely around at the disorder, the ransacked food shelves—old boxes standing on end, these. He bent suddenly and straightened, holding a *concha* made from a silver *peso*. A tiny bit of rawhide string still clung to the slots of the ornament. Lance came over to look.

'Several men,' he said slowly, looking at the dirt floor. 'Maybe we can get a line on how many, and where they went. I used to be a tolerable trailer.'

'I'm a sight better'n a *tol'able* trailer, right now,' Tom drawled. 'I see Mex work in this. Only two pair of boots in the whole business— and one of 'em belonged to *him* over there. The rest of the feet wore Mex' *calzados*. Le' me look.'

He took the candle and began to move about, studying the floor. Lance made a cigarette and waited, looking at the still figure opposite him. The grizzled cowboy had been both shot and stabbed. Apparently, he had retreated from the door and made a desperate stand where he had fallen, his back to the wall.

'Probably been dead for several hours,' he said to Tom. 'He's stone-cold.'

'Uh-huh,' Tom answered, but without much interest. 'Now, I want a looky outside.'

He went out and Lance followed, watching.

'Got something,' Tom reported. 'Which way's the house? I can see the direction they rode off in.'

He made a sweeping motion and Lance nodded.

'That's the way to the house, all right.

There's a beaten trail to it. Let's take a look at that and see if they took the easy way.'

The hoofprints were in the trail and, sure of this, Lance pushed forward at the trot. It was strange, he thought, to be so much a stranger on his own range that he could not say how many men would be in the C Bar bunkhouse; what resistance these killers had faced.

They rode at the slinging trot through early morning darkness toward the great, fortresslike 'dobe house built by Lance's grandfather and added to by that dour old Scotchman's son, Lance's father. As at the line camp, he went automatically across the well-remembered miles. At a wire fence he moved without need for thought to open a gate.

'It's a big outfit, huh?' Tom said slowly. 'Craigs've been in this country a long time?'

'Quite a while. Quite—a—while. When the *casa grande* ahead was built, all this country for many a mile in every direction was Indian range, Mexican range, no matter what the state thought. Lance Craig took up this location. My grandfather. But the Craigs were in Texas in 1831. The first Lance Craig on this side came from Scotland to Boston in 1740.'

'Don't tell me *that* was your grandpa!'

'No. But his son was. He'd been a preacher and stock farmer, back East. Came to Texas before the Revolution. I take it he was a fighting parson. Anyway, he was at Gonzales in '35, when the Texas men kept their cannon.

Old as he was, he went with Collingsworth to take Goliad fort and into San Antonio with Old Ben Milam. Caught a slug in the leg there, and that kept him from passing in his checks at the Alamo. But he made San Jacinto!'

He swept his hand out in a wide gesture, as if Tom could see the range about them, in the darkness.

'He rode a horse and preached and ranched around here until, right ahead of us, his horse stumbled and threw him. He crawled back on, somehow, with a broken leg. That killed him. Yeh! We've been here quite a while.'

'And it does look to me like, if this Oscar Nall can make the play he aims to make, *his* grandchildren'll be telling strangers how Grandpa Oscar come to own the C Bar,' Tom grunted very dryly. 'You reckon this is Jake Hopper's gang we're trailing, Lance?'

'Can happen. But, we've always had more or less raiding from over the river—and some from this side. When I was two or three the *Jefe* and his cowboys shot and hung six from the Tenedor neighborhood. They buried the thieves at the main ford south of here. Put big white rock slabs up, over the graves. Any raider coming across had to pass those white tombstones. The story was spread all over the country, so a thief passing by would naturally think about the C Bar way of handling his kind. It was a good warning; it certainly did work—while the *Jefe* was alive!'

They came at last to the corrals behind the big house. Lance sat Gray Eagle in the darkness and looked about and listened—and smelled. He shook his head frowningly. He was glad to be back; depressed at thought of his father's death and that of kindly, impractical Orval Kane; worried about the C Bar's present state; anxious because of that murdered cowboy on John Creek—all in one. Tom's impatient 'Well?' jerked him straight in the saddle.

'Too much ahead,' he told himself grimly, 'to look any other way, right now.'

He stared at the lightless bulk of the house; the long bunkhouse to his right, behind the *casa grande*. It was silent and, in spite of the naturalness of that at this early hour, Lance found the quiet disturbing.

'Somebody ought to be in the house—a maid or two, anyway,' he whispered to Tom. 'And no matter how poor the outfit is, somebody ought to be in the bunkhouse. Let's go see. Try the bunkhouse first.'

They crossed the yard, past the end of the 'dobe bunkhouse, to turn toward its door. Lance stumbled and stepped back with a quick, startled grunt. Close behind him there was the dry rustle of leather to tell that Tom had whipped a Colt from his holster. Lance stooped and groped.

'Another dead man!' he whispered instantly.

53

CHAPTER FIVE

'I AM THE PATRON NOW!'

They stood with guns waist-high, alert as two wolves, looking from left to right, ahead and behind them, listening for any tiny sound that would indicate men moving to attack them. Then Lance pushed his Colt into his waistband and ventured to squat and strike a match.

'I don't know him, either,' he said, after some study of the dead Mexican's swarthy face. He dropped the match and flickered another into flame. 'Some *vaquero* hired since my time, I reckon. Shot pretty well to pieces.'

He held the match without thinking, until it scorched finger and thumb, then snapped it away and came erect to stare toward the house. He took a step in that direction and Tom came softly after him. Out of the darkness by the bunkhouse someone called hesitantly:

'Señor! Oh, señor! None is alive here on the C Bar, tonight, except me. All others have been killed.'

Lance whirled to face that boyish-sounding speaker.

'And who are you? And who killed our men?'

'I am Arminio Salazar. It was the *ladrones*, the thieves from south of the Bravo in Tenedor, who killed Gabriel there—and Lucas who now lies within the bunkhouse door—and Wong the Chinaman who was *la patrona's* cook.'

'Thieves from Tenedor,' Lance said slowly. 'You mean—men of Jake Hopper?'

A vague, small figure came out of the deeper dark to stand before them. His breathing was loud, almost a panting.

'That is my thought!' he said in a shuddery whisper. 'It was perhaps four hours ago that they came—riding as if they carried the Devil himself upon their horses' necks. They killed Gabriel when he came out to look at them. They killed Lucas as he stood in the door yonder. They killed the Chinaman on his mat, where he slept in the kitchen of the *casa principal*. They shot at me, but in the darkness I ran twistingly, knowing that death was behind.'

He made a groaning sound.

'Ah! If only the son of our *patron* would come! The Señorita Lucy has said it so many times, like the rest of us who have been men of the C Bar for all our lives. If *he* came, all would be well again. For I remember him. Oh, very well I remember him, though I was but a child when he killed a killer and quarreled with his father and left the C Bar to go out upon the ocean in a ship. No more than nine years I had, then. But I remember him! Tall—and very wide of the shoulders—and afraid of neither horse nor man nor anything else that might walk—and most beautiful with eyes like the sky and hair yellow as corn dried—'

Tom suddenly whooped his amusement and Lance snarled, but it was drowned in Tom's delighted laughter.

'Shut up, nitwit!' Lance yelled at Tom. Then, to the boy: 'Who are you?'

'Arminio Salazar of the C Bar! Son of Arminio Salazar of the C Bar! Grandson of Arminio Salazar of the C Bar!'

'Then *I* remember you, *hombrecito!* So let those ears of a Salazar labor for a change while the Salazar tongue has rest. I think that I am hardly beautiful. It may be that I have fear, sometimes, of some horses and some men. But I am Lance Craig! I am the *patron* now—'

'The *patron!*' Arminio gasped. 'The *patron!* You have come back to us. My candle burned before Saint Brendan was well burned! Now we men can do something about these things we have suffered. We—'

'Where did the thieves go?' Lance checked him impatiently. 'Could you see the road they took?'

'They went from here toward the pasture of the horses. But before going they drove from our corral, here, twelve of our finest geldings—horses which *la patrona* would have sold within the week to a trader. I thought as they went yelling off, those thieves, that they meant to take from the pasture the horse herd which would pay and was intended to pay many

56

dollars of our mortgage.'

He came closer and stared up through the dark at Lance.

'And you are the *patron*, come to be *amo—the Jefe*, as was your father and his father. Now, if you wish a man to ride on your right hand in this fighting which will surely come, then—*por dios*! I, Arminio Salazar, say to you that I am that man! But tell me what to do and it *is* done or I die.'

'Can you find a horse?' Lance asked him, looking around the yard, seeing nothing, yet seeing everything, of the well-known scene. 'Mount yourself. Then you may ride with us, the Señor Tomás and me. I knew your father, Arminio Salazar, when I was no higher than the loading gate of a Winchester carbine. If you are a man like him, you will do. Get a horse! We ride now to the pasture. Depending on what we find there, we fight or we cross the river. Does that suit your stomach?'

Arminio laughed and vanished with a scuff of racing feet in the *caliche* dust. Tom grunted a wordless question.

'It was a raid, of course,' Lance answered softly. 'A raid brought on by those horses Lucy meant to sell, maybe. Or—Ne' mind that for the minute. When the kid comes back—and there never was a Salazar foaled on the C Bar who couldn't produce a horse out of thin air like a stage magician pulling a rabbit from a hat—we'll have a look at the horse pasture.'

He made a cigarette and smoked silently, thinking, trying to plan. He had just tossed away the stub of it when Arminio came thundering out of darkness and slid to a stop at their elbows. Lance mounted, and Tom.

'Now, this way!' Arminio called. 'To the pasture. But *you* know the road as well as I.'

They rode fast through the last of darkness and came in the first gray light of dawn to a wire fence. Arminio pointed to the gate that swung wide open. He led the way into the pasture and guided them to the water hole which was favored by the herd. But there were no horses there—none anywhere in the pasture. In so small an inclosure, even darkness would not have made too difficult the work of driving the herd. And within an hour they found the gap in the wire where the horses had been pushed through.

Tom swung to the ground and studied the trail. Lance hardly looked down. He was staring blankly into the south. At last, he drew a long breath. Those driven horses should lead him across the Bravo and on to Tenedor. At the Mexican *plazita* he should find Jake Hopper and, no matter who might have set him to his work of murder, Hopper was the man credited with the murders of John Craig and Orval Kane. Lance shifted restlessly in the saddle and his hand went down to touch the smooth stock of his new carbine.

'A' right!' Tom grunted at last. 'They're

headed for the river. Let's go!'

'They are many,' Arminio said presently. It was a flat statement, without any note of worry. 'And in Tenedor will be others to stand beside them. So—how do we kill them?'

In spite of himself, Lance grinned. Tom laughed outright, looking at the boy's calm, inquiring face.

'That we will see when we come up to them,' Lance replied. 'I could perhaps call upon the Spear L and the 99 and the Flying W for help in killing them. But two days of hard riding would be needed to gather those men. Even if'—he recalled the effect Oscar Nall had seemed to have upon Manny Todd and those others who, years before, had always been honest and stiff-necked cowmen—'they would throw in with the C Bar. Which, maybe, they would not do.'

It was easy trailing, and fast, as the light grew stronger. They topped a ridge and Lance looked into the east, expecting the sun to show an edge over the hills there. Then from the foot of the slope that fell away ahead of them came a volley. Lead whined past them and they jerked the horses around to jump them behind the ridge. Once covered, they dropped to the ground and pulled the carbines off the saddles. Arminio had an ancient single-shot rifle, a Mauser that must have come from some Mexican trooper, wound about with bailing wire. His huge cartridges he carried in a pocket.

Bareheaded, flat upon the ground, Lance looked over the ridge. He saw movement in the greasewood far down the slope. He fired four shots very rapidly and the dull green bushes jerked spasmodically and someone yelled agonizedly. On each side of him was shooting, where Arminio and Tom seemed to see targets. Suddenly, men showed briefly, stooping, running farther down the slope.

'Let's go! Head around 'em,' Lance suggested. 'I don't know how many there may be, but three or four could hold us here, while the horses went on with the rest.'

'Looks like they didn't make much time,' Tom grunted. 'Never expected to see 'em this soon.'

'It looks like a surprise on both sides,' Lance said. 'They didn't expect us, either. Else they'd have drilled us when we skylined ourselves. Probably, somebody turned and happened to sight us.'

They mounted and rode at the gallop over the rough country to the left. Nobody followed them.

The sun came up as they rode. Lance looked frequently behind but found no sign of pursuit. He swung again toward the river and with sight of the dark line of *bosque* shook his head bodingly.

'If they're scattered, we're going to have some fun to tell the grandchildren about—if we're alive to tell. For we are going to be wide open, crossing that flat down there, a long time before we can see *their* ears!'

But they made the *bosque* and turned into the tangle of it over stock-trails, working back toward that ford where Lance thought the horses would be crossed.

They had covered a long mile when the first shot rang out in the willows and cottonwoods before them. The slug cut a branch from the tree over Arminio's head. He ducked instinctively, then instantly straightened with young face grim. Tom shoved his Winchester forward. He snapped two shots in the general direction from which that lead had come.

Instantly, the whole *bosque* ahead was aflame with firing. They whirled the horses and ran for it. Lance and Arminio were in the lead, going stirrup-to-stirrup. The roar of firing became heavier, steadier, behind them. As by a trick, a red patch jumped out on Arminio's gray sleeve. He jerked in the big-horned saddle and showed his teeth like a young wolf. Lance saw that the wound was nothing but a scratch.

'It is not of import!' he yelled encouragingly. 'We can wait. The time will come when you take a man's head for that burn, *hombre*. Now—we must ride!'

'I—I will take two heads!' Arminio yelled in reply, grinning. 'Now, down this trail, *amo*! It shelters us from their bullets.'

They jerked around a corner—an elbow in the twisting maze of trails. They stopped, Tom drawing in beside them, to wait and listen. The firing died. Minutes passed. Then hoofs thudded on the soft delta earth. Lance pressed a knee against Gray Eagle and moved a step nearer the sound. He leaned a little and saw a dark little man—cowboy by the look of him—coming like a Comanche warrior upon their trail. This one held his rifle overhead, and looked alternately at the trail and over his horse's ears.

Lance pushed his carbine past a shielding branch and shot twice, aiming deliberately. The dark man came from the saddle over the horse's rump and the horse galloped forward, to be stopped by Arminio.

There was a tall man, black-hatted, stubbled with gray beard, just behind the first pursuer. Lance fired at him and saw dust jump from the buttonless vest that flapped about the man. Tom's carbine was rattling and the heavy bellow of Arminio's old Mauser all but deafened him. The tall man jerked at his horse, but he was already swaying drunkenly. His horse reared, dropped head, and began to buck. The man's feet whipped out of the stirrups. He was lifted high out of the saddle to crash into a tree.

There were others behind him, but the firing seemed to have alarmed them. They swung left and right, thrusting their mounts into the brush that walled the trail. Someone among them yelled savagely, a command in English to 'go around!'

'Too many for us!' Lance decided. 'If we stick here, it's going to amount to the front porch of a first-class funeral. Come on!'

But Arminio's rowels banged his bay's flanks. He shot out past Lance and Tom and dropped from the saddle. He scooped up the two dropped Winchesters, jerked shellbelts from the dead men. Burdened with his loot, he scrambled up again. Tom laughed shortly.

'He'll do!' he said. 'If he lives!'

Again they ran, this time heading toward the river. They made a ford that seemed clear of quicksand and got into the rolling sand dunes on the Mexican shore.

'One thing,' Lance grunted. 'We're ahead of that bunch and the horses can't be far off, now.'

'Those men we killed,' Arminio said suddenly. 'You do not know them? Or you, Don Tomás? Well, then! I know them both: The little man like an Apache, *he* was Olin Berry. The other was called Curtain and, for his size, "Big" Curtain. Bad ones, both. They were of those who drink and gamble at the Dos Banderas, the Two Flags of Manuel Nabor. It may be, *patron*, that not so many of those on the C Bar, yesterday, were Mexicans!'

Lance nodded. But it seemed to him that the discovery of two hard-case Anglos riding with horse-thieves proved little—except, perhaps, that Jake Hopper rather naturally drew his recruits from both sides of the river. It was an ancient practice for a Mexican gang to post spies and helpers on the Texas bank.

'That may be,' he admitted to Arminio. 'But now, I believe that we must ride to find the road to Tenedor. For I think that will be the road which they follow with our horses. It is our chance to strike these thieves, these murderers, a hard blow. Perhaps'—he grinned tightly at them both—'all of us will not see the C Bar again. Perhaps none—'

'Such a hell of a lot of talk!' Tom groaned. 'Come on!'

They made the well-beaten trail that drove south into Mexico from the *bosque* and the wind-carved dunes and led to the vicious little village of Tenedor. One glance at the Tenedor road and they knew that they were too late to ambush the thieves. There were the hoofprints of numerous horses, driven fast.

'The woods are full of 'em!' Lance cried amazedly. 'Why, they must have split up in little bunches; stopped at three or four places to look out for anyone on their track.'

Then he hit Gray Eagle down the shoulders with the ends of his reins. They went at the pounding gallop toward Tenedor, but before crossing high points of the trail they halted to look south. Within two hours they saw the cloud of dust rising behind driven animals.

'*Yaaaiiaaah!* Come on!' Lance yelled— quite unnecessarily, for as Gray Eagle lunged forward Tom and Arminio jumped their horses and came, one to either stirrup. 'Scatter!'

A man came riding fast toward them, a tall Mexican with much of silver twinkling on hat and belt and saddle. He pulled in with sight of them, shading his eyes under the wide sombrero rim with cupped hand. Then he came on at the trot, lifting in the *tapidero'd* stirrups to look at them.

'He takes us for some of the gang,' Tom called. 'Bet you he figures we're Berry or Curtain or one of the others. He—*Ah-ah!* Smells something, now! Le' me do this!'

He pulled in swiftly—as the Mexican, apparently warned by some wolfish instinct, began to whirl the big black and bend with elbows lifting. His carbine came up and the tattoo of his fire was almost like a drumbeat.

The man straightened in the saddle and his hand tightened on the reins. The black swung about and faced them once more. The rider rolled like a sack but somehow kept his seat as the horse came galloping wildly toward them. Tom watched with a sort of grim detachment until the man came finally out of the saddle and crashed face-down upon the ground.

'And *that* is a job of dusting!' Lance cried.

'I would say right off that I can't play the fiddle,' Tom drawled. 'But Winchester music's another kind of tune and I can certainly wake it up. Still—hitting him without killing a horse worth a hundred like him was pure accident.'

He looked at Arminio and gestured toward the horse.

'*Un caballo—cumplido—para Uste', hombre.* A horse, complete, for you.'

CHAPTER SIX

'WHAT SHAPE IS HELL?'

No other riders came from that dust. Lance thought that this dead man had been sent to see what delayed the rearguard. Arminio spurred out to catch the horse and drop from his own ancient hull. He stood grinning, head on one side, admiring his new possessions.

Tom and Lance rode up to the man. Lance thrust out a pointing thumb and indicated the belt ornamented with silver *conchas*. Arminio was transferring his extra carbine from one saddle to the other.

'If he didn't actually kill that cowboy at John Creek line camp,' Lance told Tom, 'he was certainly there. *Mira!*'

He got out of a pocket the *concha* found at the camp. There was a gap in the line of *conchas* on the dead man's wide belt. When Arminio rode proudly up on the black, Lance flipped him the *concha*.

'More for you,' he said. 'His belt and hat. It

is good to wear a dead man's clothing—when that man was a *ladron*, a thief, and killed like this.'

They searched him, finding twenty-odd pesos in his pockets, a new Colt .44 in a holster, cigarettes, a slim, sharp dagger next his skin in a beaded scabbard. Arminio appropriated the lot, but the man's rifle, an ancient Remington, he broke scornfully across a boulder. Lance looked south.

'Let's go! We've got twelve-fifteen miles, between this and Tenedor, for our fighting. Wonder how many are there?'

They went fast after the diminishing dust cloud and when they came close enough to smell the acrid dust overtook two men in the drag of the herd. These appeared like jacks-in-boxes, Mexicans both, who turned their horses about to stare. Tom threw his carbine to the shoulder. Lance was hardly slower—or Arminio. Their fire blended in a flat roar, and fifty yards away a man and horse went down under the shredding lead and the second rider jumped to the ground and fled toward a bunch of boulders, but dropped within two steps.

The three spurred forward and passed these drag-riders. Lance thought that one was dead, the other only wounded. He heard the pound of Tom's horse and Arminio's. But he did not look back. This was the kind of war he liked, the kind he would have chosen for his return-blows at the men who had raided the C Bar and killed his father and Orval Kane. Arminio, too, seemed to have something like that thought. For he was chanting shrilly a sort of battle song, each improvised line about '*Don Lanza, the patron*,' being on the warpath, to kill like the lance he was named, ending with triumphant '*Ai! Ai! Aiiih!*'

They passed the horses and saw them waver; begin to scatter. Three men rode point, ahead of the herd. Lance yelled savagely and Tom and Arminio echoed the high, fierce cry:

'*Yaaaiiiaaah! Yaaaiiiaaah! Yaaaiiiaaah!*'

The point-riders seemed to have no desire for battle. They looked toward the galloping, yelling trio, then leaned over their horses' necks and their arms rose and fell, rose and fell, as they quirted their mounts toward Tenedor.

'We'll collect 'em!' Lance yelled at Tom and Arminio.

For a mile it was a race. But Gray Eagle was both fast and tough. The miles he had traveled since leaving Mesquite seemed to trouble him not at all. He outdistanced Tom's stocky roan and the black Arminio had confiscated. He ran up steadily on the rearmost horse of the thieves. Under an arm the man looked desperately at Lance, then twisted to fire a pistol empty. The slugs went wild, very wild. Grimly, Lance shoved the big gray into a final burst of speed. He came up so close to the man that he could have touched him. His Colt was rammed into the other's shirt when he changed his mind and spurred still a little nearer.

He lifted his pistol and brought it smashingly down to club the Mexican from the saddle. Almost without looking at him, Lance spurred on.

The two men ahead suddenly decided to make a fight of it. They whirled, some fifty yards away, and came back shooting. Gray Eagle charged at them and Lance, twisting him deftly, sent the Gray's heavy shoulder cannoning into the nearest horse. He had one glimpse of a dark, distorted face. A pistol flamed so near his face that his cheek was burned by powder. Then he pushed his Colt into the man's body and let the hammer drop. He pulled clear of the horse as Tom and Arminio opened fire from behind him and fairly hailed bullets at the remaining thief. Suddenly, the three of them drew rein to gasp and stare at each other and at the two dead men.

'We could—leave 'em lie,' Tom panted. 'For that hairpin, Jake Hopper, to see. Kind of like—your pa's tombstones—at the C Bar ford.'

'There's one to talk to,' Lance said quickly. 'I saved him for that.'

He jerked Gray Eagle around and went back at the gallop to where the first man overtaken was sitting up, hand to bloody head. He stopped just above the Mexican and regarded him grimly. Shrewd, dark eyes came to his, then shuttled to the ground. Lance grinned and put his pistol back in his waistband. Out of the strap he took his rope and shook out a loop. His hand jerked and the man's neck was encircled by a tightening noose. Another hand-twitch and Lance had dallied the rope taut on his horn. The Mexican made a choking noise and began to scramble up.

'Stand, *hombre!*' Lance ordered him. 'You come with us. Arminio! *Aqúi!* Here! Can you drive the horses to the river, using the old, the upper, crossing? It would seem that most of them have turned back, already. I think that it will not be hard to keep them going toward the C Bar. And if you head them toward the old ford the thieves we left in the *bosque* will hardly come into your road.'

'And what will we do with this one?' Tom asked in Spanish, scowling ferociously at the prisoner. 'Hang him? But I think that too much trouble. It is far to a tree. Better if we hold him between two lariats and set the horses running.'

'It may be that we hang him. But there is also the possibility that he will prove a man of some brain and, so, go free. Arminio! Ride, *hombre!* And if on the trail you see any men coming, let the horses run while you gallop to the old ford and there wait for us. Do not try to fight! Wait at the ford—if you lose the horses—until noon of tomorrow.'

Arminio nodded sulkily and went off with a whoop to push the scattering horses north.

70

Lance kept his rope tight and watched until he saw that the boy had the herd moving. Then he turned Gray Eagle south, and the prisoner—both hands holding the loop to keep it from tightening—followed at a stumbling trot. For a half-mile the three crossed a greasewood flat, the Mexican staggering over cactus and sharp rocks, always keeping his desperate grip upon the manila noose.

'May help him to get into the notion of talking,' Lance said ominously to Tom. 'He'll talk or—This is a C Bar war, and so far as I'm concerned it's "no quarter" on our side, any more than it is on the other side!'

In a shallow arroyo Lance stopped and sat comfortably to look at the gasping man.

'Do you wish to die?' he asked tonelessly.

'I—do not wish—to die! But I am not—afraid.'

'There is a way to escape death. One way. Where is your leader, the man Jake Hopper?'

'I know of nobody with such a name. My leader is Ramon Razo, whom men call the Little Tiger. Where *he* is now, I cannot tell you. For I do not know.'

Lance jerked the rope and the man came to his knees, panting. He got up again, with slackening of the lariat. Again Lance put the question about Hopper—and got the same answer—and jerked the prisoner to the ground again. Over and over the process was repeated. At last Lance turned curiously to Tom.

71

'Could it be that he's telling the truth?'

Tom shrugged, studying the man's twisted face.

'Far be it from me to say! But you wouldn't expect a man to stand choking like that, if he could help himself by talking a li'l' bit. It *might* be that he's 'way down in the gang; don't know his real Big Auger; talks to this Razo.'

Lance turned back to his prisoner and began to question him about the raid on the C Bar. Now, the man answered frankly enough: He lived just outside Tenedor and to him had come word, an order, from Ramon Razo. It concerned the horses of the C Bar. So he and a half-dozen others of Tenedor and Razo had ridden north and crossed the river. There, other men had joined them. He had not seen these Anglos, in the darkness. The band had scattered. He had heard that several had been killed, fighting on the ranch. But he had seen no killing, being one of those sent to the horse pasture before reaching John Creek.

'You know me?' Lance demanded suddenly. 'You know that I am of the Craigs who own the C Bar?'

'I do not know you. I know none of the name. But, then, I am only a man of Ramon Razo. What he tells me to do, that I do. *El Tigrillo* does not say to such as me what he thinks or plans.'

'And in Tenedor there is no man called Jake Hopper, an Anglo who was once a great thief in Texas, a robber of the bank and the train? Remember! Your life is in that loop!'

'I do not know of such a name. But, in Tenedor, are some Anglos who do not use, it may be, the names by which you called them in Texas.'

There was something like grim humor in his eyes. He looked straight at Lance and shrugged.

'Even in Mexico,' he added, 'men have changed their names—for good reason.'

'Then—who is *Jefe*? Who rules in Tenedor?' Tom demanded abruptly.

'Why, Ramon Razo, I think. *El Tigrillo* is *un hombre valiente*; a man of much brain and bravery. None that I have seen says "no" to our Little Tiger.'

'I'm going to Tenedor,' Lance said slowly. 'Somebody is lying. Maybe this fellow, maybe somebody else. But I'm going to find out about it.'

'And a lot of good it'll do you to know it all,' Tom said dryly, 'when you're lying out on the cold prairie with your neck all unbuttoned below the chin.'

'Well—it's all I can see to do! And I'm a stubborn man; I came over to have a looky at Mr Hopper, not just to take our horses away from the gang. If Arminio gets the horses over the river, that'll be a damn' sight more than anybody else has done for just a hell's while. But I am going to see Jake Hopper before I'm through—or bust a hamestring!'

'All right! All right!' Tom groaned. 'But I wouldn't bet a nickel we'll see him, now. Anyway, let's start. I'm in no sense a stubborn man, but I reckon I assay a wide streak of plain, damn foolishness.'

They found an arroyo in the hills above Tenedor and waited out the daylight hours. The prisoner was no longer noosed. Lance only kept his feet tied together and they passed him tobacco and papers and matches, and he smoked and talked calmly during the day.

With dark they moved slowly down upon the *plazita*. Now the Mexican's wrists were lashed with a saddle string and he walked between their drawn pistols.

Tenedor was well lighted when they slipped quietly into the village and edged along house walls toward its center. From windows and doorways light streamed to dapple the white dust of the single street.

Ramon Razo was in Tenedor tonight, Lance thought—or should be. For the prisoner had said that Razo, once sure that the horses were safely on the road south, had left the raiders to return here.

'He has a new girl,' the Mexican had told them, grinning. 'He was quick to leave us.'

There was always the chance that Razo had ridden out of Tenedor, to see why the horses had not reached the place. But that, Lance told himself, was not likely. If left alone until

74

morning, Razo would surely go or send someone. But hardly tonight.

'He's lying here and lying there,' Lance decided, of the man between their pistols. 'There certainly were more men on that raid than he tells us. Maybe he was lying about Hopper, taking a chance that we wouldn't kill him; that we couldn't check on his lies.'

Past the noise of households getting ready for the night, they went toward the biggest building of Tenedor, a great 'dobe which, according to the prisoner, was the *cantina* owned by Ramon Razo and a partner and which was Razo's headquarters.

Guitars twanged in the place. Yells of drinkers carried to them. They moved more and more slowly, Lance keeping closer watch upon the Mexican. They got to the back of the *cantina* and edged up to a square window that stood open. Lance lifted cautiously on his toes and looked over the sill at the crowd inside, gathered at bar and rude tables. At that moment the prisoner and Tom fell against him and Tom gasped. The Mexican lurched clear and ran down the wall.

'He—he kicked me—in the belly!' Tom gasped. 'We—better hightail! He's going—inside!'

Lance looked quickly through the window and saw the Mexican running toward the bar, yelling, pointing at the rear door through which he had entered. Men gaped at him and at his bound hands. But the one who drew Lance's stare was a little man who seemed to have drawn shining, plated pistols before hearing more than the warning yell. But after a word he pivoted to glare at the back door.

'Razo!' Lance grunted savagely to Tom. 'I see Razo.'

He lifted himself a trifle more so that his elbow rested on the windowsill. He fired twice at the little man and saw him drop, then jerked his hand out of the opening.

'Now we'll fog it! I hit him both shots.'

They ran back as they had come, down the backs of houses and toward the horses. Behind them Tenedor's doorways fairly erupted men. The village was like a hornet's nest roused. But they had the cover of darkness and, coming to that corner beyond which they had left Gray Eagle and the roan, they stopped without need for words to send shots at the massing crowd.

'That ought to hold 'em a minute or so,' Tom said grimly. 'But from the noise, that bunch is *right* aggravoked.'

They went on at more leisurely gait to mount and ride away from the huddle of 'dobes. Once clear of the place they spurred toward the river. After a quarter-hour Tom shifted and looked back.

'Now, they're coming,' he said. 'Hear the horses? Well, you're right sure you got Razo, huh? But how about Jake Hopper? See anything that'd look like him?'

'No, I didn't. And I took the time to look. Maybe my look was a li'l' fast, but it was plenty hard. Couple Anglos at the bar, but it was Razo rodding that spread. He looked all that our man said—the Big Auger of Tenedor. The others just gaped. This little man was about to *do* something when I dusted him. No ... I'd be willing to swear that, if Jake Hopper was in that bar-room, he was under the bar.'

'Now—what?' Tom inquired, after a further time of galloping, and when the hoofbeats behind had been lost.

'See if Arminio got the horses over. Then try to gather some new hands for the C Bar, I reckon. Couldn't have been many on the place before this lick. Now—'

'Where'll you *get* hands, decent hands, in a den of rattlers like Mesquite has got to be?'

'*Quien sabe?* There's not only the job of getting the men, but the little business of paying 'em, too. Reckon I have got to sit down with Lucy for that heart-to-heart talk. She'll have to admit that we got back the horses. We'll see!'

They saw nothing of their pursuers. They made the river and rode along the fringe of *bosque* to the old ford, and there Arminio waited. He had *not* lost the horses. They were heading toward the C Bar, he said. But he had met a man on the way and he was too triumphant to hold his tale.

'He was surely a man of Jake Hopper's,' he

said. 'For he saw me before I could see him. He shot at me as I came over a ridge. So—I left my hat for him to watch and I went like a—a puff of smoke; as if I had no feet. I came to the other side of him and there I spoke of his father—guessing as to who might have been his father. When he turned to me, I killed him.'

They complimented him and he swelled. Then Lance looked up into the starlit sky. He was tired; hungry. He had not found Jake Hopper. But he was pleased, nonetheless. He grinned slightly.

'We will let our horses find the road back to their home pasture,' he said to Arminio. 'You will ride, now, to Mesquite. Find *la patrona* and tell her of the small things we have done. Say that I am looking to the hiring of new men and to making of the C Bar a place thieves will ride around. Don Tomás and I will go to Las Esquinas. There we may find riders who have filed from their pistols the front sights, and who use their spurs only to send their horses into the fights.'

'What's this-here-now Corners?' Tom asked Lance, as they rode at the long, hard trot, north and east.

'Hell!' Lance answered briefly, simply. 'At least, it used to pass for one of the seven doors of Hell.'

'One door'd do me,' Tom grunted. 'What shape *is* Hell?'

CHAPTER SEVEN

'WE NEED WOLVES'

Lance laughed in spite of himself as he repeated Tom's question.

'What shape's Hell? Eight-sided, of course! But one side's only got a li'l' bitsy window that the Devil uses to booger out of. You can take my word for it, young fellow. That's just one of the lots and heaps of things I know all about. I never told you, because I'm a modest soul and I do hate anything that even seems like bragging. But I'm practically just the same as an educated man, yes, sir!'

'G' on! G' on! It ain't the Devil you got boogering now. It's me, Fi—Tom Ziler. Get on with the tale.'

'It's no tale. When I was young and lovely, better looking than I am now, even, if that's any way possible, and with all the tender bloom still on my fair cheeks, was a health-seeker hit the C Bar. Yes, sir, a young fellow from Philadelphia that's in Pennsylvania. The *Jefe* chunked this Kearny into the bunkhouse and told me to make some kind of hand out of him. Well, I reckon we educated each other.'

Tom snorted incredulously. The flame of the match he struck to relight his cigarette showed his grin.

'Yeh, I taught him the Three R's of the cow-country—Ridin', Ropin' and 'Ranglin'—and he unloaded his box of books on me. Used to rope me and sit on my head and twist my mouth open and ram Helen of Troy and Charlemagne and Omar Khayyám and folks like that down my young neck. He'd been a college professor, you see, and old habit was strong in him. First thing I knew, I was reading his books instead of looking at the pictures in Montgomery Ward's sheepherders' bible. Why, even today, if the light's good I can make out to read a newspaper. Local news, of course. If the light's *real* good.'

'I—see,' Tom said dryly. 'And—who was it taught you to slap leather the way I notice you doing, kind of like greased lightning—lightning, anyway? Your professor?'

'No. No-o, that was a gift from old "Iron Hat" Connolly, that was foreman about the same time. But it was Professor Kearny that showed me how to hold down and hit something after I'd got the cutter out of the bundle. Ye-es, I'll have to credit Kearny with showing me how to kill a man. He killed a tough-breed horse-wrangler one day, as neat as anything you ever saw. After it was over—this breed was supposed to be something fancy with a hogleg and he leaned on that rep'—Kearny told me how he managed it. He said: "Keep your mind on what you're certainly going to do to the other factor of the equation, ignoring entirely what he may expect to do to you!"'

'Barring the way he said it, which I don't give a damn about, that's the right idee. Once—it was up at Landusky—a kind of *average* cowboy got tangled and snarled up with a fast gunfighter. Got hit by the first slug in that session, too; knocked flat on the floor. But he was thinking about all the things he wanted to do to this gunslick. So he got his gun up and— Funny! That cowboy's riding around today and the gunslick's in Landusky Boot Hill.'

'Cowboy's riding a roan horse,' Lance said with perfect understanding. 'Siding a bent-to-busted young cowman. Well, about this Las Esquinas ... It used to be the toughest little place between This and That. Wilbur Logan's Spear L range runs on one side of it and old Socrates Morrill's Pig-on-a-Fence outfit's on the other. That reminds me: If we happen to run into Soc' at the store, there, let me do the talking. Soc' is a tough old rooster, but maybe I can argue him out of killing the two of us. Out of killing me, anyway.'

'Fine!' Tom applauded him. 'The more I ride with you, the more I'm practically roped and drug by the way you think about me and my interests. But if you don't mind, will you kind of toll this Fence-under-a-Pig tornado off to the side till I wrap myself around some sardines and crackers and kind of tuck in the edges? Last time I had my head in a *morral* was about four yesterday. If I got to die, I got to die. But I'd like to do it on a full belly. It'd make me balance better, in my coffin.'

'They don't use coffins, in the Corners!' Lance informed him cheerfully. 'But I'll try to persuade him. I did talk him out of a murder, once—my murder. Happened when I was just a kid. The *Jefe* sent me up here about some horses we'd bought but never had got around to branding. They had strayed onto Soc's range and we fell out about the business, in the store. Soc' was holding down on me and I asked him about Fair Helen, the gal whose face is supposed to have sunk a thousand ships—more or less. Soc' only knew one Helen and she was over at Lanak and she wasn't fair, anyhow, being a cross between a Canuck muleskinner and a Cherokee mamma and just downright godawful brunette. So—I told him about the other Helen and I got a chance to whang him over the head with a bottle and take his pistol—he'd taken mine away from me ten minutes before.'

'*Amor de dios!*' Tom cried. 'I never heard about anybody having a ship between the Gulf and El Paso, much less any such foolishness as a thousand of 'em. What *I* bet happened was, you got started gabbing and you got the man so weak he couldn't pull back the hammer. Likely, it would have been a good notion if he *had* killed you, then. Unless you're aiming to take up the law.'

They were riding, now, across greasewood flats stubbled with mesquite and desert willow, spiny with cactus and ocatilla, rising toward the low mountains. Lance waved a hand up the slope toward a blur of yellow lights. He grinned, but with tight mouth.

'Las Esquinas—the Corners,' he said. 'And, maybe, plenty of trouble. You really ought to take that hammer-head of yours off, out of the way. Shame to drag you down to a horrible death this way. It's just business, with me...'

'Trouble,' Tom drawled. 'Goodness me! Fella, turn your wolf loose—and tell me he ain't just a cub!'

They rode on toward the little trading point of the mountain ranches, where—as Lance well knew—law was of the sort which hard-handed men made for themselves, limited for the most part of whatever one efficient man could do to another of his own self-contained sort.

'Quinn Jackman runs the Corners. He's the storekeeper,' Lance explained. 'At least, he runs Las Esquinas if the Rangers or some hard case haven't shot his name off the sign.'

'I'll grease my holster,' Tom grunted without alarm. 'I never did crave cashing in on a snow-white bed with a gang of medicine bottles around me. I hate castor oil too bad.'

There were three houses, beside the store, in the tiny settlement. Lance rode up to the first of the scattered string, and at his call the door opened to frame a tall, gaunt, and stooping woman, who remarked acidly that any drunken cowboy looking for supper at this ungodly hour would get more than his constitution could endure.

'Why, Mrs Purdy!' Lance cried. 'You wouldn't accuse *me* of being drunk! And I've thought about your pies for seven years and more; clear across the world and up and down. It's just pure luck, you being awake.'

'Who's it?' she snapped. Then her voice changed, softened. 'Pies? Clean across the world—Don't tell me it's Lance Craig! Why—come in, son! Ain't a thing in this shack Big John Craig's boy can't have, *I* tell you. Light!'

'We'll put the horses away, if your shed's still there. And feed 'em. They—deserve it.'

'Ever'thing's about the same around the Corners,' Mrs Purdy assured him. 'Except, of course, some that was *ain't*.'

They unsaddled and stabled and fed Gray Eagle and the roan in the pole-walled shed behind the house. Lance laughed when Tom put a question.

'She's the widow of one of Mesquite's old sheriffs. And the best cook you ever met in all your unsaintly life. I'd ride five hundred miles to eat one of her venison-mincemeat pies and count the time to education charged, as Kearny used to say. The *Jefe* loaned her the money for her place here, after Purdy was killed on the river by rustlers.'

Inside the cheerful living-dining room they sat down at a table covered with a bright red cloth and the gaunt, leathery-faced widow regarded Lance with head on one side, sharp black eyes narrowed.

'It is and—it ain't,' she said at last, while they ate enormous steaks and plates of fluffy biscuit and baked beans and 'greens' from the Purdy garden patch. 'There ain't the size to you by a third there was to Big John. Not that you ain't big enough, Lord knows! But you favor your ma a lot, Lance. Still, you got Big John's way about you and'—her angular face hardened—'there's plenty need for his way, son, around Mesquite these days!'

She put questions to him, gave him local gossip, in a steady outpouring of speech. He had opportunity to return only the briefest of answers, and it was not until he leaned back 'stuffed like an anaconda,' as he told her, that he could make a cigarette and light it and ask questions of his own.

'Ain't seen Soc' in a week,' Mrs Purdy told him. 'He won't eat with me; says it's too different from what he eats on the Pig. Just as o'n'ry and cantankering as always—and the best friend I got in the country. Quinn Jackman still runs the store and somehow he keeps in with ever'body, no matter how much they fight among 'emselves. He's friends to Soc' and Wilbur Logan both, and both of 'em hating each other. I reckon the Corners ain't much different, Lance. Hard cases come in quiet and sometimes they stay quiet—and stay permanent. We likely got the biggest graveyard for our size of any place in Texas.'

Lance considered his private problems. But he was tired and sleepy and the prospect of meeting whoever might be in Jackman's store had no appeal. Tomorrow, he thought, would be time enough. He said as much to Tom, who nodded.

'We'll roll up on your porch,' he said to Mrs Purdy.

'Fine!' she answered. 'You're really sticking, this time? And—how's that with Lucy? From the talk—and what I see in Mesquite times I wander over—looks like if the Craigs and Kanes can hang onto the C Bar you're going to partner with Oscar Nall. And I can't see you and him teaming it. I—well, I reckon I always used to look at you and Lucy and sort of—'

Lance moved his shoulders uncomfortably, nodding.

'Yeh. Maybe I had notions that way, too. Now—oh, it's bound to work out all right. If I can get the C Bar back to something like what it was, we'll pay off the mortgage. Lucy is bound to see Oscar Nall the way everybody else sees him. He's a coward and a schemer and downright mean inside him. She's *bound* to find that out!'

'But maybe not till after she's married him,' Mrs Purdy said dryly. 'You don't give Oscar credit enough. About that Hopper, now—'

'I told you we couldn't locate him in Tenedor. But that is no proof we can't, one time or another. I know it's a big order I'm taking on: To straighten up the outfit and pay off what we owe the bank; to pay Jake Hopper for those murders; and to keep Lucy from marrying Oscar. But I'm going to hang and rattle and I think I'll do every one of those things. After that, I can sit back and ramrod the C Bar the way Craigs always have done. Now—'

He got up, yawning. He and Tom made their hard, but sufficient, beds on the dirt floor of the porch. They slept late, and waked to eat a breakfast as enormous as their supper of the night before. Lance told Mrs Purdy of their errand in Las Esquinas and she shrugged.

'Well, it ain't for me to say. But *I* wouldn't want the kind of wolf that usual hangs around Jackman's bar riding for me!'

'We need wolves more than plain cowboys, these days,' Lance said carelessly. 'And if they come tougher than their boss, that's just my hard luck and I might as well find it out first as last.'

They left the horses in her stable and walked the two hundred yards to where Jackman's log-and-stone store stood beside the trail, its back against a steep cliff. Before they reached it they saw horses at the hitch-rack and heard someone chanting unmusically. Lance listened and nodded.

'Sounds like Socrates Morrill. Quite a bunch inside ... Seven—eight—nine horses. Well—'

'Don't y' monkey with my Lulu gal,
Or I'll tell y' what I'll do:
I'll shoot y' with my pistol
An' cut y' with my razor, too!'

The harsh voice lifted to a roar, and Lance knew that the singer was Socrates Morrill. He and Tom stopped in the wide door to look at the dusky, cluttered room. Part of the long counter was given over to Jackman's liquor, and that end was crowded. A dozen men were drinking or talking there. At the end nearest the door stood the Pig-on-a-Fence owner, short, very wide, rocking on run-over heels. His hat was on the floor, and he swayed his gingery head in time to the hammering of a bottle on the bar. He did not look around, but the one-eyed man behind the counter stared at the newcomers without expression and three or four of the drinkers turned to look.

Lance went in, Tom a step behind him. He walked up beside Morrill and pushed in to twist his head and look intently into the sun-reddened face and pale gray eyes and cluck tongue against teeth reprovingly. He spoke softly:

'I thought it was you! For the last forty miles I was almost sure of it. You never could sing,

88

Socrates. I cracked you over the head about that—or about something—years ago. Of course, I was young, then, and full of vinegar. Now, we're both old and feeble. But your singing's worse—'

Socrates Morrill shifted a little and stared. He blinked little eyes and shook his head. Then, suddenly, he lifted his chin and howled wolfishly.

'The Craig kid! Big John Craig's outlaw colt come home! By—Judas! Lance, I'm glad to see you. Where y' been?'

He flung a great arm around Lance and banged his bottle harder on the bar.

'You—Quinn Jackman!' he yelled. 'Y' know this boy. Y' ought to. Bring up y' whisky—or what passes for whisky in the place. Y' remember the day he got me boogerin' about some gal name' Helen Somebody an' took my gun off me, right here at this bar, by Judas!'

'Hello, Lance,' Quinn Jackman greeted Lance tonelessly.

He came down with a quart bottle and two glasses and poured drinks for the three of them. Socrates beamed on Lance and nodded genially to Tom.

'I reckon y' know about all the troubles y' got,' he said. 'If y' come through Mesquite, y' ought to, even if Oscar Nall *is* runnin' the county these days. Pa bushwhacked. Orval Kane done the same. C Bar stripped an' badgerin' deeper in debt allatime. Hell of a fix!

89

Son, if y' aim to do ary thing, y' got to do plenty. By Judas! Y' got to rise up nineteen foot high an' land on them thieves allasame cyclone. Wipe 'em plumb out.'

'Something like that has been rolling around my head,' Lance assured him. 'You hear about the last lick the thieves hit the C Bar?'

As he told Socrates of the raid and their recovery of the horses, three men moved out from the bar and went out. Mechanically, Lance watched them, a very tall, blond man of sloping shoulders who had an odd, stiff-legged, pigeon-toed walk, a grizzled cowboy with liquor-bloated face, a foxy-faced, dark little man. All were wearing pistols openly, the blond man having two. He went on talking.

'We need hands on the C Bar. Somehow, I'll scrape up money to pay 'em. Six or seven straight cowboys who can stand to see trouble through the smoke.'

'I can git 'em for y'. An' one, Ples Cahill, is plenty good enough for fo'man. He could run the C Bar an' run her right. I sent him over to talk to Lucy Kane, once, but Oscar shoved in an' she wouldn't hire Ples. If he'd been managin' the place, y'd have a sight more to come back to.'

'Fine! If you'll send Cahill over, tell him he's hired. Same for the others. Cahill goes on for range boss. If I don't happen to be on the place when he lands there, tell him to just move into the bunkhouse and start riding for me. I may

90

be somewhere else, you see. There are se-vei-ral things I have got to straighten out, before I can settle down to being a nice, quiet, respectable cowman like you!'

Socrates threw back his big head and bellowed at that picture. Lance and Tom drank again, clinking glasses against that of Socrates. Then Lance straightened.

'We've got to hit the road,' he said. 'Mesquite. Lucy is due for a long, hard talk with me. Thanks a lot, Soc'. With this Cahill and some of his kind on the place, to side Tom and me, I do think that the old C Bar is going to sit up and get over its bellyache. Sorry I can't stay here a while and drink you-all under the table. But we'll be back. And the C Bar won't forget what the Pig-on-a-Fence is doing.'

They went out and turned toward Mrs Purdy's. As they passed the house beyond Jackman's, those three men who had left the store came out in front of them. The blond man was grinning. He had his hands on his pistols. The boozy cowboy and the dark little man, also, gripped their Colts.

'The C Bar kid,' the blond man drawled, with a grin for both of them. 'Well, well! Funny—runnin' into you at the Corners. For we was sort o' lookin' for you yesterday. Me an' some others out o' Mesquite. But we never found you. An' now—here you are!'

CHAPTER EIGHT

'SOMEBODY—FOOLED ME!'

Both Lance and Tom had stood with hands loosely hanging at their sides. But as Lance looked flashingly, at these three and understood instantly, perfectly, the situation, he snapped hand to waistband.

Then a shot crashed at his elbow—and a second shot. The dark little man, whipping out his pistol, whirled as if on a pivot and began to run, but sprawled with arms out before he had taken more than his first long step. The blond man staggered—and staggered again with impact of Lance's bullets. Tom shot twice again and the last of the murderous trio, only one of them to loose a bullet, dropped to his knees, tried to lift his Colt, then fell upon his back. His thumb slipped on the hammer and his final shot went wild.

Lance leaned slightly, staring savagely at the blond spokesman of the three. But his hands had fallen away from his pistols. He was holding himself upright with hard mouth twisting all to the side.

'Somebody—fooled me!' he said in an angry tone.

Then he crumpled like a man made of paper.

Lance looked from one to another of them,

then at Tom. He shook his head frowningly. No more than seconds had gone and three men were dead, or dying, before him.

Socrates Morrill and others from the store came at the run. Socrates looked at Lance, then at the sprawling figures, and back at Lance. He pushed back the gingery hair from his forehead.

'Well!' he said wheezily. 'I al'ays *did* allow that the Corners was the fastest place in Texas. How-come?'

Lance looked past him and the cowboys to where Quinn Jackman stood, single eye narrow, long, thin face without expression.

'I don't know, yet,' Lance told Socrates. 'But—Quinn Jackman! Who're these would-be gunslicks?'

The storekeeper hesitated, but under Lance's grim stare and the steady regard of Tom and old Socrates, he shrugged.

'Big fella was Upton Elliott. Kind of a handy man for Oscar Nall,' he said unwillingly. 'Special dep'ty sher'f. So was Ohio Ott—him with the gray hair. Do'no' the other'n' but he was around with Elliott a lot, lately. They *was* gunslicks! Leastways, Elliott an' Ott was. But why they'd hunt trouble with you men—'

He shrugged again and Lance looked at Socrates.

'They'd been looking for us, Elliott said. Yesterday. That's interesting. It might explain—a few li'l' things, to the man with a

93

li'l' bit of idea on some subjects. But I'm still Mesquite-bound, Socrates. What's the habit in the Corners, these days, in cases like this?'

'Oh, Quinn's a justice. He'll be coroner an' settle this one-two-three! Won't y', Quinn?'

'I seen the whole thing,' a cowboy thrust in, turning to Jackman. 'Seen these men walking along the street minding their own business. Elliott walked out in front with his hands on them cutters. Ohio Ott and that mean-faced little one, they looked ready to pull, too.'

'Reckon that settles it—far's the Corners is concerned,' Jackman said slowly. 'As coroner, my verdict is they come to their death at the hands of Lance Craig an' Tom Ziler, who was actin' to the best of their knowledge to save their lives. It's usual to hire old Pedro Fernandez to bury 'em, Lance. He charges two dollars apiece.'

Silently, Lance got a gold piece from his small store and held it out. Jackman began to produce silver, but Lance waved him off and watched broodingly while men lifted the dead and carried them toward the back of Jackman's.

'Bother you some?' Tom asked him softly.

'Some. But it does seem that Mesquite County's going to force killing on us. Those were all killers, and killers of the worst kind—packing guns for hire. Nothing but killing serves such as that. So the quicker it happens to 'em, the better for everybody. Let's get out of

94

here! See you some more, Socrates. And— thanks again!'

They went on their interrupted path to Mrs Purdy's. She was a woman in a thousand, for she had seen the encounter from her porch and now asked only the names of the three who had stopped them. Lance told her and she nodded grimly.

'Good enough! County's a sight better off with the like of Upton Elliott in Boot Hill. He's done a shady killing—or six—up an' down. The others probably was like him. Son—he was Oscar Nall's right bower in some things. Don't you kind of expect Oscar's got some more like him? An' don't you reckon Elliott wouldn't ever have come at you without Oscar knowing all about it?'

'Can happen!' Lance admitted. 'I have had the same notion for some minutes, now. Well, we have got Oscar on our li'l' list, for a visit. But Lucy's first.'

When they were riding silently out on the Mesquite road Tom looked several times sidelong at his friend. But Lance was seeing—he could not help seeing—the tall Elliott with his sneering grin, standing, then falling. He looked grimly straight ahead. No turning back, now! Every generation of Craigs, it seemed, had to clean the home-trail. It was his turn and, unless he died as his father had died, he would eventually look across C Bar range that owed nobody a dollar and over which none would ride but with his permission. If the Elliotts, the Razos—and the Oscar Nalls—had to be killed before Mesquite County was peaceful again, they would be killed, and they could blame none but themselves. Tom began to sing in a husky voice a Mexican song Lance had never heard before:

'Soy novillo despuntado
Del rancho del Homobono, uy!
  Ay! Ay!
Y a más de cuatro vaqueros
Les he quitado lo mono, uy!
  Ay! Ay!
Que risa me dá!

I'm a blunt-horned steer
From the Homobono Ranch, oh!
  My! My!
And I've made more than four cowboys
Quit their funny ways, oh!
  My! My!
How they make me laugh!'

Then he began to talk to this and that, very careful to avoid mention of anything connected with Las Esquinas. Lance understood his efforts. He shook off his depression.

'Certainly glad we found old Soc' Morrill,' he said. 'His Cahill sounds like a real find. Somebody who can handle things if you and I happen to stay out late of nights.'

'That Morrill!' Tom grunted. 'And you, too. It's blame' funny that when I sock people over the head with bottles, they always seem to get peevish about it. But when you swing at 'em, they turn around and write letters about how you're the best friend they ever had. It might be a gift, huh?'

Lance laughed and pushed away the picture which had been riding with him.

'He's a warrior and a fighting man's what he likes. No dogies ride for the Pig-on-a-Fence! Everyone in *that* herd is a bull and a fire-snorter. Now, if you don't have to be so damn' conversational, we'll try to figure this Mesquite trip. Better slide in after dark, I reckon, and get to Judge Oakes's without waking the sheriff.'

'Going by the C Bar?' Tom inquired. 'Those dead men, you know, something ought to be done about 'em.'

'I thought we'd ride to Mesquite that way,' Lance said. 'Because Lucy might have left town—I don't think she has, but it's possible—and because of the men.'

'That'll mean Mesquite tomorrow night, then—unless she's come out. Who'd bring her? Or would she come by herself? If she run onto the *vaqueros* in the yard and the bunkhouse and that cook Arminio told about, in the kitchen, she *would* have a jolt!'

'I don't know. I just don't know what she might do or how she'd go about it. There's going to be lots happening around here, before

97

the old range is what I remember, run in the old way. But let me get settled in the house with a good bunch covering the C Bar range and I believe we'll get back to the old ways. Then, if Oscar Nall wants to see Lucy, he can do it in town!'

He looked forward over Gray Eagle's ears. But all the rolling country was no more than frame for the picture he saw—Lucy Kane, older, but much lovelier than he had ever seen her in their childhood, steady hazel eyes meeting his...

'Not much use in trying to keep something from you,' he told Tom slowly, with small, twisted smile. 'I've always had a soft spot, just about my only soft spot, it may be, for that "sixty-fifth cousin" of mine.'

'She feel the same way? Before you left, I mean.'

'I don't suppose either one of us ever thought about it—about how we felt—in those days. We were around each other so much, we just took it all for granted. I was busy on the range; she was running the house with her Mexican servants ... Then I pulled out. For years I'd think about home—when I had time to think about anything but what I was into at the minute! And—I began to think about her a good deal more than about anything else. I—'

He shrugged irritably and made a cigarette. When he spoke again it was in a grim voice. 'I thought the world and all of the *Jefe*, even if we did happen to be so much alike that we didn't get along too well. And Lucy's father, Orval Kane, he was one of the finest men in the world. No driver like the *Jefe*. Not so much at rodding things and making money, but the kind that enjoyed living. The *Jefe* would look at a mountain and see something he had to cross. Cousin Orval saw it the way he'd see a picture. The *Jefe* watched the sun rise or set and figured what kind of weather it meant. Cousin Orval would see the change of color in the sky.'

He laughed reminiscently.

'How many times I've listened to the two of 'em, riding together! Orval would point ahead and say: "Look at that sunset, John. Look at that sky—gold and a blue that's not really a blue; more a kind of lavender..."

'And the *Jefe* would snort. "There ain't a pound of beef—lean *or* fat—in that foolery of yours!" he'd rip out.

'And Orval would tell him: "There's something written about a man not being able to lived by bread alone, John, and I reckon that goes for beef, too."

'"You're blame' well right a man can't live on bread and beef alone!" the *Jefe* would say. "Plenty of times he won't live if he hasn't got a good Winchester, in *this* country!"

'Cousin Orval ... I liked to ride with him; listen to him talk. He'd sit at the table with us and keep Lucy and me on the edge of our chairs when we were little, making the forks and spoons disappear and come back in queer places; doing card tricks and sleight-of-hand with coins. And now he's dead—murdered. Jake Hopper...'

'And—Oscar Nall?' Tom drawled.

'I don't know. But this I do know! If Oscar's little schemes for putting a brand on Mesquite County—his brand!—have led him into any kind of dealing with Jake Hopper and those Tenedor thieves, I'll kill him just as I'd kill a rattler and think nothing of it.'

'That business at Las Esquinas was funny! All you did in Mesquite was spread a deputy sheriff over the floor. But Ull Varner gathered up a posse like you'd done a murder. A shooting posse. Upton Elliott was Oscar Nall's killer. He certainly aimed to rub you out.'

'I've thought about that—and about everything else. But it does seem to me that my first play is to find Jake Hopper. I don't know how he came into this business, but I have heard about him ever since I got back. So I want to see him. Damn' well I want to see him! Maybe he was the toughest train-robber in Texas. But—one or two places in this wicked world would say that Lance Craig has been tough, too, when he had to be.'

'I believe you!' Tom grunted, staring. 'I do believe you, now!'

They rode on steadily through the day and came into C Bar range. Before dark they made the quiet yard of the *casa grande* and looked about. There was no sprawling body where Lance expected it. The bunkhouse, too, was empty. Tom jerked a thumb toward a patch of flooring which was cleaner than any other part of the long room.

'Somebody's scrubbed it,' he said, 'Arminio, you reckon?'

Lance shrugged and led the way to the kitchen. Here, as in the bunkhouse, there was evidence of recent cleaning. A heavy green linoleum covered the kitchen floor, and it was spotless except where their dusty bootprints showed. They went through the big house. In the long living room, the dining room, the several bedrooms, furniture and furnishings showed what Lance thought were effects of the raiders' hunt for valuables. These rooms had not been put in order by whoever had removed the bodies of *vaqueros* and cook and washed away the bloodstains in kitchen and bunkhouse.

'Might have been Arminio,' he said at last. 'Or Lucy might have come out with somebody, cleaned up a little, and left again. Or there may be a hand or two left on the place; somebody in one of the camps missed by the thieves. *Quien sabe?* But yonder, on that slope where you see the motte of cottonwoods, is the C Bar graveyard. Let me borrow your glasses for a look.'

When he had the binoculars from Tom's

alforjas he looked at the distant slope from the long front veranda, and nodded with sight of four fresh mounds.

'Somebody buried them all, including the cowboy from John Creek. Well—I'm glad that's done. We might as well have supper and sleep here. I don't want to hit town in daylight, so there's no use starting until noon tomorrow.'

'Somebody!' Tom grunted suddenly.

They went around the house quickly and found two stocky, middle-aged *vaqueros* sitting C Bar horses before the bunkhouse. These stared at them, keeping hands upon their pistols. Lance knew neither of them and approached cautiously.

'I am the *patron*,' he told the men. 'Are you riders of mine? I have been long away. I found that thieves had stolen C Bar horses and killed our men—'

'We are men of the C Bar,' one *vaquero* answered slowly. 'We are Gregorio Montes and Felipe Anza. I am Montes.'

They had been on the Flying W, returning horses borrowed from Nathan Wingo. They had come back by way of John Creek and there had found the dead man, whom they called Hervell. They had brought him to the house, not knowing how he had been killed. They had found the other murdered men in bunkhouse, yard, and kitchen.

'We did not know what to do,' Montes said

stolidly. '*La patrona* was not here. We thought of riding to town. But it seemed better to bury them and wait for her to come and say what should be done. So we made their graves and washed the blood away. Then, because we did not like to stay here, we rode to look at the pasture of the horses, the cattle on the range. The cattle are where they should be. But the horses are gone. So we thought of Jake Hopper.'

He stopped, watching Lance. Anza, who had said nothing, but only stared fixedly, suddenly grinned, nodding:

'You are the *patron*! You are the Señor Lance of whom Arminio Salazar has told us. I have seen a picture of you as a boy. You are different, but now I know you. What do we, about these thieves? Arminio has said that when you came back to be *Jefe*, the C Bar would kill those thieves of Tenedor as in your father's day they were killed. So—'

'Something like that we have just done,' Lance told him. 'The horses are coming back, Felipe, Gregorio. As for those who took them and killed our men—'

They listened with fierce grins to the tale of battle and recovery of the horses. Anza swung down and looked around the yard cheerfully.

'I do not mind staying here, now,' he said. 'All is changed, somehow. It is no longer a place of quiet and fear. Arminio, I think, was right!'

103

He and Gregorio put the four horses in the corral and hung up the saddles. All of them ate in the kitchen and sat there, smoking, drinking the last of Tom's whisky, afterward. From the *vaqueros* Lance drew a fairly accurate account of affairs on the ranch, with tally of stock and its condition.

'Not so bad as I'd expected,' he told Tom, when at last the *vaqueros* had gone out to the bunkhouse and left them to make beds in his old room. 'If we can just hang on to what's left, I think we can make out to pay our interest.'

Tom grunted, where he stood before a faded photograph in frame of candle cactus stalk.

'I see what the Widow Purdy was talking about,' he said absently, staring at the group. 'No trouble to pick out your pa and Cousin Orval and Lucy. It's you behind the spurs, of course...'

'Won 'em at Lanak,' Lance answered, coming over to look. 'Bronc' riding. First prize at a shindig over there. Gold and silver plate. Still wearing 'em. They've been all over with me. Kearny, the professor, made the picture with his big camera. He went home, cured, right after that. Ye-es, I do look like the *Jefe*. I can see it, now.'

But he stared at Lucy who, in that picture, smiled at him.

CHAPTER NINE

'WHAT OF JAKE HOPPER?'

Noon of the following day found them on the road to Mesquite going at a leisurely running walk toward the county seat. The horses were back in their pasture. Montes and Anza had their orders to ride steadily over the range until Lance's return, or arrival of Ples Cahill and such hands as he might bring. Lance whistled as they rode.

'Things, my pious friend and drunken companion,' he told Tom, 'they are shaping up nicely. They are that. The way I figure this affair is thusly: Ramon Razo was Jake Hopper's *segundo, caporal,* Panjandrum of the Rustling. Now, Razo is either dead or a ve-ry sick man. Hopper will have to pick him another vice-ramrod or lead his gang himself. If he comes over, we'll keep him—right on the river with a white rock over him such as the *Jefe* marked his thieves with. If he only sends a gang, we'll abolish 'em, what with Cahill and some rough, tough-sticking cowboys.'

'She *is* a pretty girl,' Tom drawled, unmoved. 'But to have all this effect, just from a *mira* at her picture when she was admiring you and the Sears Roebuck spurs—ah, me!'

But he had to listen to more of enthusiasm,

as the two sat comfortably in the *bosque* outside of Mesquite, waiting for darkness. With night, they resaddled and rode around the backs of houses, to draw in where they had stopped before, behind the house of Judge Oakes. Again Tom waited.

At the kitchen door Lance listened for Maria-of-the Five-Husbands, but she was not in the room. He leaned to look and faced the slender, white-haired judge himself, where he stood in a corner oiling a double-barreled shotgun.

'Well!' Judge Oakes said pleasantly. 'I didn't get a chance to speak to you, Lance, on your other visit. Come in and have a drink. I'm practically an orphan. Nancy and Lucy are out at old Johann Zemel's. And even the courthouse has been deserted, today. The sheriff and his force are out on some business or other.'

'Zemel's,' Lance said slowly. 'I wanted to see Lucy. I—there are a good many things I want to tell her, talk over with her. When are they coming back?'

'Oh, tomorrow or the next day. They went out with Johann and a couple of his girls, last night. He'll drive 'em in. But you'd better have a drink. Lord! Doesn't an old man get any consideration, any more? I want to hear all about you.'

'Thanks. Of course I'll come in. Let me bring in a good friend of mine, first. He's out back, but if the sheriff is out of town, he might as well come in.'

He called Tom and explained. They put the horses in the judge's stable and joined him in the kitchen. He led the way to his study, a big, book-walled room with game trophies and English sporting prints on the walls above the shelves.

Over their Scotch, Lance found himself talking freely to the gray friend of his father and Orval Kane. The judge put occasional quiet questions, but for the most part he drooped in a big chair, wreathed with cigar smoke, blue eyes narrowed behind his spectacles.

'And Upton Elliott tried to kill you,' he said at last. 'Ye-es, I admit that does look a good deal like a play of Oscar Nall's at you, Lance. But you'd have trouble proving it. And if you decided to omit proof and kill Oscar, you'd possibly hang, certainly learn to make shoes at Huntsville. Ull Varner is Oscar's creation—as much as if Oscar had carved Ull out of a clothespin. And you may have noted Ull's more than passing resemblance to the aforesaid clothespin? Well, in addition to Ull and certain other lesser lights, there's our young county attorney, Hale Baggley. Hale is both energetic to a fault and—another of Oscar's creatures. Bad!'

'If I get this proof I spoke about—that Oscar had a connection with Jake Hopper—I'll risk the rope and Huntsville,' Lance told him calmly, grimly. 'I'll kill Oscar and—Ull Varner and anyone else who looks to be off that coil. Lucy doesn't seem to agree with me about Oscar. But even a girl ought to be able to see that it's damn' peculiar when a high-and-mighty, upright citizen of Oscar's caliber manages to associate with sneaks like Varner and killers like Elliott and Ohio Ott. I'm not saying that Oscar is our boss thief, or anything like that. But I say it seems downright queer that he seems to be bossing some almighty tough cases.'

'True. Quite true. I—have entertained ideas about Oscar. But he is clever. I dislike him thoroughly, but I must admit his brains. His mental processes are crooked. His way of doing any business is crooked. But he keeps within the law and—I'm sadly afraid, Lance, that Oscar is far too clever for you—'

'On his own ground!' Lance broke in savagely. 'But I'm going to be on *my* ground! I think he had something to do with the *Jefe's* death, with Cousin Orval's, with everything that's happened to hurt the C Bar. I honestly believe that, somehow, it's Oscar's doing that the C Bar is mortgaged and until I got back was on the way to his pocket. I'll certainly kill him if I find that my suspicions are facts!'

'Pre-cise-ly! And for the rest of your life be in serious trouble. A murder charge, probably. Hale Baggley and Ull Varner will see to that. It won't do, Lance. It just won't do!'

'Maybe it won't do, but—it certainly will happen!' Lance said grimly. 'I won't take all this backing off. Now, Judge, I think I've got too much on my hands to be sitting around. Pleasant as the company is! You know everything that's happened. Can you think of anything that might be used by the noble ring here as base for a charge against me?'

'Anything!' Judge Oakes said calmly. 'Anything that's happened can be so interpreted as to constitute a crime. But I'll watch for signs. In a small way I still have some influence. And some small gift for stating facts in an alarming manner, also. Where are you going now?'

'Out to Johann Zemel's, to see Lucy. We have got to straighten ourselves on the management of the C Bar.'

'Yes, you have to settle that. Try to be diplomatic, Lance. Lucy has a temper and she has, also, the feminine characteristic known as mulishness. Rub her the wrong way about Oscar Nall and she'll say more in his defense than she really means or believes, just to disagree with you.'

'I'll try not to raise a riot,' Lance promised, without much interest. 'But this is bigger than Lucy's silly notions about Oscar. She'll have to admit that her handling of affairs hasn't resulted in anything but losses—and that I do have an interest in stopping those losses.'

They had a final drink with the judge, then went out to the stable. Lance led out the gray and mounted, to sit considering what he had best do. Tom scratched a match and set the flame to his cigarette.

'We won't take the road,' Lance decided. 'The Dutchman's place is on the Lanak road, and that's pretty well traveled. Too, it winds. We can cut across open range and cut off miles.'

They rode out of the judge's yard and Lance led the way through the darkness. Tom looked at the overcast sky and forecast rain. Lance laughed.

' "In Texas," ' he quoted, ' "only nitwits and newcomers prophesy about the weather." Surprised at you, Tom. But I'll go this far with you: there's not much chance of a moon, and it ought to be a good night for Oscar Nall and Ull Varner and their kind. Yeh! Good night for a murder.'

They had gone only two or three miles on the way when Tom pulled in and stopped Lance with quick, soft grunt.

'Somebody's ahead of us,' he whispered. 'Hear them hoofs hit the ground! Sounds like a bunch, too.'

'It does. And if Oscar Nall had more than Elliott and Ott and that other killer looking for me—no telling who it is, or how many. Are they coming or going?'

'Stick here a minute!' Tom said softly.

'Nobody knows me for more'n a roving cowboy, riding the chuckline. I can go here, there, or anywhere without anybody taking a second look. Keep quiet till I come back!'

Lance began objecting, but Tom was already moving away, going down the slope. So Lance swung off and squatted with reins in hand, carbine across his arm, listening. The hoof-beats could not be heard, now. He wondered why those riders had halted—or if they had halted. Minutes passed—many minutes, he thought. Then from the slope below him came the rattle of shots.

He came erect and listened tensely. But only a yell—then a chorus of yells—sounded. There was no way of knowing whether Tom had been discovered and fired upon or if those men down slope had hunted and found someone else.

'—or if Tom opened up on them and hit hard, or if he's wiped out!' Lance finished in furious uncertainty, impatience.

He mounted quickly and held in the chafing gray. Then out of the darkness hoofbeats pounded straight toward him. He lifted the carbine. A dark mass surged up the slope, barely darker than the night itself.

'More than one horse!' he thought. 'And that's about all I need to know, tonight. Except—'

He called Tom's name; called it twice. When there was no reply he hesitated no longer, but shoved the carbine forward and brought it to his shoulder. Whoever came, except Tom Ziler, was an enemy in Mesquite. The galloping men were shooting at him before he fired, but he had the advantage of steadiness. The staccato drumming of his shots was the sound of a stick rattled along a paling fence. His targets yelled, and before he had emptied the Winchester they had stung right and left to miss him.

'Tom!' he yelled again. 'Tom! Come on, boy! The sons are yelling *calf rope!* We'll run 'em—'

But there was no answer; no sound except that of horses running away on each side of him. He pushed down the slope and went deliberately for a hundred yards or so, to the rim of an arroyo. The gray bunched himself and jumped, to land with rattle of stones in the watercourse. That noise was signal for three or four shots; how many, he did not know, because he ducked over the horn with the vicious whine of lead past him. He spurred the gray into a gallop. There was more shooting, but farther ahead.

As he went, he thought of Tom Ziler rather than of being shot. A man needed a friend, he told himself. A man found that friend, found a Tom Ziler, then let him die.

All the shooting stopped. He pushed on and a faint, thin voice lifted:

'*Lancito! El señor Lancito!*'

He listened incredulously, for that sounded like Arminio and he could not understand

112

Arminio's being here. Then he answered in Spanish and the voice was raised again, nearer. Lance waited until a horse made stumbling noises among the rocks and he could see it and its rider as one gigantic blur in the darkness.

'*Don Lancito!* This is Nicolas, brother of Arminio. I—I have to tell you—the man Jake Hopper—*Dios!* I have stopped a bullet. I—I think that I die. The man Hopper—'

'What of Jake Hopper?' Lance cried. 'Where is he?'

'He waits—says Arminio—at the old house. The house—'

Lance spurred forward. He felt, rather than saw, the boy swaying from the saddle, caught him and held him.

'The old house—of the Blues. He waits— waits for—'

Then he sagged against Lance, who dismounted awkwardly still holding him and squatted beside him. There was neither pulse nor heartbeat that he could find.

'The old house of the Blues,' Lance said softly, staring straight ahead. 'Blue Briggs's hangout. And Jake Hopper is there, waiting for somebody. A great many candles will burn for you, Nicolas Salazar, because you told me that much. A very great many...' He was using Spanish, as if the dead boy could hear, and the language seemed to shape his thoughts. 'I have lost a father and a cousin who was a second father and a friend who was the best of friends.

113

And good men, not the least of whom is you, Nicolas. And Jake Hopper waits—and it will be Lance Craig who comes to him!'

He came tigerishly to his feet and reloaded his Winchester. Then almost soundlessly he moved down the arroyo in that direction from which Nicolas had come, hunting those who might be left there, of Oscar Nall's men, or Jake Hopper's. He had gone no more than twenty or thirty quiet steps when he stumbled over a moveless body. He squatted to rake the head of a match along his overalls. In the small light he saw a freckled face, unmistakably one he had seen in Mesquite in the shadow of Ull Varner. He moved the flame and it twinkled upon a deputy's badge.

So the sheriff, too, had hunted him. And he, or Tom Ziler, or Nicolas Salazar, had killed this deputy.

He wondered where Tom might be; if he had fallen somewhere around here or if he had somehow ridden clear. But he could not wait to hunt for Tom. Not when Jake Hopper was in the house of the Blue Gang in Murder Cañon.

He went back to the gray and mounted. Looking down at Nicolas he shrugged regretfully. Tomorrow, if he were still alive, he would care for the boy's burial. Tonight—

He rode out of the arroyo and turned automatically toward the entrance of Murder Cañon across the flats.

CHAPTER TEN

'ONLY ONE OF US LIVES!'

Lance considered, as he rode steadily over well-known country, all that he had ever heard of that ancient stone house which all Mesquite County knew, the ruined cabin in which had been done more of violent death than any other house of Texas had ever seen.

The old stone house ... He remembered how every boy in the county had firmly believed every tale told of it; how the site of it had been an Indian camp and the scene of a massacre; how the Blue Briggs Gang had used the deserted cabin as hangout and, getting drunk after a stage-robbery, had managed with Winchester, Colt, and knife to kill each other off—eight of them, in all.

Every boy—and many grown-ups!—had heard the Mexicans tell of luminous, floating figures seen in the dark, and of shrill screams and bellowed oaths heard on stormy nights around the roofless walls.

'There'll be screams, tonight,' he thought grimly, 'if Jake Hopper's there. I won't promise ghosts that look like floating Japanese lanterns, but Jake Hopper will scream—if he happens to be the screaming kind!'

The mouth of the cañon passed, he went

more slowly, forcing himself to be careful, watchful, to travel deliberately. The gray rounded a bend of the wide cañon and he saw the old house—not the shape of it, but three thin lines of pale yellow light, evenly spaced, seeming to hang in air.

'Sacks nailed across the windows...' he muttered. 'Anyway, that shows somebody's hand. Somebody's there.'

He dismounted and went toward those shrouded windows, keeping close to the wall of the cañon which widened, here, to become a narrow valley. Step by step he tested the ground before him. He was no longer impatient. Only past him could anyone leave the cañon and—nobody would pass him.

A startled grunt not two yards ahead of him was the first warning of another's presence. He had hardly stopped when a shot came out of the darkness by the wall, the flame blinding him, powder particles stinging his face and neck. Instinctively, he punched at the man with his own carbine and let the hammer fall, flicked down the lever, and fired again. He heard the clatter of the other's gun on the rocks at his feet, then a gasping sound.

'I—I think I die!' the man rasped. 'I—'

He fell. It was like a segment of the wall toppling. Lance bent quickly over him, after one look at the house. He knew that this guard was a Mexican. He said quickly in Spanish:

'You are alone? Alone, here, to watch?

116

Where is Jake Hopper? Speak! Where is Jake Hopper?'

'Dead!' the man whispered painfully. 'Why—do you ask—that? He died under the knife—of Ramon Razo—'

Lance ventured to flick a match into flame and hold it cupped in his hand over the thin, brown face.

'He died—within a week of—coming to Tenedor. He—*Cuerpo de dios! Patron! Patron!* Don Oscar! Don Oscar Nall! Watch! He who killed Ramon Razo has—has killed me—also! He—knows you—'

'Knows—what?' Lance snarled, shaking him until the shrill voice died in rattling gurgles. 'Knows what?'

'Knows you,' the man mumbled. 'Knows you—for chief of us all—killer of his father—cousin—he is here—'

Lance glared incredulously down through the darkness. The match had been dropped, burned out, seconds before. Only those yellow lines of light showed on the wall of the house.

'No Jake Hopper! Just Oscar Nall. He was clever enough to set that tale going, to cover himself—'

He came to his feet in a single quick, smooth straightening and went in wolfish quiet toward the house. At the corner he listened and, hearing nothing, moved down to the first sack-curtained window. He moved a corner of the sack and looked into the firelit room. Standing by the rude hearth, strained faces, wide eyes, turned directly toward him, were Lucy Kane and Nancy Oakes.

'Who could it be?' Nancy said in a low voice, without looking at Lucy. Lance could barely hear her.

'He'll find out!' Lucy answered. 'He— Nothing to be afraid of, honey. Don't worry!'

Her voice shook, as Nancy's had shaken. Lance went on, past the other windows and to the corner. Around that was the door. Whoever 'he' might be, investigating the shots, there was no sound of him ahead.

He could not understand the girls' presence, unless Oscar Nall had kidnaped them. And that seemed incredible.

He slid inside the door and Nancy Oakes screamed with sight of him. But he was not concerned with that; he looked to right and left flashingly and saw nobody else in the room. Then, out of a window opening at the end of the room a shot came. The slug glanced off the wall so close to him that he felt the vibration through his shoulder. He whipped the carbine a little farther up and fired twice at that window; saw the sack whip under his slugs; heard Nancy scream again. Then he was outside once more, jumping through the doorway.

'*Patron!*' a voice whispered, down the wall. '*Don Lancito!* This is Arminio! He is yonder! He ran from the window after your shots.'

Lance looked right and left, fumbling for shells. He reloaded the carbine.

'Go that way. I go this,' he told Arminio. 'Keep to the ground, *hombre!* Then, if he hears you and shoots, he will send his lead above you. He does not know that two of us are here. Drive him back upon the muzzle of my gun!'

Arminio laughed softly and slipped away into darkness. Lance inched down the wall to the corner. Suddenly, Arminio yelled shrilly from behind him. He spun about and a gun flamed. He fired at the flash of it. Before he could jerk the lever and fire again a man cannoned into him and pinned his arms to his sides in a bearlike grip.

Lance's carbine dropped and he wrestled furiously to free his hands. He butted forward and with the impact of skull upon face the other's grip was slackened. He used the ancient backheel and fell upon his opponent, slamming his fist, left and right, to the head.

'Got you—Oscar! Got you—dead to rights!' he gasped.

'I—who is it?' Oscar Nall demanded painfully. 'Who is it? If you think—'

Lance thought of his pistol and drew it. He got Oscar's.

'Up you come! I've got you covered. Make one move I don't like and I'll kill you without batting an eye. I'd a little rather kill you than not. You'd better remember that!'

'You have him, *patron*?' Arminio called

softly. '*Bueno!* I heard him. I called to you. I—What do we, now?'

Lance drew a long breath, keeping the pistol jammed into Oscar's side, holding the hammer back.

'Lance Craig!' Oscar said in a surprised tone. 'Why—I thought it was one of Jake Hopper's crowd. You can take that gun off me, Lance. I thought it was one of those outlaws, or—'

'Shut up!' Lance commanded grimly. 'Arminio, as you must know, inside are *la patrona* and her friend. Bring them out. Find horses for them. Take them away.'

'I know where stand the horses on which they were brought here. I will see that *la patrona* and her friend go safely.'

'If either of those horses are not so good as the horse of that man I killed in the cañon, or the horse of this one, bring the best of the four. For presently Don Oscar will have no need for a horse. Go. Get the girls out of the house.'

He prodded Oscar farther away from the door.

'Now, listen, Lance!' Oscar said in angry voice. 'Don't play the damn' fool. I don't know what crazy idea you're nursing, but those girls are in the house because they were caught on the Zemel place and carried off—by men of Jake Hopper! A man of mine saw that they were being taken toward the *bosque*. He rescued them; brought them here because I was here for the night and—here they are! They'll

120

tell you the same thing. And when I saw you in the room a while ago, without recognizing you, naturally I took a shot at you. I—'

'I know all about everything,' Lance checked him tonelessly. 'I don't need to hear Lucy and Nancy tell what they *think* happened. Be still! Be very damned still! If you open your mouth again, before they're gone, I'll let this hammer drop and cut you in two.'

The girls came through the door, almost running. And Lucy's voice rose angrily:

'Lance Craig! What are you doing to Oscar? What do you—'

'He's playing the fool!' Oscar cried desperately. 'Accusing me of kidnaping you. He'll kill me if you don't—'

Lance let the hammer of his Colt down— gently. He whipped it up and sideways to Oscar's temple. With Oscar's groan and the thud of his falling body, Nancy Oakes screamed. Lucy ran toward the sound; caught Lance's arm furiously:

'If you hurt him, I'll personally see that you suffer for it! You stay away for years, when you ought to be here; then you come back and try to lord it over those who *have* worked and those who helped; you—'

'Arminio!' Lance called flatly. 'I told you to take them away. Come take them to the horses.'

'Lance!' Lucy said in altered tone. 'Listen to me, now! We were caught on Johann Zemel's

121

place, by men of Jake Hopper's. One of Oscar's men—'

'There's no such man as Jake Hopper—alive! Ramon Razo killed Hopper before he'd done a thing in Mesquite County. It was Oscar Nall who killed the *Jefe* and your father and stole the C Bar blind. He used Hopper's name as a blind—'

'You're crazy! Absolutely crazy! And you can't touch Oscar without paying for it! You—'

'She's right, Lance!' Nancy Oakes said shakily, running to stand at Lucy's side. 'A man of Oscar's saved us. Lance! Listen to us! You're wrong about Oscar—all wrong. You—'

'Take them away, Arminio!' Lance ordered the *vaquero* inexorably. 'By the arms, if you have to.'

'You're going to kill Oscar?' Lucy whispered. 'Murder him? If you do, Lance Craig, I'll never rest until you hang!'

Arminio's hands closed upon their arms. He pushed them forward, struggling to turn back on Lance, Lucy crying over and over again that she would see Lance hanged.

When they were gone Lance bent to catch Oscar by an arm and drag him into the house. He hardly thought of Lucy. What was in his mind was the grim fact that, within five minutes, one or the other of them would be dead.

There was an old table, rough, very rickety, in a corner. He brought this out to the center of the room, opposite the hearth on which the fire still blazed. Upon it he put his Colt and Oscar's, setting them a foot apart, parallel in position, butts reversed. Oscar stirred and groaned and Lance went to stare down at him fixedly. He stirred Oscar contemptuously with a boot toe.

'I'm going to give you a chance to kill me,' he said evenly. 'I think I'm going to kill you. But I'm going to give you the chance you didn't give my father or Orval Kane.'

'I didn't kill them! I swear—'

'I know you killed them. Don't bother to lie. It won't get you an extra second of living. You killed them. You rodded the gang that stole stock all around. Now, it's payday!'

'I'll make it up to you! I'll clear the C Bar mortgage. I'll give you what the place would have earned. I didn't tell the boys to kill them. I—'

'Your gun and mine are on the table. We'll take opposite sides. When I give the word we'll reach and start shooting. Only one of us lives!'

CHAPTER ELEVEN

'SOME FOOLS I LIKE!'

Oscar propped himself to a sitting position, then got unsteadily to his feet and stood, swaying, mouth gaping, smooth face ash-colored. His jetty eyes, which Lance had always seen so level, fixed in stare, were rolling wildly, now. Lance got tobacco and papers from a pocket and rolled a cigarette almost without knowing what he did. He lighted it and drew in smoke, watching Oscar. He blew a thin cloud out, inhaled again, and flipped the cigarette away.

He went to the table and stood behind his gun. Trail's end ... For one—perhaps for both—this was the end of a hatred that had begun when they were six or seven.

'Come on!' he said shortly. 'Come stand behind your gun. Come on, I said! All your life you've talked—lied—yourself out of tight places. But this is the real quill, and you might as well realize it. Whining will get you nowhere. Come over here or I'll kill you where you stand! I'm giving you as good a chance as I've got!'

With the lagging feet of a man climbing gallows steps, Oscar came to the table. He looked once into Lance's face, then his eyes went to the guns.

'When I say—' Lance began.

Oscar's hand darted to his Colt; snatched it up cocked. Lance punched him with left hand, sending him backward while he clawed at his own gun. Oscar fired and the slug burned across Lance's neck. He fired again and there was a searing pain in Lance's side. But he leaned a little across the table and drove two slugs into the taller man, one into the body, the second into the face. He sent the table over with a crash and rushed at Oscar, who was toppling, sagging, at the same time. He kicked the dropped Colt into a corner of the room and looked down at the moveless figure.

How long he waited he had no idea. Oscar Nall was dead—that was the important thing. Oscar Nall was dead. Jake Hopper had died twice, once in Tenedor, again tonight, here. He and Oscar seemed to be alone in an enormous space. The walls of the room were far away. So was the shrill voice that cried:

'You did murder him! You did! And you'll hang!'

He turned slowly. Lucy and Nancy were in the doorway. He shook his head to clear away the faint haze before his eyes. Mechanically, he began to move toward them. They vanished from the door so quickly that for an instant he believed he had been mistaken; that they had not really been there. Then Arminio sprang into the room.

'*Patron!* You must hurry! Men are coming

125

across the flat toward the cañon. The sheriff and his killers, I think. *La patrona*—do not blame me, *Don Lancito*. She rode so quietly, turned so quickly, rode back so fast—But you must hurry—'

'Hurry to be hung!' a thick, savage voice said, from a window. 'Stick 'em up, Craig! We got a rope for you!'

Slowly, Lance turned to face that window. The tow head of Homer Ripps was there. The deputy's pale, cold eyes were shining. He held a pistol on the stone sill and his mouth was drawn up in one-sided grin.

'Yeh, got a rope you can stretch,' Ripps said slowly. 'But, on the other hand, I owe you one, personal. And ropes cost money. So—'

His head jerked. His chin struck the sill. The Colt in his hand made roaring sound in the room but the slug thudded into the dirt floor. Then the gun dropped. Again his head jerked and he came in a froglike dive over the sill to sprawl on the floor. Tom Ziler's face was framed in the space between sack and stone.

'He's quite a talker,' Tom grunted. 'Thanks be!'

He clambered into the room and stood looking about.

'Why—that's Nall!' he said.

'As much Jake Hopper as Oscar Nall,' Lance told him wearily. 'Hopper was killed within a week of landing in Tenedor. Killed by Ramon Razo. Is Ripps, there, dead?'

126

'Just knocked cold. I bent my gun around his skull. There's a bunch of visitors coming, Lance. What about it?'

Lance stared from Nall to Ripps.

'Lucy Kane and Nancy Oakes will swear that I murdered Nall in cold blood; that he was rescuing them. Ripps will swear to the same thing—'

'Thin chance you'll have of hearing 'em testify,' Tom said grimly, 'if Ull Varner and that shooting posse of his corners us here. They won't even ask us do we want to give in. They'll just buttonhole us.'

'I know a lot,' Lance told him slowly. 'I know that Oscar was all I suspected he was—and more! But I can't prove it! I can't even prove that he shot at me before I shot at him; that I gave him the chance of a duel and he ran true to form even then—cheated; grabbed up his gun first. I can't stay here, Tom. I've got to run.'

'You certainly was a damn' fool to hand him the chance to kill you. But—some fools I like! If you want a *compañero* on the road to Mexico, I'm your hairpin!'

Lance nodded. He had to go. He could never prove Oscar Nall's direction of Mesquite's thieves, his clever murder of any who stood in his way. Stay here, and he would be rail-roaded to penitentiary or gallows by Lucy's testimony, Nancy's testimony, the lies of Homer Ripps—whom he could not kill, now. He had to go.

'And the bank will foreclose on the C Bar,' he said drearily. 'Lucy will be broke, same as I'll be.'

'Maybe not,' Tom drawled. 'After I got separated from you and had to skip around, I got pretty close to town again. And a notion popped into my head. I rode right fast and quiet into town and found Nall's house and—got inside. I'm right good at that ... I looked it over. I'm good at that, too ... There was a hole in the bedroom wall under a picture and a sizable iron box in the hole. I brought the box outside of town and opened her up. I'm—more'n tol'able, at that ... I have got enough to lift that C Bar mortgage and leave some over. You can send it back to—oh, Judge Oakes—'

Lance stared, then shrugged.

'I'll take it! Because of Lucy. Arminio! Will you ride into town, taking this money to Judge Oakes? Saying only that it came from me and is to be used for *la patrona's* benefit? Then, until these matters quieten and I can come again to the C Bar, stay close to her, guarding her, working with the men who will come from Socrates Morrill—'

'I will take the money into town. I will stay beside her—and I will tell her the truth of tonight's affair,' the boy promised earnestly. 'And you will come soon? Where will you go, first?'

'To Campoblanco. It is well to the side of Tenedor. It has the name of hardness, a *plazita*

128

where men ask no questions one of another. *Sí!* I will go to Campoblanco. From there I will keep watch and when I can come back to the C Bar—listen for the hoofs of my horse!'

Homer Ripps stirred and groaned. Arminio went over to him, grinning. He picked up Ripps's pistol and struck him deftly with the barrel. Ripps lay still again.

Tom crossed to the door and went out. Arminio, with a grunted word, followed. Lance stood waiting until Tom came in with a canvas bag that jingled and rustled. They heard the hoofs of walking horses outside. Arminio called and they went out to him. He put the canvas sack in an *alforja* and they mounted.

'Remember! Watch over *la patrona*,' Lance said.

'I will remember. I will watch. And—I will talk!'

'Too damn' much talk!' Tom grunted. 'Let's hightail.'

They got out of the cañon quietly and on the flat turned toward the south, going at the walk. The hoofbeats of trotting horses carried to them through the darkness. Tom laughed softly.

'I'd like to see Ull Varner's face, when he looks at that house! And—Ripps's face, when Varner works it over.'

They rode steadily through the night, up and down slopes, in and out of arroyos, until the *bosque* swallowed them. By winding stock-

129

trails they made the Bravo and splashed across.

'Campoblanco...' Tom said to the silent Lance. 'I've heard considerable about the place. Now that we're safe on the safe side of that creek—Ever hear of Fine Upham? Used to be quite a train-robber, after he quit being a young, foolish cowboy that got into his first stick-up when he was drunk. Used to have a li'l' bunch of his own. Then that bunch got killed off and this Fine Upham, he was shot up so complete that it disencouraged him. Yes, sir! He decided to cut out the robbing business. But when this Fine Upham got outside Oscar Nall's house, and inside the house, and looked at that iron box—I was kind of glad, Lance, I'd learned some things.'

'And so am I, Fine!' Lance said sincerely. 'The robber robbed ... Thanks! Thanks a lot. One of these days this trouble will blow over. The C Bar's out of debt, thanks to you. I can go back; take it over. Campoblanco's only a hundred miles or so. Close enough to let me keep an eye on Mesquite. We'll go back, *viejo amigo*. We'll go back together.'

'Right now'—Fine Upham was yawning— 'where I want to go is into my hot roll. I'll split a pint with you—I found it where I found the iron box. Then turn in.'

They found a sheltered arroyo and when the horses were unsaddled and picketed they drank the whisky and smoked, lying comfortably on their blankets. Fine laughed suddenly and flipped away the stub of his cigarette.

'I was just thinking,' he said. 'What I told you in the old house—about being a damn' fool. That makes two of us.'

'Right back at you,' Lance told him. 'Some folks *I* like, too. Well—Campoblanco about day after tomorrow.'

CHAPTER TWELVE

'HE'S AN OLD WOLF'

Campoblanco accepted the two strange Anglos without show of interest. In the ragged street, the two stores, the *cantina*, Campoblanco folk spoke briefly and courteously when addressed, but made no attempt to begin conversation.

'And that suits me down to the grass,' Lance told Fine, as they explored the *plazita*. 'What I need, right now, is a chance for my second wind. I'm pleased to think that my unfinished business is all ahead of me. Let's go sit in the Early Moon, *amigo*. That Ofelia in there represents the most important thing in sight. She and the drinks. How's about it with you?'

'Fine! Like I told you, I was taking one of them vacation things when I hit Mesquite. Retired from crooked trails. I was plumb decided not to rob trains and banks and things, never no more. What with this and that—Rangers, specially—that kind of work didn't look so good. Maybe my heart wasn't ever really in the robbing. Sometimes, I thought that.'

They went into One-Eye Villa's Early Moon *cantina* and sat at a corner table. Fine looked seriously at Lance.

'Hell, though! The way you're a road-runner. I hate to think of you being down on the reward notices for murder.'

He shifted his stocky figure in the rough chair and Lance regarded him affectionately. Cowboy every inch of him, he was 'one to ride the river with,' this dark efficient. Now, he waved at 'Ofelia' and the pretty Mexican girl hurried toward the table with flashing smile. Fine looked past her and grinned.

'Comes that-there tintyper again,' he said. 'That "Jerky" Xavier. And if he ain't the biggest bundle of mixed-up and assorted scares ever I put eyes on! Scared of Mexicans. Scared of Mexico. Scared of being killed. Scared of dying in the porehouse. Scared of—well, if there's ary thing he's not scared of, he just neglected and forgot to tell me about it, while he was trying to take my tintype or fix me with spec's or pull one of my teeth.'

'His name's not really "Jerky," of course,' Lance said lazily. 'It's Xerxes. I read about him in a book, years and years ago, when I was a

132

tender li'l' innocent with long, curly yellow hair. The Old Original, I mean, not our dentist-spectacle peddler-tintyper yonder. That one was a Persian king, and he held forth maybe twenty-five hundred years ago.'

'Now that I take another look at our tintyper, I can see he's not that old,' Fine conceded. 'But if he's so scared, what's he doing on this side the River? Campoblanco's supposed to be right salty. That's all right for you and me; we probably can hold up our end and maybe kick the middle while we're doing it. But the likes of him—'

The wandering photographer-optician-dentist was short and fat and amazingly red of face. Evidently, he had set up headquarters in the Early Moon, after a day of inspecting Campoblanco. Shabby camera and tripod were beside a box of cheap spectacles and an old-fashioned dentist's foot drill. Xavier was talking animatedly to three *vaqueros* and one nodded and produced silver. Xavier took the money and turned to his camera. Lance and Fine watched while 'Ofelia' brought drinks to them.

Then Lance's thoughts drifted, back across the miles to Mesquite. Half-owner of the C Bar though he was, he could not set foot in Texas without danger of being recognized, arrested.

'I'm a wolf and nothing but a wolf. That range is barred to me. And yet—I don't see how I could have done anything but what I did do. A man plays the cards dealt him—'

A stranger came slowly, quietly, through the street door, an incredibly tall and gaunt man, a cowman, a Texan, by the look of him. He was elderly, somewhere in middle fifties. His skin was tanned like leather. And there was a sweaty streak across his overalls to tell the practiced eye of a sagging shell belt just taken off. There was also a bulge under his shirt to tell where he had pushed that pistol into his waistband. He looked around the room with fierce, steady eyes.

'There's somebody!' Fine breathed. 'I bet you he's an old wolf and his teeth ain't wore down much either.'

The tall man came farther into the room and seemed to study the line of Mexicans at the bar. Then he crossed to a corner table at rocking horseman's gait and sat down. There was a hard-faced and taciturn cowboy among the Mexicans before One-Eye Villa's bar. Except Xavier, this towhead was the only Anglo Lance and Fine had seen in Campoblanco, and he only grunted when spoken to. His name was Ron Oberman. So much Fine had learned from Xavier.

'I'm wondering if Oberman knows the stranger,' Lance said underbreath, 'or if he just sees something interesting about him. He's kept his eyes on us, but he's really staring at the old boy.'

Oberman suddenly blanked his face and

reached for his drink. Xavier came over to Lance and Fine.

'I swear,' he complained, 'it just ain't worth the time I take to talk these folks into toothing or tintypes or spec's. They beat me down on the price, and I can't even start to say something without they put their hands on their knives or their pistols and they git me so shaky I just about give 'em whatever they want. And if I *was* to make a couple honest dollars, likely I'd have my throat cut on the way back to Texas. I never claimed to be terrible brave. And if I had guessed what kind of country this is, I never would've crossed over.'

'Why don't you go back, then?' Lance grunted, without interest. He was watching the hard-faced Oberman. 'Road's supposed to be open north and south.'

'Because I ain't cleared a penny, yet. I'm a nervous man, like I said. And these people make me nervouser. But I ain't cleared a thing and I got to eat.'

Five Mexicans, very colorful in *charro* jackets, wide-bottomed *pantalones*, and embroidered sombreros, came from the street and Xavier looked hopefully their way. The slender, youthful figure in the lead was more ornately dressed than his followers. More of silver embroidery was on his sombrero and jacket; his sash was wider; tiny bells tinkled on his spurs. All of the group were armed, but this youngster had twin pearl-handled pistols thrust into his sash, and handily across his arm was a neat Winchester carbine.

'Look at the Old Wolf!' Fine whispered tensely. 'That's what he was looking for. That bunch.'

As Lance turned slightly to look, the tall man came wolfishly to his feet. There was a pistol in his hand, pointing at the Mexicans.

'Candelario!' the man yelled savagely. 'The Devil reaches for you, Candelario! This is for Donovan, *El Toro*—for the Hacienda Gerónimo. I, Lee the *mayordomo*, say it!'

He began shooting. But, if he were the wolf Fine Upham had called him, the slender Candelario was a cat—and now moved like one. He twisted and lifted the carbine almost with the first sound of Lee's yell. The Winchester report blended with the shot Lee sent at him.

Fine and Lance were under their table—and with Colts forethoughtfully drawn. Ron Oberman, too, had dropped to the floor. Where Xavier the nervous had gone, Lance had no idea. The tintyper had seemed to vanish into thin air, with the first yell from Lee. The *cantina* had exploded into pandemonium. Men were yelling, Candelario's followers were shooting, drinkers were jumping the bar or running for the doors.

Lance saw dust jump from Lee's faded denim jumper. But Candelario sprawled on the floor with arms outflung. So did another of the group behind him. From over the bar men fired at Lee. Then a slug banged the table over Lance's head. A stray shot, he counted it. But when lead began to hammer the floor on each side of the table and he had a flashing glimpse of a dark face above a pistol he raised his own Colt. For that pistol was pointed at him and Fine and at nobody else.

'They're after us, too!' he yelled. 'Let's take cards. Back old Lee. They'll rub us out anyway!'

He drove two shots at the man who fired at them. Face and pistol disappeared. But others were shooting their way. Lance looked sidelong at Old Lee and found him down across his table, only his hand lifted, clicking his empty gun. He slid to the floor and Lance went on hands and knees across to him. Fine came after Lance. A yell carried from Oberman:

'A' right! I'll play with y' all!'

Lance squatted beside Lee. He heard Fine and Oberman shooting. Lee was hit in arm and thigh and there was blood on his lean neck. He swallowed noisily.

'If—if I had a loaded gun—'

'Cover us!' Lance yelled generally to Fine and Oberman. 'I'll pack him! Through the window!'

He picked up the gaunt figure bodily and trotted to the square opening on his left. He shoved Lee out and fairly dived after him, careless of how or where he landed. For there was the *thut-thut* of shots on the wall about him, and it seemed impossible that none had struck him. He scrambled to his feet and ran, leaving Lee on the ground. For his horse and Fine's were in the brush-roofed shed twenty yards behind the *cantina*. And their Winchesters were on the saddles.

He snatched his carbine from hanging saddle and whirled back toward the *cantina*. Fine and Oberman were outside now. Fine turned to shoot through a window from an angle that sheltered him.

'Bring Lee!' Lance yelled. 'Bring him on out. I'll cover you. Here they come!'

Men crowded the back door but gave back under the lead he rained around them. Fine and Oberman caught up Lee between them and trotted toward the shed. Lance stepped to the side and continued to shoot at the door and at the corners. When his carbine was empty he got Fine's.

'Take care of the saddling!' he called.

'Take care of the shooting, then!' Oberman answered grimly. 'And we'll be leaving town!'

CHAPTER THIRTEEN

'OUR SCARED TINTYPER!'

But 'leaving town' was not so simple! Campoblanco men were spreading out, now, moving from the Early Moon to houses on right and left of the shed. They encountered scattering fire before—with Fine and Oberman supporting Lee on his horse between them— they had galloped forty yards.

There seemed to be an efficient skirmish line between them and the rugged hills which walled in that side of Campoblanco. It was getting hot in the *plazita* for four Anglos, and—Lance thought grimly—there was good chance that it would be still hotter.

He looked fiercely left and right, hunting a path that might take them out of the line of fire. But wherever he turned there was shooting. Then, from the flat roof of a house, a heavy rifle sounded. Instinctively, he placed it as a .45-70 or .45–90—and he knew the size of the hole one of those big slugs made in a man.

But, as instinctively he hunched in the saddle, expecting to feel the numbing impact of the bullet, Fine twisted a little and yelled at him. And he saw a Mexican in the open drop as if hit with an axe. Two others ran for shelter.

'Why—why, it's Jerky!' Fine yelled. 'Our

scared tintyper! On that roof!'

Then, with a drumming of hoofs, a man galloped up behind him. Lance had never seen him before, this slim youngster, smooth of face, wobbling awkwardly in the silver-trimmed saddle cinched to a big and nervous black. He had a rifle in his left hand, a pistol in his right. He grinned excitedly.

'Go ahead!' he yelled. 'I'm with you! We can ride right through 'em!'

And they went hellbent through the last thin line of the opposition. There was no opportunity to more closely inspect this stranger of apparent friendliness. Out of Campoblanco they galloped, up the first slope of the Blanco Hills. On a level patch of trail they drew in to let the horses breathe and to look almost dazedly at one another.

'My name's Downes,' the youngster told them cheerfully. 'Tommy Downes, from Laredo.'

'Laredo?' Fine drawled, rubbing a burned arm. 'If you're a Laredo man—'

'Laredo last,' Tommy Downes admitted. His quick grin flashed. 'Originally from Newark. New Jersey, you know.'

'I didn't. But—you certainly wandered along when we looked like needing friends— and boiler-plated pants and li'l' things like that. So we're glad to meet you, Tommy. How's the old man, Lance? Bet he's got a bootful of blood.'

He leaned to get a pint of whisky from his saddlebag and draw the cork. Lance took the bottle and put it to Lee's mouth. Lee drank and drew a long, painful breath.

'I—I'll be all right. I shorely thank you boys for gitting me out of the Early Moon. Looked like it was all up for a while. Got something you can kind of tie me up with? I—got to find somebody.'

'We can take time to fix him up,' Lance decided. 'Right here, we could stand off a young army.'

They let him sprawl on the ground and Lance got the remnant of a clean white shirt from his *alforjas*. The bullets had gone clean through Lee's arm and thigh, missing arteries. He had lost much blood, but Lance thought he was not in danger. The wound in his neck was no more than a graze.

'Well!' Lee grunted, when he was bandaged. 'One more jolt of that red-eye and I'll be set. Been one of you young sprouts, likely you'd be dead by now. But the kind of Texas, me, I come out of, a fella figured to die in bed when he was two hund'd just because he was tired of the same old things. I'll be all right in a day or two.'

Fine gave him the whisky and eyed him curiously.

'What was the idee in taking on that whole Candelario bunch? You know, you look like and you act like a reckless hairpin. You damn' near got the whole bunch of us killed. When that crowd started shooting it did look like you made 'em peevish and they aimed to wipe out every *gringo* in sight.'

Lee tilted the bottle and made gurgling noises. He said '*ha!*' in a satisfied tone and motioned toward his horse, a tall roan with plain narrow-fork saddle and one-ear bridle.

'If you'll set me into my kak, now, I'll be good for riding,' he said calmly—and evasively, Lance thought, watching the grim face intently. 'Hope I see you all again—'

Ron Oberman moved on the outskirts of the group. He stood with thumbs hooked in the belt of his leggings, head on one side, hard face softened by mocking grin.

'You damned old billygoat!' he said without preface. 'You nitwitted old *macho!* You never did have two thoughts above ary old gray goose my grandma raised. You ain't learned a thing in the six years since I rode for Gerónimo. Maybe you can fool these men, strangers, but you can't fool me! I know how-come you tied into Candelario: He was Luis Sebas's *mandador*. He—'

'Shut up!' Lee snarled at the cowboy. 'Which you waggle that horse-collar mouth of yours the same as always—too much! You mind your own business, if you got any. You—help me up onto that hawse and—'

'Campoblanco's turning out like a nest of hornets,' Tommy Downes announced, his young, smooth face split by a pleased grin. 'If

142

they catch up with us we're going to have fun.'

Lance looked down the slope. Some twenty or thirty riders made a ragged column on their trail and, as Tommy Downes had said, they were riding fast.

'Listen, Lee,' he grunted. 'I don't know a thing about your affairs and, if you don't want to talk about 'em, that's all right. But we've got to hightail. And you're in no shape to be riding alone, no matter what you think. You're pretty badly shot up. After a while you're going to be a sick man. I don't see any point to yanking you out of Campoblanco and leaving you here to die on the trail or get killed over again.'

'Looks like you're right,' Lee admitted. 'Le's go!'

They mounted him gently and his leathery face was expressionless. But a white line on each side of his grim mouth told of the pain he bore.

'Who would that be—special—chasing us?' Fine asked Ron Oberman. 'Some of Candelario's friends?'

'Maybe Pancho Nasco,' Oberman hazarded, with side-glance at Lee. 'Nasco's a good friend of Luis Sebas's—and he's a colonel in the army . . .'

Lance looked at Fine and shrugged. It was all quite complicated. He had no idea concerning the extent of Oberman's knowledge. But that the cowboy knew all about Lee and the Hacienda Gerónimo there was no doubting. However, he thought the important matter of the moment was getting away from the men of Campoblanco, no matter who they might be, or what their reason for chasing Candelario's killer.

They pushed on fast into the hills, with Oberman slipping naturally into the lead. They followed him into arroyos and out again, twisting and turning over rocky soil that would hardly hold a trail. At last he pulled in his horse on the crest of a high divide and reached for tobacco and papers.

'Not much chance of 'em following up to here,' he said. 'If that's Colonel Nasco, *he* knows how easy it is to walk into Serious Trouble in these hills. Hey, Quintus Lee?'

Lee was swaying in the saddle. His face was white under the tan of years. He nodded wearily with the question. Then, from somewhere below them in the welter of cross-arroyos, there came a shrill wolf-howl, repeated again and again.

'It's the Kid—Dolores,' Lee muttered. 'But, how she knowed where to find me—'

'Dolores!' Oberman cried. 'Why—she was in school, in San Antonio! What's she doing down here? I knowed about Bull Donovan being killed, but—'

'She brought me down. Brought down Glenn Winters and Vane Warren. Onliest old Gerónimo hands we could locate when she got this notion. It was Luis Sebas—and

144

Candelario that was his range boss—that murdered Bull Donovan and run off the hands and grabbed the place. Dolores wouldn't stay in school after she heard about it. I was in Texas buying bulls when it happened. She hunted me up, month or so back. She had some diamonds and things and she sold 'em and brought us down to hit Sebas. She says she'll take back Gerónimo or she'll die. My notion is, she'll die.'

'And how long have you four plumb nitwits been down here?' Oberman demanded, staring.

'Couple weeks. And we hit Sebas some! But he's got too much money, too many hands, too much pull with the *políticos*. They been running us to a frazzle. So, when I heard about Candelario going to Campoblanco today, I sneaked off from Dolores and went in to kill Candelario. And yonder's Dolores, with Glenn Winters and Vane Warren.'

Lance watched the slim, boyish figure, coming on the chestnut gelding, followed by a very tall man, a very short man. He found himself much interested in this girl from a San Antonio school, whose experience so oddly paralleled his own, a girl who had enough iron in her to send her riding the blood trail.

Dolores Donovan pulled in on the ridge and stared. She was vividly pretty, dark of hair and eyes, with olive skin and full-lipped, determined mouth. Her clothing was as disreputable as that of Winters and Warren, who sat grimly with Winchesters across their laps. She wore an old Stetson and waist overalls jammed hit-or-miss into puncher boots. A shell belt was about her slender waist, holding up a man size Colt .44. The only feminine note about her was the beaded Cheyenne vest she wore in lieu of coat—out of a pocket of which dangled the tag of a tobacco sack.

From face to face she looked quickly, then spurred over to face Quintus Lee with narrowed, troubled eyes.

'Quint, you old reprobate!' she cried. 'You haven't ever gone and got yourself shot, now? I *knew* you were up to something when you disappeared. But—what is this? Convention?'

'These boys—was in One-Eye Villa's—when the fireworks started with Candelario,' Lee said painfully. 'They—took up for me—saved my bacon—and—'

Oberman caught him as he fainted; held him easily.

'The old sidewinder! I swear, Dolores, if you ain't got the blamedest bunch of nitwits with you! Quint killed Candelario. Tried to take on the whole town. And if it ain't Glenn Winters and Vane Warren. Found 'em in the Old Cowboys' Home, I bet you. I knew it was them when I heard their old bones a-creaking on the hill. Ah, me! Come on, you two; gi' us a lift with Quint. He's bad-shot, Dolores; arm and leg, both. We got to put him somewhere to get over it. Question is: Where?'

For all her bold appearance, Lance saw something like hopelessness come into the girl's face, and he realized how young she really was.

'You're right,' she told Oberman. 'We've got to get Quint somewhere. But—where can we take him? We've lived like so many scared wolves for a week, with Luis Sebas's hands harrying us up and down. We haven't had a night's sleep. We've been chased away from our fire when we tried to cook a strip of beef. We—I don't know where to put Quint, to keep Sebas's men from finding and finishing the job.'

'Over the River,' Oberman suggested. 'You bit off a lot, Dolores. I know about Bull; and how Sebas finally glommed onto the Gerónimo. I *sabe* how you feel; how you want to hit him midway between mind and mouth. But it looks more'n you can handle. Now, I'll put my marbles with yours; throw in with Glenn and Vane. We can make the River and cross it—'

'I won't!' she stopped him fiercely. 'I came over to jar Luis Sebas loose from Gerónimo. I'll stay until I do that little thing or—or get rubbed out trying. But one way or another I'll take care of Quint.'

'Miss Donovan!' Tommy Downes broke in eagerly. 'I don't know anything about this holy war between you and Luis Sebas, except what I've picked up today. But I'd like to enlist under the Gerónimo flag. I'm Tommy Downes from Faraway and Effete New Jersey. I haven't got a thing to do with my life except see that it interests me. I'd like to ride with you!'

She studied him, then shook her head.

'You'd just get killed. I can't have that on my hands.'

'But I came across into Mexico looking for fun!'

'I reckon I'm a Gerónimo man again,' Ron Oberman drawled. 'And if I do get killed, it's no more'n I've expected time and again. Anyhow, I'm riding with you. Because of Bull.'

CHAPTER FOURTEEN

'WE'RE GERÓNIMO'S ARMY'

Lance looked at Tommy Downes's stubborn face, then at Dolores, and last of all at Fine Upham. Fine grinned.

'Go ahead! Say it! Us, too.'

'I think we're all your recruits,' Lance told her slowly. 'I'm Lance Craig; this is Fine Upham. Probably we won't have to tell you that we're Texas men. We are footloose and fancy free, right now. And we're in just as hot water with the Campoblanco crowd as if we

148

owned Gerónimo. Too, this Luis Sebas sounds like the kind of gunie I like to land on. And I ought to know how you feel. Pretty much the same thing happened to me in Texas, but in a smoother way. And that's why I'm in Mexico now. We'll side you!'

'But—but Lord only knows when I can pay—if ever!' she said brokenly. 'I sold my jewelry to get grub and horses and shells for this raid. There's almost nothing left. We've been beefing Gerónimo steers, between licks at Sebas.'

'We'll take our chances! Fine and I aren't quite broke. But we'd better settle about Lee. He needs doctoring; needs nursing. We'd better see to that, then take on Sebas.'

'Tecolote,' the tall, grim Glenn Winters grunted. He had only looked with little jetty eyes from one to the other. 'The Old Owl'll take Quint in. And his woman's a good nurse.'

'Tecolote!' Dolores agreed. 'Of course! I never thought of him. But that's the answer. Nobody will ever find Quint in the Hermanas Hills. But, how'll we get him up there?'

'Well,' Fine said judically, 'from the way he acted a while back, my bet is if I uncork this whisky and wave it before him, he'll rise right up and follow me any reasonable distance. Up to forty miles, say.'

'It's nearly twenty miles,' she remarked frowningly. 'But if we bolster him up with it and one rides on each side—'

They dribbled whisky down Quintus Lee's throat, and when he opened his eyes asked if he could ride to Las Hermanas, the Sisters. He grew angry at the question. He could ride indefinitely. So they hoisted him into the saddle again and for the rest of the afternoon, the forepart of the night, they went at the walk, taking turns two by two at holding Lee in the saddle. Out of the Blancos and down upon grassy flats and so into the Sisters Hills they went. Dolores and Oberman, Warren and Winters, all rode as by instinct over the trails.

They came in brilliant moonlight to a little tableland, a mesa in the rugged hills. There was a stone cabin on a shelf of the cañon above the mesa. Dolores rode forward and hailed the house. Presently she was answered harshly from a boulder above it. When she gave her name, Tecolote, the Owl, came into the open. He listened to the girl, nodding.

'I was a *vaquero* of Gerónimo before I became crippled and a herder of goats,' he said simply. 'I will tell Maria. She is very good with shot-wounds. We will take my old friend Queent into the house and it will be his house, as it is your house.'

When Lee had been taken inside and the wrinkled old woman had re-dressed his wounds, Tecolote sat with them before a fire in the cañon above the house. He had brought such food as he had, goat meat and *tortillas* and fat, brown beans and coffee. While they ate Lance studied the girl as she talked with the old man.

'We have done a few things,' Dolores told Tecolote. 'We took from the herders of Luis Sebas nearly two hundred of big steers. The *vaqueros* fought and two of them were killed. Then we pushed the steers into the broken country of which you know—and of which Sebas and his thieves know little—well into the western range.'

'And you killed two!' the old man said, leaning forward. His face, Lance thought, was like that of some old Aztec god—the god of battle, at a guess, because of the fierce shine of Tecolote's narrow eyes, the feral twist of thin lips. 'Good! Very good! Luis Sebas will yet learn that it is one thing to steal, another to hold that which is stolen; one thing to kill, quite another to keep from being killed. *Por dios—* yes!'

'This,' Tommy Downes said very softly, touching Lance's arm, 'is *exactly* the kind of thing I came hunting. I don't know how you feel about it, Lance Craig, but I can't think of a place I'd trade this one for.'

He waved his chunk of broiled goat. Lance grunted non-committally and Dolores turned his way.

'Well,' he said evenly, 'we're all Gerónimo men. A little more than that, even—we're Gerónimo's army. I hope we have got quality and lots of it. Because we certainly haven't got quantity. Now, what, exactly, are we going to do? Tomorrow, say? I've listened to you people and I think I've got a rough notion about the layout:

'Luis Sebas is pretty well up in affairs around here. He can even call on the local army officers if he has to, to hit at you—at us. I suppose you own some ideas, besides the general notion about smacking Sebas and his hands wherever and whenever they're found?'

'Not very many,' she confessed. 'You see, I was in a San Antonio school when I heard about father's murder and how the ranch had been taken over by Sebas and that murdering foreman of his—Candelario. All I could think of was getting down here and killing Sebas and Candelario to pay for Bull Donovan's murder; and—somehow—driving the Sebas crew off Gerónimo. So, Quint Lee and Glenn Winters and Vane Warren and I crossed over. We've recovered some steers. We've killed two or three of Sebas's fighting *vaqueros*. Quint killed Candelario and with your help perhaps wiped out two or three others. But—what do you suggest, for tomorrow?'

'Five of us—not counting you...' Lance said slowly.

'Not counting me? Well, count me! Wherever Gerónimo rides these days, I ride! Understand that right now. I'm not going to be held back because I'm a girl. Gerónimo belongs to me—if we can get it back. I'm more

152

involved in this war than anybody else.'

'We can argue all that later on. I think we'd better slide down onto Gerónimo range tomorrow for a look around. Reckon this Colonel Nasco of the army will be down there, helping his friend Sebas?'

'He blame' well might be!' the tall grim Winters grunted, speaking his first word for two hours. 'He's standing in with Sebas. Likely, he gets paid off for backing the grab of Gerónimo. And he's plenty salty, that Nasco!'

'Plenty salty,' Warren, the other Gerónimo hand, agreed. 'They say he ain't no Mexican, a-tall. Spanish. That he used to be in one of them foreign legion spreads across the ocean. Anyhow, he's the best horse-fighter *I* ever see in a Mexican uniform. Keeps his *soldados* right up to the minute. That outfit of his are the real quill.'

'And how many hands would Sebas have— about?' Lance asked generally, of the girl and the two veteran Gerónimo men.

'Twenty, maybe,' Winters hazarded. 'We run the spread with around ten. Reckon Sebas'd double that.'

'And how many soldiers'd Nasco have?' Fine inquired purringly, dark face lighted by the swelling coal of a cigarette.

'Forty-fifty,' Winters answered slowly. 'Maybe a few more or a few less. That's about what he used to have.'

Fine laughed softly and rolled over on

his back.

'Say—sixty,' Lance said cheerfully. 'A dozen to one. Ah, well! Twelve to one's not so bad *if* you can keep 'em out of your back hair. What's so funny, Fine?'

'Don't let Baby Face fool you, Dolores,' Fine drawled, blowing smoke upward. 'What he really *wants* is about a dozen in his back hair, with the chance to reach around and yank 'em out and whack 'em against the ground. I know! I ought to, considering I just sided him in a young war over in Mesquite County and he like to got me killed and kept me scared stiff allatime.'

'Ne' mind "Windy" Upham,' Lance said. 'Does it sound all right, taking a *paseo* down to your range tomorrow and—seeing what we can see?'

A chorus of approving grunts ran around the circle.

'How about shells? You-all got plenty? Fine and I are all right. We brought what we had left from our war.'

'We've got enough to deal misery to Sebas,' Dolores said.

'And I've got enough to stock a young army,' Tommy Downes put in, energetically. Lance noted how the boy watched Dolores fascinatedly—and how she seemed hardly to see him.

'I—I want to thank you,' she said now, moving closer to Lance on the blanket. 'It

154

doesn't seem so hopeless. When I saw old Quint reeling in the saddle and knew that he was out of the war; when I considered that every man lost to Gerónimo was irreplaceable—everything seemed black ahead.'

'We may do a deal of running,' Lance drawled. 'But there's no law against shooting over your shoulder when you do run—and turning around now and then. Don't worry, Dolores. We'll try to make Sebas wish he never had jumped Gerónimo.'

They turned in—Dolores in the house, the rest of them in the cañon. They were up in darkness to eat more goat meat and *tortillas* and drink more inky coffee. Then they saddled and rode down to the flats. When the sun rose Dolores, at Lance's stirrup, made a sweeping gesture.

'Gerónimo! The range runs for miles toward those hazy mountains. Up there in the hills there's a village, Pepita. It's a tough little place but people aren't friendly to Sebas. That's handy to remember, if we're chased! Quint and the boys and I *were* chased, last week. We went through Pepita. A woman, Estrella Morro, runs the place.'

'Funny,' Lance said. 'Never heard of a woman doing that.'

'When you see this one, you'll understand how and why! She's as big and strong as a man. She wears a pistol. Mostly, the men of Pepita keep clear of her.'

'Where's your *casa grande*—your big house? Your line camps? Has Sebas pulled the cattle up closer, since you began hitting at him? Where's the horse herd?'

She described the range in detail and he nodded, placing with cowboy eye the landmarks she cited.

'He can't keep the cattle close to the house,' she finished. 'Not enough pasture. He probably counts on a close guard of the range. Horses are different. They'll be close.'

They rode alertly over the great pastures, stopping before each ridge to look across the range ahead and to left and right. Near noon, Winters pointed to cattle grazing.

CHAPTER FIFTEEN

'IT'S RUN OR DIE!'

The cattle were far away across a flat. Dismounted, the 'Gerónimo army' stared.

'We can handle that bunch, easy,' Winters grunted.

He pointed out the way by which, in two parties, they could move by arroyos toward the cattle and, if men of Sebas were guarding the pasture, take the cowboys from two sides. Winters, Warren, and Dolores seemed naturally to make one group. Tommy Downes looked doubtfully at Lance, then at the girl. He grinned and spurred over to her side. Lance and Fine nodded. Oberman lifted his reins.

'A' right,' he said. 'We'll take this side. Reckon I ain't forgot the old range much.'

He led Lance and Fine by twisting arroyos closer and closer to the grazing cattle. Suddenly, he pulled in. A horse was coming toward them, moving at the walk. Then—as if the rider had heard them—the hoofbeats stopped. They sat very still. The horse began to walk again—away from them.

'I—wonder!' Lance breathed. 'Ah, like that!'

For that unseen horse up the arroyo was jumped suddenly into a pounding gallop. There came the heavy report of a rifle.

'Got to git him!' Oberman grunted. 'He'll have a bunch down on us, he ever makes the next line camp.'

They spurred hell-for-leather down the arroyo and saw the *vaquero* just vanishing around a turn of the dry watercourse. He rode low over the big horn of his saddle, arm rising and falling as he quirted the stubby pony he rode.

'Le' me!' Fine grunted. He roweled his horse and jumped into the lead. 'Le' me have one shot at him!'

The others pulled in a little. Fine increased his speed. The *vaquero* was not so far in the lead, now. He looked back and Lance had a glimpse of dark face split by snarling teeth. Then the man whirled his pony and sent it scuttering up a sloping place in the arroyo-wall. Fine jerked his horse back on its tail, lifted his carbine, and fired rapidly. Pony and man came in a backward somersault down into the arroyo. The pony got to its feet and trotted off, limping. The man lay still where he had dropped.

'Gashed him, that's all,' Fine announced, when he had swung down to stoop over the *vaquero*. 'Now, I reckon we better take a look for his friends. We—Listen!'

From the direction in which the others should have turned, there was firing. They left the *vaquero* with his creased scalp and went out of the arroyo by the trail he had essayed. Far across the pasture three men were riding, coming straight their way. Behind them in a thin skirmish line were Warren and Dolores, Winters and Tommy Downes, riding like Indians with rifles or carbines waving overhead.

'Why, *we* can take cards in this,' Oberman said with a slow grin. 'Reckon if we could just git Sebas's bunch headed out on a straightway, where there wasn't no help for 'em, we could about run 'em clean out of Mexico!'

When the Sebas men saw the riders pop up before them, they whirled off to right and left, quirting, spurring. From Winter's party came more shots. A Sebas horse went down. The man threw himself clear and sprawled on his belly, shooting. Fine Upham loosed a volley, but all the others were shooting, now. It was impossible to say whose bullets hit which man.

Down in a huddle went horses and men. Hoofs lifted and thrashed; men jumped up and cleared themselves of that death tangle. From two sides the yelling Gerónimo warriors closed in upon Sebas's killers.

A *vaquero* came to his knees like a hurt wolf and raised his carbine. With the report of it Tommy Downes's hat jumped on his head. But the boy spurred on and leaned from the saddle to thrust out his long gun as if it had been a pistol. He held it in one hand, shoving it past his horse's head. He fired twice while the *vaquero* continued to shoot at him. Then the man fell back and Tommy's black jumped over him.

That was the end of it. Two of the three *vaqueros* were dead, the third dying. The Gerónimo side drew breath and looked at each other. Dolores was pale, but her red mouth was set hard. Lank Winters made a growling sound in his throat.

'A good lick!' he said grimly. 'I know 'em all. Ever' last one was a picked killer—picked by Candelario. Ever' last one was in on Bull Donovan's murder. A mighty good lick!'

'We dropped one back there before you started shooting,' Lance told him. 'Fine dropped him. Left him. Just gashed. Back in

159

that arroyo.'

Winters lifted fierce, dark face wolfishly and stared in the direction indicated.

'Come on,' he said to Warren drawlingly. 'We'll take a *mira* at him. Nah,' he added, when Lance and Fine began to turn their horses, 'me'n'him is plenty. Rest of you might start them cattle moving. Up toward the old Indian Rock, Ron. You know the pass good's I do.'

He and Warren pushed toward the arroyo. Lance stared cautiously at the girl but she had already turned toward the grazing cattle. Fine met his eyes, looked after the pair riding fast toward the arroyo, and shrugged. They followed the girl. For a hundred yards they rode, then out of the arroyo carried the faint sound of a shot.

'Two shots,' Lance corrected himself. 'Well—it's war! And I reckon Winters and Warren remember some ugly things.'

Dolores continued to stare straight ahead, but it seemed to Lance that her face was paler, even, than when she had looked down at the *vaqueros* dropped in the open. None spoke for a while. Then Dolores waved toward rugged hills.

'When we get this bunch rounded up, we can line 'm out for Indian Rock and the pass,' she told Lance. 'It's not a big bunch. We can handle 'm easily.'

They began to start the cattle forward. They were wild and some broke to left and right, and there was riding to do to keep them headed in one direction. Lance watched mechanically the movement of the others, as Ron Oberman and Tommy Downes, with Winters and Warren, who had come back from killing that *vaquero* in the arroyo, worked in a shrinking half-circle.

Then Dolores rammed in the spurs and dashed after a black bull. She twisted across the flat after it, jumped her horse into an arroyo on its right. But it zigzagged back toward Lance. He was already riding to head it, the tall gray running like a quarter-horse. They crossed two more arroyos before Lance overtook and turned it. He yelled and the bull raced back toward the other cattle. He waved to Dolores—and found her staring under shading hand at something distant.

She jerked her chestnut around and came galloping toward Lance, motioning at something behind her. He plunged that way. Still he could see nothing. But shots—a very volley of them—came from the flat where the cattle were.

'Sebas!' she called. 'His men, anyway! A little army of 'em. They're between us and the others. They—'

A half-dozen riders topped out of one of those arroyos they had crossed. With sight of Lance and Dolores they yelled savagely and began to fire.

'Come on!' Lance commanded the girl. 'We've got to run for it. So do the others have to run.'

'But we can't leave 'm! We've got to get back to 'm!'

'It's run or die!' he assured her. 'They'll run, too.'

She came with him, then, stirrup-to-stirrup, racing before the yelling Mexicans. But both chestnut and gray were tiring, while the horses behind seemed fresh. Steadily, within a half-mile, the Sebas men crept up on them. Lance watched from under his arm. At last, he called to Dolores:

'Keep going! I'll give that bunch something to remember us by! Keep going—around that hill yonder. I'm going to pull in for a couple of shots.'

He spun Gray Eagle around and stopped him; lifted his carbine and fired fast at the ragged approaching column. He could see no hits made, but the Mexicans also pulled in. He whirled the gray and raced after Dolores, riding low in the saddle. He heard the splatter of shots behind him and lead buzzed viciously close, but the Sebas men were no more accurate than he had been.

Dolores waited for him around the shoulder of the little hill. He looked quickly at the place, but it could not be held against a half-dozen rifles. He tried a long shot and knocked a man from the saddle. But the others came on steadily. So he reloaded and Dolores, too, rammed shells into her Winchester. Then they pushed the lagging horses on.

'If we can get a couple of miles farther along, into the hills,' Lance said pantingly, 'we'll have a chance of losing them. If we make out until dark, we're all right.'

They kept ahead, but with decreasing lead, for a mile. Occasionally, Sebas's men tried shots, but without coming near. Then, on the rim of a deep and narrow cañon on the edge of the hills they had set as their goal, the chestnut groaned and staggered. Lance saw blood streaming from the horse's wound. He pushed quickly up beside her and put an arm around her waist.

She cleared her feet and twisted as the chestnut dropped to its knees, to swing behind Lance. But Gray Eagle was only trotting, now. Lance spurred him and looked desperately left and right. He found a pile of boulders.

Bullets went past them. Dolores grunted and flinched. They had still fifty yards to go, to that jumble of rocks. A bullet sang in Lance's ear like a mosquito, burning the lobe. He rowled the gray furiously into a lope. They made the first boulder and dismounted.

Lance stood beside the great rock and drew a long breath. The *vaqueros* had scattered fanwise. He lined his sights on one and drove three shots at the man's belt and saw him hang desperately to the horn of his saddle. Two others jumped from their horses and sheltered themselves behind rock or bush.

Then from behind Lance came the rattle of Dolores's firing. He looked around, over the rim of the cañon and down a hundred feet of almost sheer rock, that had only a few stunted bushes clinging to it here and there, then at the boulders that sheltered them.

'It's a trap,' he thought. 'We can hold 'em off, but we can't get away except by riding straight through their line. Not so good! In fact—*not* so good!'

CHAPTER SIXTEEN

'THE TEXAN LEAVES YOU!'

Dolores called to him presently, while he waited for a shot. She said that those on her side were too well covered to hit.

'Same here,' Lance answered. 'But take a shot or two at the cover, just to discourage their notions.'

She fired three deliberate shots. Lance caught sight of a black spot that moved, beside a bush some fifty yards away. He watched it, saw it move, then fired to the side of it. A man came convulsively to his knees behind that bush. With a second shot Lance knocked him down again.

After that, as the sun slid down the sky, there was quiet for a time. Lance turned toward where the girl stood. He had suddenly remembered how she flinched against him under that hail of lead, as they raced toward this shelter. Now, he saw the red stain on her shirt sleeve, near the armhole of the beaded Cheyenne vest. He looked quickly out again, to where the Indian-patient Mexicans held their cover and—doubtless—waited for darkness. He went over to Dolores.

'Let's see that arm,' he ordered. 'I'd forgot you jumped.'

'It's nothing. Just a nick. I put a bandana around it a while ago,' she objected. 'I wonder if the rest of our bunch got away. They had to ride across the flat ahead of Sebas's men. But they had more chance to see Sebas coming than we did.'

Her mouth tightened and there was trouble in her eyes.

'I—I never should have done it,' she told him in a low voice. 'Tried this attack on Sebas, I mean. I had no right to drag Quint and Glenn and Vane—and now you and Fine Upham and Ron and that nice tenderfoot, Tommy—into my private troubles. We haven't got a chance, here, you and I. For me, that's no more than fair—in a way. But I've pulled *you* into this place. As soon as it's dark, they'll crawl up and—no matter if we do kill some—'

'Ho!' Lance stopped her, grinning. 'You didn't pull Fine and Tommy and Ron and me into anything. It was just our dispositions that

165

did the work. No more did you drag Quintus Lee and the other old Gerónimo men. No ... There's just something about a blame' cowboy that makes him do the things he does. I tell you, I know; I've studied the animal. Before I went off to be a sailor, some seven years back, I had plenty of Cowology in my schooling. A cowboy works for his spread and he fights for it. If he gets licked and run off the ground, the way your men did, all he wants is a chance to wipe off the blood and come back fighting some more.'

'But you and Fine and Tommy—and Ron, too, for he quit us years ago—what about you? *You* hadn't been run off Gerónimo.'

'I tell you, it was our meddlesome and quarrelsome dispositions. That is, in my case and Fine's. Tommy is having the time of his young life. He bought himself a Buffalo Bill suit and came out West to fight Indians. He came on across to Mexico hunting excitement. All right, he's getting it. If he gets killed, he'll die happy. Serving a lovely lady and all that.'

'But—you and I!' she said fiercely. '*You!* We haven't got a chance against that ten or a dozen out there. If *I* get killed—'

'Shoo! We're not going to get killed,' he assured her comfortably, with certainty he by no means felt. 'When dark comes, we're going to move. Old Eagle's rested, now. You wait. I'm a most notionate man, and right now I've got plenty of notions.'

166

He got tobacco and papers from a pocket and made cigarettes, one for each of them. Then he turned, to be sure that the besiegers were not trying to come closer. When he turned back she was facing him, dark eyes very soft, smiling slightly. She put out a slender, tanned—and very dirty—hand to his arm.

'I thank you,' she told him softly. 'You—I never met a man just like you. One who can fight and punch cows and—and—'

He laughed with something of a forced note. He had never known a girl like her, either, and he was not sure that he enjoyed the experience. The way she faced him made him somehow uncomfortable—and made him think of Lucy Kane...

'Not so many cowboys had books hammered into 'em by a health-seeker professor, then kicked around the Seven Seas,' he said. 'Well, we'd better be watching those hairpins. No telling but there's a notionate man out there, too! One might entertain a notion to drop right into the middle of our back hair.'

'What was it Fine said about that?' she called after him as he moved quickly back to his position. 'That you *liked* to have people drop into your back hair, so you could yank 'm out?'

'Ah, that Fine!' he answered. 'Biggest liar I ever met—even among cowboys and sailors. He's the bullhead of our partnership. Me, I'm long on scheming, so I won't have to fight.

Give 'em another shot or two, just to make 'em chew the dirt!'

Twilight came, without attack from Sebas's men. At the first of darkness, Lance moved quickly over to his big gray and tightened the latigos of the saddle. Eagle nipped at him; evidently, he was rested. Lance shortened the leathers.

'Come here,' he called to Dolores. When she stood beside him he explained his plan:

'It's like this,' he said quietly. 'We can't hope to make a sneak with both of us on one horse. They'd ride us down—and it's going to be moonlight, too. So, you'll get aboard Eagle and I'll slide out now, before the moon comes up. Those fellows have got horses back yonder out of range. I'm going to collect one of 'em. Here's the picture: You get on Eagle, but you don't run for it—yet! They'll try sneaking up on foot. I'll get through 'em and to their horses. When I'm ready I'll let go two quick shots. That'll be your signal. You'll come out splitting the breeze. And don't worry about anybody catching up with you. Those hairpins out there have got good horses, but I'll back this ugly *caballo* against any of 'em.'

'But—but suppose you run into some of Sebas's gang before you get *to* the horses!' she objected. 'You're taking all the risk, Lance. You—'

'It's the only way! Now, don't give me trouble. We haven't got a lot of time, anyhow.

168

Get on Eagle. I've fixed the stirrup-leathers. They ought to fit you. I'm going out, now. You stay here behind the rock. If they sneak up on you before you hear my shots, make a run for it. Oh! In case we're separated, where can we meet?'

'At Pepita. On the outskirts of Pepita. If you can find the village, from here.'

'I can find it. I know the general direction, even from here. Now, I'm gone, before the moon gets up over the mountain.'

He was turning away when she caught his arm and checked him. Before he guessed what she was intending, she had pulled his face down a little and kissed him. He straightened quickly and said shakily:

'Here! Here! None of that, child! You get on Eagle and—and—Oh, get on him and be ready to fan it!'

As he moved on, carbine across his arm, he shook his yellow head bewilderedly. She was an odd mixture, he thought; very young, and yet—

'She's got what it takes; what you'd want to find in a man's backbone,' he told himself. 'Still, she knows the trick of making a man do whatever she wants. Her looks, the way she puts her hand on his arm, the way she—kisses ... What if Lucy had kissed me that way—even once? But she didn't. She never kissed me at all ...'

He put them both out of mind, and
169

concentrated on what lay before him. Standing where he had shot at the *vaqueros* of Sebas, he looked out into darkness. The low moon was still behind the ridges of the hills. But he could hear if he could not see. And there were little rustlings, pantings, mutterings of voices, to tell of men out in the flat on the cañon rim and beyond it.

He stepped noiselessly forward and, step by slow step, walked toward the place where he had killed or wounded the man in the black shirt. He thought this would be a spot empty of Sebas's men. Certainly, he had seen no sign of any effort to carry that man away.

There was the little noise of something moving just ahead of him, after he had gone twenty yards. He squatted, putting down the carbine and drawing his pistol. The noise stopped. He waited. Then, without warning, a dark figure materialized, coming up over him.

'*Hah!*' a man gasped. 'El Tejano—'

Lance jumped to the side without rising. He fired; guessed that he had missed; fired again. The man crashed to the ground and Lance leaned to snatch up his Winchester. Men cried out in Spanish, over to his right. He ran straight ahead. The *vaqueros* of Sebas had put their horses in a little hollow, fifty yards away, when dismounting to take cover. He ran toward the shallow depression.

A man loomed ahead and yelled at him and Lance answered in Spanish that the *Tejano* was trying to escape, then ran on. He was almost at the place where the horses stood when he heard the pound of hoofbeats behind him. And a man, jumping up, caught him in gorillalike arms, swung him from the ground, and fell on him. His warning yell to Dolores was stopped before it began.

He fought furiously against that amazing grip, but the Mexican held him and tried to butt forehead against his face. Lance still held his carbine. It was close against him, between him and the other. Somehow, he hooked his toe under the buttplate and jerked upward. There was a grunt of pain as the muzzle punched the Mexican. The locking arms relaxed and Lance rolled, breaking that numbing hold. He smashed at the man with his fists, for somewhere he had dropped his pistol. The Mexican groaned and was motionless.

Others were running toward the horses, now. He could hear them telling each other that they must get the horses; that the two behind the boulders had somehow got away.

Lance groped until he recovered his Colt, then went down into the hollow and with skilled hands began to examine horses, running a hand down their noses, expertly judging the shape of heads to find the scrubby Spanish ponies and reject them. Only the best of these animals would serve him, tonight! He found a Texas saddle and it was cinched to a horse bigger than the others. Behind him the voices of the Mexicans were louder. He rammed a toe into the stirrup and swung up. Very much, he would have liked to stampede the other horses, but there was no time. Already, the Sebas men were jumping down into the little hollow. One of them seemed to have the eyes of a cat.

'*Quien es*?' this one yelled. 'Who is it?'

'*El Tejano*!' Lance answered in a yell. 'The Texan leaves you!'

He spurred the horse; jumped him into a gallop. There were shots from the Mexicans, orange flames that stabbed the darkness. But the lead was wild, high over him or singing off to right and left. He raced away and, as he galloped, he wondered if Dolores had got past the men. She must have mistaken the double shot with which he had dropped that Mexican, he thought, for the expected signal.

He heard yelling around the horses that indicated quick pursuit. He had to ride like a jockey, because the stirrup-leathers of this stolen saddle were much too short for him. But he kept the horse at the gallop for a mile, then turned off to retrace the trail he and Dolores had ridden from that flat where the cattle had been.

The moon lifted above the serrated ridges. He heard no hoofbeats, so he pulled in to the long, hard trot that eats miles. Now, he could locate himself; pick out the peaks which Dolores had shown him, marking the

172

mountains which held the village of Pepita. The horse he had taken was a dark bay, a fourteen-hand animal which—very evidently—had good blood in him. The moonlight showed his intelligent head, the shape of him. As for the Texas saddle—

'Probably some Texican waddy's looking at the daisies from the root-end, now,' Lance told the bay grimly. 'He had a saddle some of those killers wanted, so—he's under the grass, now ...'

He was on a ridge when he saw a tiny pinpoint of light far ahead and to the left of him. He sat the bay, frowning. That would hardly be Dolores. The girl would know better than to make a fire, and there was no house in all this wide and savage land, from what he had been told. He nodded slowly, shifted the carbine a trifle, and rode that way. It was a mile or more away, that fire; he lost it and found it again, saw it flicker and blaze up a half-dozen times before, coming at the cautious walk, almost soundless, he looked into an arroyo and shoved carbine forward.

CHAPTER SEVENTEEN

'I SLANG A FEW SLUGS'

The fire burned before the opening of a little hollow in the arroyo-bank. There was no sign of life anywhere—of man or animal. Lance studied the camp, wondering if his approach had been heard; if the camper was hidden somewhere watching him—or watching for him. He sat the bay for three or four minutes, listening, staring. Then out of the darkness of that hollow, the cavelike opening in the arroyo-wall, a short, thick figure came, to put a stick of wood on the fire. Lance stared hard, then:

'*Como le va*, Mr Xavier!' he called to the tintyper. 'How goes the world with you?'

Xavier jumped back into the dark with agility amazing in his fat body. Lance laughed.

'This is Lance Craig,' he said. 'The man you helped out of Campoblanco, along with some others. Don't tell me that my beautiful features and graceful figure have been forgot already! Come on out, man. Come on out. I'm an *amigo*.'

'Craig! You—why, of course!' Xavier grunted. 'Come down to the fire and make yourself at home.'

'Uh-uh! *Uh-uh!* No fires for me, tonight,'

174

Lance told him humorously. 'I just left some gentlemen of the same persuasion as those who chased us out of Campoblanco. I think I've shaken 'em off, but I wouldn't bet you a nickel against a gold twenty that they aren't on my trail. I'm headed for Pepita. If you want a word of good advice, you'll douse that fire and pull your ears down between your shoulder blades. If those men of Sebas's come up on you they'll probably make a sieve out of you first and apologize later on—sometime when it's convenient. I—think they're pretty riled about the way they've been hammered lately.'

'My sacred stars!' Xavier grunted, bobbing out into the light. 'I'm always gitting into something, not knowing! I—'

He bent and scooped up dirt to throw upon the fire. Lance watched, grinning. Since Campoblanco he had been under no illusion whatever about the kind of man Xerxes Xavier really was. There was plenty of lean to the bacon of *that* fat man. His action at Campoblanco had proved it.

'Where's your horse?' he asked, when the arroyo was lighted only by the moon and Xavier was a chunky silhouette skipping nimbly about with his bundles. 'Better collect him.'

'Ain't a horse. Mule. Me and horses don't somehow understand each other. But mules, now, is different. We git along. She's up the arroyo a-piece—about a whoop and a holloa.

I'll git her. Where you going? What you been *doing*—to git Sebas's gang on your tail?'

'I'm headed for Pepita in the mountains. Know where that is? No time, now, to tell you all the things I've done, or helped to do, that roused Sebas's worst side and put him on the warpath. Better collect your *mula* and hit the trail. And you'd better miss the low spots and just skip from peak to peak. It's that bad, Xavier, my friend!'

'I'll git her. Yeh, I'll git her and I'll hit the trail. Hell of a country! Honest business man ain't got a chance—'

His muttering became indistinct as he ran up the arroyo. Lance shook his head and grinned. He waited until Xavier came back, leading a quick-walking little saddle-mule. Xavier saddled swiftly, expertly. Lance nodded to himself. Tintyper the fat man might be, but he was no pilgrim. He watched the sacks strapped on behind the saddle. Then Xavier swung up with grunts and pantings and snarled at his mount.

'Come on, you cross between Original Sin and the Burro that wouldn't go on the Ark. *Andarle!* You' worse'n the *macho* I rode across Spain, one time—and *he* was sold to me by a gipsy! *Andarle!* Up you go!'

The mule scrambled up the arroyo-bank, to stop beside Lance's bay. The tintyper looked swiftly, shrewdly, at the horse, then at Lance. His red face was plain in the moonlight, now.

176

'Oh!' he grunted. 'Been in real trouble, huh? You rode a ugly gray out of Campoblanco. Now, you got a bay—and it ain't your saddle, neither. That's a woman's saddle, from the size of that tree. Well?'

'I'm going to Pepita. It was like this—' Lance began.

'Let's go! Pepita suits me right now. Tell me on the road.'

And as they rode stirrup-to-stirrup, the fat man swaying in his swellfork hull to the mule's easy singlefoot, Lance told the tale of the fight on the flat and his run with Dolores before the Sebas men. Xavier made rumbling noises at the end.

'I slang a few slugs, whilst you was gitting away,' he said. 'Wouldn't be too s'prised if I *hit* two-three of 'em. Anyway, there was some ready for the *campo santo* by the time you-all had rolled on in your cloud of dust. Some— several! Me, I just skipped back down from my roof, leaving the Winchester up there to gather when I had more time and quietness.'

'Nobody saw you?' Lance demanded incredulously.

'I thought not. That's what I'm about to tell you: I was back talking tintypes and tooth-pulling and spectacles before the cloud of smoke had got good blowed away. Seemed to me nobody guessed I'd been in on that li'l' bitsy fracas. Then in comes an *hombre* that had seen me. But I smelled him! I had my mule saddled,

177

too. I got out with some of 'em dusting my pants. They chased me hither and yon and up and down before I could shake 'em. I swear! It was like being in the Rangers ag'in!'

Lance laughed helplessly.

'It's certainly a warm country!' he said. 'Fine Upham and I fogged it over here to cool off and sort of get the smoke out of our hair. And in walks old Quintus Lee, bringing a war in his hands—as you saw! And before we know what's happened—'

Briefly, he told of their meeting with Dolores Donovan and her gladiators. Xavier grunted and nodded.

'Yeh, I know a lot about that. Heard some of it before I crossed, the rest in Campoblanco and around about. She's one blame' fool and—to *my* mind—you and your Upham and the rest are off the same bolt of calico. You ain't got a chance to lick Sebas. Not with him having the soldiers behind him. You can hell it up and down. You can kill off some of Sebas's killers. But in the long run the bunch of you'll either take your foot in your hand and hightail it over the River, or you'll meet a southbound slug whilst you're a-going north. Sebas has bragged it around he is going to stake out all her men on anthills—maybe with rattlers wrapped around their necks. The girl—she's half-Irish, half-Spanish, they say—he'll take home with him to cook his beans.'

Lance shrugged. But there was much of

sense in what the fat man said. The same thought had come to him, and still another—that with Colonel Nasco's troopers on the scene, it would be easier to recover the Hacienda Gerónimo from Sebas than to hold it afterward. They rode silently through the night, heading toward the mountains. Xavier grunted at the last.

'I ain't been up here, at Pepita,' he said, 'but I was aiming to head that way eventual. So I got directions. And I been enough places in fifty year, one side the water and another, to figure out country. We swing left, now.'

At dawn they were in the hills. Xavier brought food from the bundles which seemed to hold everything necessary to his existence in a barren land. Water trickled from a hole in the cliff against which they sat, making a little *tinaja* in a basin of slick stone. Xavier nodded toward it.

'Reminds me of Cottonwood Spring, near El Paso,' he said reminiscently. 'I rangered in that country, years back, before I was so fat and old and timid, and tired of having a tincupful of lead shot at me ever' time I lifted my head over a rock. That is pretty country. So's this. And my advice to you is to take a long, good look at it, young fella! You ain't got much longer to *be* looking!'

He got up and inspected his mule. Lance stared at the saddle on the bay. Suddenly he shook his head. The back of the cantle was beautifully carved. Within a carven oval were the initials *D.D.*, flanked by the Rafter G brand. Some of those *vaqueros* had evidently found Dolores's dead chestnut and stripped it of hull and bridle and saddled this tall bay with her outfit. He wondered where the girl might be, this morning, and it puzzled him that he felt so keenly about her.

'She's all right!' he told himself impatiently. 'She knows the country and she was on Eagle. If they had caught her I'd have known it. She's all right! She just rode hellbent away from there when she heard me kill that hairpin.'

They went on by steep trails, higher into the mountains. Xavier rode with the long Winchester across his arm.

'Lucky I had a minute to snatch this off the roof,' he said grimly. 'Never was much with a short gun, though I have had to use one a time or six. Pepita oughtn't to be awful far ahead.'

And as if the words were signal, a rifle came thrusting over a natural breastwork of stone, twenty yards up the trail. They were caught in the open. Before they could whirl their animals and try to make cover fifty yards down that bare trail, the rifle could blast them from the saddles. Lance yelled frantically:

'*Amigos!* we go to Pepita!'

'Perhaps!' a slow, deep voice answered. 'And perhaps you die there in the road. That is as I say. Lift your hands and keep them from the pistols; put your rifles in the road. Then

180

I will consider.'

There was nothing to do but obey—or charge the rifleman, who showed only as a tall-crowned sombrero and glittering dark eyes above the Winchester. They let the long guns slide to the ground and drop. Lance considered the possibility of snatching out a Colt and taking a snap shot at the head. But he lifted his hands, instead. The fact that they had not been killed instantly seemed to be in their favor. Too, he recalled what Dolores had said, of the hostility borne by people of Pepita for Sebas and the folk of Campoblanco. If this were one of the Pepita men...

'We were driven out of Campoblanco,' he said smoothly. 'We heard that in Pepita those who are enemies of Luis Sebas are welcome. So we rode this way. It is as you say: We come on or we die here.'

'As I choose,' the slow voice agreed. 'I am Estrella Morro, *Jefe* of Pepita. Why does Luis Sebas call you enemy? Are you one of those who follow the *tontita* Dolores, trying to do that which she cannot do—take back the Hacienda Gerónimo from Sebas? I have seen her and the three men she leads to their death. They were in Pepita before I went out on *negócios* of my own. Three old men at whom my oldest woman would not look. You—*por dios!* You are not like them ... The fat man of the so-funny face, there—he is of their kind ... Come with me. Take up your rifles. I have decided to let you come to Pepita, whether you ride with the *tontita* or not.'

Lance nodded gravely and swung down. He handed up Xavier's Winchester, then picked up his own carbine. Xavier was whistling cheerfully. His red face wore a grin.

'That's what it is to be beau-ti-ful!' he grunted. 'Now, me, she'd likely have shot me right up off this mule. But I do hope you ain't a married man...'

Lance mounted, and they rode around the end of the ledge of rock. He stared curiously at the woman who stood waiting. She was as tall as he, but slender, dressed in *charro* jacket and bell-bottomed pantalones of green wool, with silver buttons at the seams. A pearl-handled pistol was thrust into her crimson sash beside a silver-hilted dagger. But the rifle held accustomedly across her arm was as plain and businesslike as his own. She had a square face, skin as brown as an Indian's, mouth full of lips but tight. Suddenly, she smiled at him.

'You *are* one of handsomeness!' she cried. 'Wait and I will get my horse. You will ride with me. And it is good that you met me! For if you had gone two miles more along this trail you would have died in the open without knowledge of the bullet striking you. From this side we expect war—and so we watch for it.'

She jumped up to a rock, then to another, cat-quick, light, graceful. She disappeared into an arroyo. Lance stared after her and

182

shook his head.

'Something tells me that trouble's ahead,' he grunted.

CHAPTER EIGHTEEN

'IT'S TIME WE MADE PLANS'

PEPITA, which they gained within a half-hour—and without seeing the sentries Estrella had said were watching—was a site well chosen for defense. Mountains almost enclosed it, but so slanting were their sides that the village was not endangered by their height. The single trail that crossed a small tableland dived steeply and ran straight from both north and south, coming each time through a pass that one man could have held against an army.

'My village,' Estrella told Lance, as they dismounted in the tiny *plaza*, to be surrounded by curious villagers. 'Our fields are across the mountain. But the field my people like best to plow is that of Don Luis Sebas. He—'

Suddenly, she broke off to stare and Lance, turning to see what attracted her, caught sight of the group coming from a house—Dolores and Tommy Downes, Oberman, Winters, Warren, and Fine Upham. Fine yelled at him:

'Well! That's a sight for sore eyes!'

'*La tontita...*' Estrella said with something

183

like grimness in her tone. Dark eyes were narrowed, mouth compressed. '*La tontita*, in my village...'

She moved directly toward Dolores, walking with the long strides of a man which, yet, had the catlike grace Lance had noted in her before. So the two women stopped within a yard of each other, Dolores smiling, the taller Estrella keeping expression from her dark face.

'*Buenas días*,' Dolores greeted her. 'I have come here to find shelter from Luis Sebas, as once before I came to Pepita. Is it good?'

'I cannot refuse help to any enemy of that *chucho*, Sebas. You and yours may stay in Pepita for a while.'

Then Estrella looked at Tommy Downes and the others—longest at Fine Upham. He grinned cheerfully at her and she moved up to stand directly before him, head on one side, as if he had been a horse for sale.

'And you?' she said suddenly. 'What are you named? I have not seen you here before today.'

'Fine Upham,' Fine told her. 'From Texas. But now I ride with *la señorita* on business of Gerónimo. I thank you for the freedom of your town.'

'I will see *you* again. We will talk,' Estrella promised.

Then she turned abruptly and the crowd of villagers made a path for her. Lance looked at Dolores, who smiled at him.

'This *is* a relief!' he said. 'I let go those two

184

shots because a man jumped me. I hoped you'd ride clear. Oh! I found your saddle on a pretty good horse. You take him and I'll ride Eagle again. Well? What's the notion, now?'

She told him briefly of mistaking the double shot for his signal; of riding fast through the Sebas men and making for Pepita. Tommy Downes listened, his perpetual grin in evidence.

'We had a grand little fight, down on the flat,' he said to Lance. 'We had to run, of course, but two or three who had better horses than the others and caught up with us are—sorry, now! Well?'

'Let's go somewhere and have a powwow,' Lance suggested, looking from Xavier to Dolores. 'It's time we made plans—some real plans—and started carrying 'em out...'

She frowned slightly, meeting the grimness in his face, then nodded and pointed to the long house from which her party had come.

'That's the *cantina*,' she said. 'We can find a corner to ourselves. Come on.'

They crossed the little *plaza* and Lance and Fine brushed elbows as they went. Tommy Downes was with Dolores; Oberman walked with Winters and Warren. Xavier brought up the rear. Fine looked sidelong at his friend:

'What's it?' he grunted. 'You don't look too pleased.' Lance shrugged:

'Hell! I want to *do* something! Something that'll mean something. I—have got the

185

making of an idea, I do believe. It's a kind of double-barreled proposition. Well, we'll see.'

Inside the dusky room that was inn and drinking place, the eight of them moved toward a corner and sat at a rough table. Dolores turned curiously to Lance.

'And what are you going to suggest?' she asked slowly.

'This! Xavier, here, said something on the road that fits my notion just ex-act-ly. We can go along biting pieces out of Sebas and he'll just throw in new men to take the place of those we drop. We'll get nowhere in the long run. Because we haven't got men to lose. He has. We can hit five licks to his one; we can take back Gerónimo cattle and hide 'em out—and still lose in the long run. So—the answer is: *Get Sebas!*'

'Get him?' Dolores said slowly. 'How?'

'Out of the whole bunch here, there are three of us who probably aren't known to Sebas—Fine and Ron and me. Suppose the three ride down to Gerónimo and drop a loop over Sebas? His gang won't amount to much without him. We'll have just the leaderless bunch to buck—'

'And Colonel Nasco and his outfit,' Winters broke in dryly. 'But there's a lot to what you're saying, no denying it. If I could line Sebas up over my front sight, we wouldn't have much to worry about. But he keeps awful well covered. No chance of picking him off. I don't see how

186

you men—'

'I'm willing to make the try!' Lance told Dolores grimly. 'By myself, if that's necessary. But if you-all could talk that she-tiger, Estrella Morro, into throwing in with us—well, we'd have as many on our side as Sebas has got.'

'It's a notion!' Fine Upham admitted.

'It's *the* notion!' Xavier said flatly. 'The only one that's come out of this business since the bunch of you come fogging it over the river to hit Sebas.'

'I don't know where *you* fit into our affairs,' Dolores told him stiffly.

'Maybe I don't fit. But that don't keep me from giving you lots and lots of good advice. I been in Campoblanco and round about. I heard plenty about all this. Craig's right. You got to hogtie Sebas or—you're nothing!'

'Sebas ain't put his eyes on me in years,' Ron Oberman said drawlingly. 'I'll take a chance and drift down with you, Lance. I know ever' foot of the range.'

'How about you, Fine?' Lance asked, turning to the stocky man. 'Ron can show us the way to the house; we'll turn up there with a yarn about hunting jobs—'

'Well, now,' Fine said gravely, 'I just do'no'. It sounds like a dangerous business. Reckless, too! S'pose this-here-now Sebas suspicions us? Why, he might kill us! No telling.'

'Ah, you—' Xavier began, then laughed. 'A' right! You had me going for a minute. Tell you

... I looked this place over when we first rode up. Looks to me like the last spot in the world I can take a tintype or pull a tooth or sell a spec'. I'll ramble along with you boys. Between us, maybe we can collect Sebas.'

'No!' Dolores cut in, fiercely. 'This is a crazy idea. If Sebas has one suspicion of you, he'll have you shot into doll-rags! And you don't owe Gerónimo a thing. I won't have it!'

'Listen,' Lance told her patiently, 'you enlisted the bunch of us, to—oh, I don't know, exactly ... To see that a thieving killer can't get away with his schemes. Well! We're playing with you, clear across the board. But if we think there's a better chance to save our skins by doing something that sounds crazy, we ought to have a right to do that crazy thing, *no es verdad*? Suppose we do get ourselves killed? It's no more than we'd be risking by riding across Gerónimo range, with the good chance of stopping a Sebas bullet, somewhere between our minds and our mouths. But, how about talking Estrella Morro into backing us? She sounds like a gal who would enjoy stripping him.'

'I'll talk to her,' Dolores said doubtfully. 'But—somehow I don't think she is too fond of me.'

'You talk to her,' Xavier suggested, grinning. 'Somehow, I think she *is* fond of you, Craig...'

'It's my beauty,' Lance said gravely. 'But
188

since she's seen Fine, my stock has gone down to about a dime on the big dollar. Fine, you go hunt up the lady and turn that grin of yours on her. I'll bet she gives you Pepita. I could tell by the way she said she'd be seeing you that—'

'You know where you can go!' Fine advised him. 'This is the first war ever *I* was in I got kind of cramped because of a lady being in it. I—'

'Two ladies,' Lance drawled. 'And if you're cramped by one and can't use all the rough language natural to you, what're you going to do when Estrella sets you up in housekeeping? Well? Is it a hen, then? Do we set her? Ron and Fine and Jerky amble down to Gerónimo with me and we see what we can do about putting Luis Sebas out on the well-known limb?'

'After all that talk about two ladies, looks to me like it's the only safe place for a man,' Fine said sourly. 'I swear! More talking around here than in Austin in legislature season. When do we go?'

'Right away,' Lance grunted. 'If you won't try to persuade Estrella to throw in with us, we'll have to leave that to Dolores and Tommy. We have got to—'

Estralla Morro came through the door, a dozen men behind her. Each of her followers, Lance noted, was armed with rifle and pistol and dagger. She crossed to their table and stood easily, surely, beside it, looking from face to face.

'And what is the plan?' she inquired at last.

189

'What do you fools know?'

'We ask that you and the men of Pepita join us,' Dolores told her suddenly. 'To end the day of Luis Sebas. I know what he did to you. I know that it was your sister he took out of Pepita, four years ago. We hate him, you and I. He took your sister and he murdered my father.'

'My hate for Luis Sebas is my affair,' Estrella stopped her. 'I will kill him for the thing he did to me. I do not need the help of you—any of you. So, why will I join those who must run to my walls for shelter?'

Dolores shrugged. Estrella looked from face to face again and stared longest at Fine. Then, under Lance's quizzical eyes, Fine Upham leaned back in the corner, head against 'dobe wall. Up and down he looked the tall Mexican girl and on his square, dark face was an expression Lance had never seen there.

'Because you want a fight, beautiful one,' Fine said slowly. 'Because you hate Luis Sebas. You would have killed him long ago, but he has had behind him the soldiers of Colonel Nasco. You have taken the men of Pepita down from the mountains; you have stolen cattle from Sebas and killed men of his. But, always, you have had to ride fast, back to the mountains, when the alarm was raised.'

Estrella threw back her head, abruptly. She laughed. They watched her, Lance with narrowed eyes, Dolores with underlip caught between her teeth, young Tommy Downes openly staring.

'You—you—' she said at last. 'Come and talk with me, Fine Upham. I think that—perhaps—we will think of something to please you. *Yo no sé!* I do not know. But—come with me. Gregorio!'

A stocky, scarred man stepped stiffly, quickly, to her side. His lips lifted in a wolf-snarl under grizzled mustachio. His hand was on the butt of a pistol.

'This *hombre americano* comes with me, to—talk!' Estrella told the captain of her guard. 'And—if any here objects, you will know what to do, Gregorio!'

'I will know!' Gregorio nodded. He half-turned his head to face the staring, stolid crew behind him. '*Hombres!* If and when I say "*fire!*" you will fire...'

'*Muy bien,*' Fine told her, grinning. 'There will be no need to shoot. I will talk to you and, when we have had done with talking, the men of Pepita will go down to Gerónimo and there will do what is necessary, to make of Luis Sebas—*nada*—nothing. *Es verdad?* It is truth?'

'Come with me,' she said in her slow, deep voice. 'Come with me and we will see what Estrella, the Woman-Soldier, can and will do for Hacienda Gerónimo ... We will talk, you and I. We—will see what Pepita and the men of Pepita will do for the little fool and those who follow her.'

CHAPTER NINETEEN

'THE WORD IS "GUERRA"'

Dusk came. Pepita was quiet, except for the sound of guitars in the *cantina* and the yells of those who drank too much of agua'diente, the fiery, colorless rum made of sugar. Lance sat dourly in a corner of the drinking place with a greasy and tattered deck of cards and laid out solitaire patterns.

Xavier came to him, finally. The fat ex-Ranger leaned to look and Lance snarled at him.

'I can't help it,' Xavier grunted. 'That ain't the right card for that line. You ought to learn solitaire before you start playing it. Oh! Seen Fine?'

'It is—and I did—and I haven't: it's the right card and I know solitaire and I haven't seen Fine since he went out to talk Estrella into helping our war.'

'Yeh?' Xavier said jeeringly. 'Well—when do we leave? I am a timid soul. There's a lot about this place I don't like. About fifteen things—all of 'em that big gal. Let's hit the trail, Lance. One thing I never did like was a woman. And, like Fine was saying we got two of 'em in this jackpot.'

'Neither do I like 'em!' Lance said irritably.

'And I'm a lot more than ready to hightail. But I've got to wait for Fine. You haven't seen him?'

'A while back. Setting out in the patio with that Estrella, in the house she's got in the middle of town. I—took a snooker over the wall. Because, like I say, I am timid and I want to know when we're hitting a place where there's just a few gunies a-shooting at me. Fine looked right happy—the nitwit.'

Lance scooped up his cards and looked about the big room. A slovenly Mexican met his eye and came to the table. Of him Lance ordered *comida*—the evening meal. He shook his head.

'I swear!' he complained. 'I don't know what kind of a jackpot this is, Jerky. But I'm in it and I'll stick. Same for the rest of us. What do you think of the Downes kid? It does seem to me he's pretty soft on Dolores...'

'He certainly is,' Tommy answered calmly, for himself, putting his head into the window above Lance's table. 'Probably, he'll get softer, too! I think she's about the finest article I've ever seen, heard, or read about. She can have me any time she's willing; she can have my neck or anything else I happen to own. And that reminds me ... Fine Upham is still impressing our gentle little Estrella. Estrella is not fond of the notion of letting him go. He sent me to find you. He says: Get out of town as quickly as possible. He'll meet you down the trail, at the place where Estrella stuck you up.'

'*Bueno!* As soon as I can find Ron, we'll be on the ground. Seen him? Or has the whole crew gone skirts-and-petticoat crazy?'

'I don't know about that last,' the boy told him, grinning. 'But—he *was* talking to a pretty girl when I saw him a little while ago. Stay here. I'll try to find him.'

'Crazy!' Lance said disgustedly to Xavier, when Tommy had disappeared. 'Give me a man, every time! These women—'

'And yet, we're putting our fool heads into the rope for a woman,' Xavier reminded him, placidly. 'You're not soft on the Dolores gal? It's not—jealousy with you?'

Lance made a wordless, growling sound. The *mozo* came to the table bringing the usual cold, fried beef and *tortillas* and brown beans and inky coffee. Xavier sat down with him and they began to eat. Ron Oberman appeared in the doorway, looked around, and came to the table. Lance pushed food his way. The shrewd eyes of the one-time Gerónimo rider were twinkling.

'Well,' he said slowly, 'it does look to a pore cowboy like the petticoatedest town ... That pilgrim, Tommy Downes, he is at Dolores's apron-strings; Fine Upham and that Estrella Morro—Vane Warren's got the fattest woman in the place cooking him some grub and—'

'And *you* were out with all the rest of the women in Pepita,' Lance finished for him. 'But,

194

ne' mind! Fine is really trying to talk Estrella into bringing the Pepita guns to fight on Gerónimo—whatever the side-issues to his love-making may be. When we've got rid of this *comida* we'll go out. Fine'll come to meet us down the trail. And if we're lucky we'll drop a loop over Luis Sebas. Where's Dolores? Any chance of sneaking out without seeing her?'

'She was having a confabulation with Winters, last time *I* seen her. It's dark enough, now, to cover us. I found out the places where Estrella has got her men staked out.'

They ate and Lance called the *mozo* over again to get *agua'diente* for them all. They lifted clay cups of the water-clear rum and looked at each other. For all that he knew his chances of doing the wild thing he planned were one in a thousand, Lance found a lift to the liquor.

'Well, after all,' he told himself, 'you get so damn' little out of this life that a drink and fight ought to be welcome. So—'

'It's dark enough,' he told Ron and Jerky Xavier. 'Let's go.'

They found their horses in a brush-roofed shed behind the *cantina*. Nobody of Pepita was there. They saddled and led the animals down the single street. If anyone looked at them from dark doorways he did not see fit to raise an alarm. Ron pushed up into the lead.

'There's a hairpin setting in that house over yonder,' he told Lance and Jerky in a whisper.

'But—that gal I was talking to is his *querida*. The word is *"guerra"*...'

When they came abreast the 'dobe house he indicated, a short, harsh challenge stopped them.

'*Guerra!*' Ron and Lance and Xavier answered, in a breath.

'Good! Go with God!' the sentry said almost without interest. '*La soldadera*—Estrella—she has many plans...'

'I hope Fine talks her into making our plan one of her plans,' Lance told the others dryly. 'I have thought a good many things about that gunie, but a woman-wrangler I never did take him for. Still, and yet, he seems to do tolerably...'

They made that breastwork of natural rock behind which Estrella had sheltered and dismounted. Xavier grunted and began to fumble in his *alforjas*.

'Sorry I'm the only drinking man in the crowd,' he drawled. 'Because as this red-eye goes it ain't bad red-eye and it looks to me like I got about a quart of it...'

'Kill him!' Ron said to Lance. 'A hairpin like that ain't got a bit of right to live. A whole quart of that spider-killer and he thinks he can handle it.'

Lance reached out, to take the bottle deftly from the fat man's hand and upend it. Ron took it as expertly from him and there were gurgling noises until Xavier groaned.

196

'Hey!' he said. 'I seen some damn' camels in my time—that was in Arabia where they got the hawses and the gals with mosquito netting over their faces—and ought to have 'em; the way most of 'em look—but if you two ain't worse'n ary camels I ever seen—'

He got the bottle and they drank in turn, afterward. For an hour, two hours, three, they waited behind the ledge of rock. Then Lance got up to stare toward Pepita.

'Something's holding up that son of a gun!' he said. 'Well, Fine probably knows the way down to Gerónimo well enough to follow us. We have got to go back to Pepita, or go ahead. My idea is to go on. No telling what he's got into, but Fine's old enough to handle whatever it may be. Let's go on down the hill.'

'My notion, too,' Ron agreed. 'Let's go on down.'

They rode quietly down the steep trail. Once more, Ron was leading. For miles they rode, while the moon came up over the peaks and made the land almost as bright as in daylight. Then Ron jerked a hand up and forward, to indicate a huddle of boulders on a greasewood flat.

'That's Gerónimo range,' he said. 'That—'

The moon disappeared, blanketed by clouds. They pulled in short and Ron said that he heard something. Neither Xavier nor Lance heard anything. They started the horses and went forward at a walk. And from the boulders came the familiar orange splash of shots, spangling the darkness.

'Sebas!' Ron grunted. 'Might've knowed he would have somebody watching the trail. What do we do?'

Lance spurred forward with a snarl. It had suddenly come to him that he was very tired of Luis Sebas, of being hunted here and there by men of Sebas's.

'Give 'm hell!' he said irritably. 'It's the only thing!'

'Who's that?' Xavier cried. Even in the darkness Lance saw the fat man whirl his horse. 'Somebody behind us!'

'Lance!' a tense voice called. 'Oh, Lance!'

'Dolores!' Lance yelled. 'What are *you* doing out here?'

'Looking for you idiots!' the girl answered.

'Stay back!' he told her. 'We're going to get us an armload of Sebas's gang. *Stay back!*'

The three of them charged the boulders. Someone fired at them and Lance emptied his pistol and knew that Xavier and Ron, also were shooting. Then there was the dim shape of a horseman running away and he sent Eagle after the fugitive. He distanced the others; only heard the faint pound of their hoofbeats somewhere behind. The man he followed twisted in the saddle and there was the stab of orange flame to mark a shot.

Then Lance came—untouched—up beside him. He swung viciously at the man's head with the barrel of his Colt, felt the steel crash through felt and hair. As the tall rider swayed, Lance caught him, pulled him from the big horse. From behind Ron encouraged him with a yell:

'Rake him, boy! Rake him plenty!'

'Got him!' Lance replied pantingly. 'Got him—plenty!'

Then the two of them went to the ground together. The man was limp in his arms as Lance fell upon him. Lance himself was stunned for an instant, but he held to his prisoner desperately. Then Ron and Xavier—and Dolores—charged past. There were other shots. Lance ventured to scratch a match and look at the unconscious one. It was a handsome head and face but streaked just now by slow trickles of blood. A hawknosed face, light of skin, with small mustache and spiky tuft of hair on the chin.

'Sebas?' Lance asked himself incredulously. 'Can it be?'

He had pistol belt and holster but had dropped his weapon. Lance searched him rapidly, then—sure that he was harmless—waited for the others to come back. It was a half-hour before he heard the hoofbeats of their horses, and before that time his prisoner had stirred and groaned. At last, he sat up and spoke inquiringly:

'Who is it? What happened—besides my fall?'

'You're Sebas?' Lance countered. 'Luis Sebas?'

'And—if I am? Who are you? You speak Spanish smoothly enough but—you are no Mexican.'

'I ride for Hacienda Gerónimo—the real owner of the Gerónimo. I am a man of Texas. And now, I think, the fight is done. Without you to lead them, your *vaqueros* cannot stand before us. And—when the men of Dolores Donovan take you, Quintus Lee and other riders of Gerónimo, who remember how you murdered their *patron*—it is my thought that you will go the way of Candelario, who died in Campoblanco under Gerónimo bullets...'

'It has a sound of reasonableness,' the other admitted. His voice was quite even. 'It was these others who charged with you against me—and who ride this way now?'

'Some of them. You can ride? There will be riding to do, tonight. It will be done, of course—even if you must be tied in the saddle...'

'I will see. My leg, I think, is badly strained. And, too, the wounds upon my skull—I am fortunate, that my head is tough and somewhat used to being hammered. I—'

He shifted position in the darkness beside Lance, making little panting noises. Then he had moved like a cat and was jumping toward the dark bulk of their horses. Lance fairly dived at him, caught his leg, and was kicked in

200

the side. But he hung to the leg and jerked and brought the man down. He held him and called to Ron and Xavier. They closed the little distance between at racing gallop and dropped to the ground demanding the reason for Lance's yells.

'Sebas!' he gasped. 'I have got Sebas, here!'

CHAPTER TWENTY

'HOW ABOUT THIS NASCO?'

They crowded around. Someone struck a match and held the flame over the pair on the ground.

'Sebas!' Dolores said softly, but with an edge of deadliness in her voice. 'Sebas! You killed my father. So I swore that I would not rest until you were dead and Gerónimo once more in the hands of a Donovan. So—'

'It would seem that your vow is fulfilled,' the prisoner conceded, quite calmly. 'Now, Man of Texas! If it is permitted, I should like to sit or stand; to have more of comfort in position than I can have with your knee on my neck.'

'It is permitted,' Lance said. 'Ron, if you and Jerky will tie him up—there ought to be some old pigging strings in my *alforjas*. Then we'd better clear out. His gang might come back and it'd all be to do over again.'

201

'Not much chance,' Ron grunted. 'We chased his gang so far down the line they ought to be out of reach of anything but a letter.'

But he went to get the short lengths of rope. When he came back he tied the calm prisoner's hands behind his back.

'Now, what?' Lance asked Dolores. 'Back to Pepita?'

'Why not to Gerónimo big house? With Sebas in our hands I don't see any particular danger. The only one we'll really have to watch for, now, is Colonel Nasco. Ron! I wish you'd ride to Pepita and bring the others—Winters and Warren and Tommy and Fine. The bunch of you can meet us at Horsehead Spring. Then we can settle everything without bothering our Woman-Soldier!'

She looked at Lance; moved closer to him.

'I *don't* like that woman!' she said viciously. 'I don't want anything more to do with her. After you left, Lance, I tried to persuade her to help us. But she was so smitten with Fine that she just pushed me aside as if—as if I'd been a troublesome kitten! So I slipped out of Tommy's sight—the boy would never have let me come without his strong, protecting arm— and rode after you. I don't understand Fine . . . But—I suppose he was smitten with her, too.'

'Maybe he likes 'em big and rough,' Lance ventured amusedly. 'No telling—and no time to worry about it. Want to do the trip to Pepita, Ron?'

'Nah! I don't *want* to, but I will. Somebody ought to bring up the others. Reckon you're right, Dolores. No sense to us all going back to Pepita and maybe ending up with a row. That Estrella's just about the uncertainest proposition ever *I* put eyes on! No telling what she'll do, next. A' right, I'm fogging it. We'll meet you at Cabeza Caballo Spring.'

They saw him go at the trot. Then, with the prisoner mounted and a lariat about his horse's neck held by Jerky Xavier, they rode toward the *casa grande* of Gerónimo.

'Horsehead Spring is in the hills about the house,' Dolores told Lance as they rode. 'The house ... Our house...'

He heard her saying the words over and over, almost underbreath. She rode so close to him that her leg brushed his. And he understood what capture of Sebas must mean—return of the great range; repossession of her home. It made him think of Mesquite County and the C Bar. He shook his head as the picture rose in mind.

'I'm where she was; I'm still there,' he thought. 'If all that Lucy feels about me is right—that I was just gallivanting around the world when my place was with the *Jefe* or Cousin Orval—then I certainly have been paid...'

He pictured Lucy's grave, lovely face, her steady, clear hazel eyes, but another picture slipped over that. He saw her as she had looked in the door of the stone house of the Blues, face distorted with fear and horror and—hatred.

'Yes, she hates me,' he admitted. 'She must have been in love with Oscar. I thought man-fashion, maybe. I thought that nobody could look at him, knowing him for what he was, except to hate him. But maybe the books are right, about love being blind. She loved him and so she couldn't see what I saw; what Judge Oakes saw. I killed him and—she hates me for it. And I'm the man who—with Fine's help—saved her last penny.'

Abruptly, for the first time since crossing into Mexico, he considered himself clearly in relation to the C Bar. He had been taking it for granted that, eventually, conditions would alter in Mesquite County, opinions would change, and he could go back to take up the work his father had been murdered while doing. Now—

'I'll never go back!' he told himself—with something like amazement that he had not seen this before. 'Of course I won't go back. No matter if conditions do change so that I won't have to stand trial for murder, she won't change. And I couldn't stand being around her, seeing that look on her face—No! It's Mexico—or farther south—maybe the Argentine—but not Mesquite County—'

A soft, warm hand closing upon his own, where it rested on the saddle horn, jerked him back to thought of Gerónimo.

'It's just more than I can realize—believe!' Dolores told him shakily, with a little laugh. 'All this! I—before I met you, the whole plan seemed wild and impossible. I know that I realized how crazy it was. I simply shut my eyes and rode fast and hard and wouldn't think. Then you pushed yourself into my troubles, Lance. You brought Fine and Ron and—and Tommy, that darling pilgrim. And *you* thought of capturing Sebas, then captured him! So, here we are, able to clear Gerónimo of his killers and start the old place working again. Thanks to you!'

'Nonsense!' he said lightly. With his free hand he patted hers. 'Thanks to yourself for hanging to your guns; to Quint Lee and Winters and Warren for backing you; to Ron Oberman and Fine and Tommy and—and even Jerky Xavier! It was pure luck, our running into Sebas tonight, my happening to loop him, instead of some *vaquero* of his.'

She still clung to his hand. The pressure, the nearness to her, worried him—and yet it was pleasant.

'How about this Nasco?' he asked quickly. 'Do you think he'll let you hold Gerónimo? Friendly to Sebas, as he's been, do you think you can handle him?'

'*El Toro*—my father—seemed to do it. Usually, you know, these colonels ride with the winner; they don't run against rope. I think we'll just have to chance it. If—if you'd stay on

205

Gerónimo, Lance—You're the kind of man my father was—more than just a fighter; a cowman, not just a cowboy. I—told you the truth, there on the cañon rim, when I thought we were certainly finished; I never met a man just like you.'

He laughed forcedly and patted her hand again.

'You're just worked up. It's natural, now the strain's slacked off. I'm a roving cowboy these days. We'll do more talking later on, when you're rested.'

'I guessed from things Fine said that you've lost a war in Texas,' she persisted—and still her hand was on his. 'You did lose a war? And—a ranch?'

'Not exactly. We actually won the war, but—'

Then he went on. Somehow, he could not help going on.

'I own half of a sizable cow-spread, but I can't stay in Texas to run it. My—partner will have to see to that. We won the war, but while we were winning it we—I, that is—lost—and—Oh, it's all mixed up; hard to talk about!'

'A girl?' she said quickly, hand tightening. 'There's a girl over there, Lance? A girl you're in love with?'

'Yes!' he answered grimly. 'I wish there wasn't!'

'So do I!' she whispered. 'Oh, so do I!'

Lance shifted in the saddle to look, first

behind him, then up at the sky.

'Beginning to drizzle,' he said. 'Well, I thought those clouds meant rain—said *The Old Sailor* confidently. Jerky! How's it? How's your li'l' playmate at the end of the string?'

'Good enough,' Xavier answered placidly. 'How much farther to that-there spring, Dolores?'

'Not far. With glasses, we'll be able to see the big house, below.'

She had loosed Lance's hand but still her horse crowded close to his. They went on, talking very little, until she led the way up to a wooded height and over it by trails now dripping with the fine, steady rain.

'There's a sort of cave over here,' she said presently. 'Rather, an overhanging ledge. It'll be the most comfortable place for us, while we're waiting. The spring is just beyond; comes out of the rocks and makes a little mouse-size creek that runs past the house.'

She laughed. Lance found a hard note in the sound.

'I used to sail paper boats in it—a thousand years ago, when I was young.'

They found the ledge and unsaddled. Xavier hunted out dry wood and built a fire on stones under the overhang. He grunted in satisfied tone and spread his big hands to the tiny blaze.

'Reminds me of one night I got lost in the Toledo Mountains,' he said. 'Going from Cordova to Madrid tintyping and pulling teeth and selling colored saints' pictures. I like to froze, that night. It was close to Christmas.'

Lance was staring curiously at their prisoner. Dolores, too, looked at the silent man near the fire. Lance thought he could read her mind. What Winters, Warren, and old Quint Lee would do to Sebas there was no doubting. And it was fair enough in this lawless land that the man who had made his own law and executed it should die because of that same law, executed by those others.

Until dawn came—without slackening of the rain—they smoked. Lance asked Dolores about the house down-slope; if it could be seen without glasses. Xavier stayed as guard while Lance and the girl went down to a bare point. She gestured downward, but through the rain they could see nothing except stock grazing close below.

'Have to wait for the rest of the bunch,' Lance said at last. 'Because—'

Then, from the direction of the house, there carried the rain-muffled rattle of shots. Closer and closer, while the two stared tensely the noise of a very battle came. Then riders showed, far away upon the flat, galloping, checking their horses as to fire at pursuers Lance could not see, then racing on again. Xavier and his charge came down. The latter stood staring at the running fight.

'There are binoculars in my *alforjas*,' he said slowly. 'But I do not need them to say that yonder are men of Gerónimo, running away. Which must mean that your side has attacked. But I did not know that you had men enough, *señorita*, to drive that score of *vaqueros...*'

Lance ran back to the horses and from the saddle pockets snatched the fine Zeiss binoculars. He ran back to focus the powerful lenses upon the battle. Now, behind the Sebas men he saw others, a long, thin skirmish line of riders.

'There's Winters!' he cried. 'And—and Fine! And—if that's not Estrella Morro—'

'We could metagrobolize 'em, kind of, from this side,' Xavier said thoughtfully. 'Dolores, could you watch Sebas whilst Lance and me took cards in this?'

She nodded, if a shade doubtfully.

'I think Sebas's men are heading for the spring over yonder,' she told Lance. 'There's the trail up. We can drive 'm back from that boulder. Jerky, if you'll get the long guns, we can all take cards!'

Xavier skipped up the slope to the saddles and came back with carbines for Lance and Dolores and his own long rifle. With their prisoner they moved down to the great red boulder the girl had indicated. Xavier lined his sights on a man two hundred yards away, a *vaquero* riding in the van of the driven warriors. With the crash of the heavy rifle, the man pulled his horse in short, seemed to gape their way, then whirled to gallop off to the left.

209

Others of his side split their line and went to one flank or other of the hill.

Lance killed a horse. Xavier fired again and the man who had been his first target dropped off, to be dragged by foot in stirrup. Behind the Sebas men came Estrella's warriors from Pepita, with Winters and Fine Upham. Man after man of the *vaqueros* fell, or was thrown from a horse killed. Within three or four minutes only the men following Estrella were in sight from the slope where Lance, Xavier, and Dolores watched. Lance began to yell and wave.

'Oh, Fine!' he called again and again. 'Fine! This is Lance—and Jerky—and Dolores—and Luis Sebas! Sebas!'

CHAPTER TWENTY-ONE

'IT IS A LETTER!'

Fine came at the gallop up to the foot of the hill and sat staring. Estrella Morro was only behind him, sitting her big horse almost down upon its tail. It was she who spoke first:

'Sebas? Now, what is this talk of Luis Sebas? We killed Sebas at the *casa grande* of Gerónimo, with certain ones of his, *Anglo* and *Méjicano*, before we drove these *vaqueros*.'

Lance turned to the impassive, silent

prisoner. Now amusement showed in the narrow, dark eyes, the lift of the thin-lipped mouth. Dolores was staring at him, also.

'Who are you, then, if Sebas is dead?' she demanded.

'I am Colonel Francisco Nasco. It did not seem wise to me to say, when you captured me, that I am the colonel called friendly to Luis Sebas. There was always the chance that I might—leave you; or that Sebas would come up with you. But now, it seems that I must make virtue of necessity. I am Nasco and—what will you do?'

Estrella and Fine rode up the slope. The Mexican girl stared heavy-lidded at Nasco. Scarlet mouth began to tighten. Her hand slid to the pistol in her sash. But Lance had seen and he took two long steps to her stirrup and caught her wrist. He held it—with an effort—against her fierce struggle, so that she could not draw the pistol.

'Sebas you killed,' he told her. 'But Colonel Nasco is my prisoner and *I* say what shall be done with him.'

'He will be killed,' she said thickly. 'He will be killed as Sebas was killed. Take your hand away!'

Nasco looked calmly from Lance to Dolores.

'If it is permitted,' he said, in English heavily accented, but understandable, 'perhaps I can make a bargain with you. I am a Spaniard, no

Mexican. Before I come to Mexico, having fought against the Moors and other people across the sea, I was for a time in your United States. So I speak English after a fashion; understand it even better.'

He looked at Estrella, who was scowling at him.

'I have listened to your talk; your thought of what is to be next, for Gerónimo; your—question about me. Now, it is true that, after Sebas won against your father, I supported him in a fashion. If the civil authorities would not displace Sebas from what he had seized, it was no affair of the military. Now, suppose I give you my word to support you, much more than I supported Sebas, in possession of Gerónimo? To, not merely leave you in possession as perhaps my successor would not be inclined to leave you, but to protect you with my troopers? Is that worth—my life?'

He shrugged and the thin smile widened.

'If I must die, then I will die. There will be no crying out about so small a thing. But I would rather live!'

'If we could trust you!' Dolores said doubtfully.

'That—I am sorry!—you must decide in your own mind. But I am sure that you have never heard of Francisco Nasco breaking his word. I promise you, not only to consider you the owner of Gerónimo, but to support you against attack with my troopers. Is

212

that enough?'

Estrella was impatient of this talk she could not understand. She jerked against Lance's hand, snarling.

'Talk! Talk! Talk!' she cried. 'I have said he dies!'

'Cut him loose, Jerky!' Lance said abruptly. 'Give him back his horse and take him over the hill. See that he gets clear. Fine! Help me with this *tigre* of yours!'

When she saw the bonds cut from Nasco, Estrella pulled and kicked and swore furious many-jointed oaths. Lance twisted her wrist and the Colt dropped. With Fine's help he pulled her from the saddle and they held her, Fine pinning her arms to her sides from behind, Lance squatting, holding her ankles, while she struggled angrily, threatening them.

Nasco went up to his horse, saddled and mounted. He lifted a hand and bowed to Dolores.

'*Hasta la vista!*' he called. 'I will put some miles between me and—such as that. I will go back to my troopers. I—am glad that they were not behind me, last night.'

He disappeared into the thickets at the gallop, riding like a part of the big horse. Estrella sagged.

'*Muy bien!*' she yielded sullenly. 'He is gone. So I say nothing more—except that it was the act of a fool to let him go. I would have killed him as I killed Sebas and the others.'

213

'Here come the others,' Fine grunted. 'Dolores, that pretty pilgrim of yours has made a Hand! Yes, sir! He's as nice a shot as you'd want to see. Says he read how to do it in a book—a book with red covers. Says everybody back in Newark—that's in New Jersey—learns to shoot and ride and punch cows out of books. But if you'll let him stay down here—'

'He's a darling, if he is a pilgrim,' Dolores said, looking at Lance and flushing. 'And if he wants to stay—'

Tommy Downes led Winters and Warren and some of Estrella's men up to the foot of the hill. The boy pulled in his black horse with a flourish, Lance noted how much easier he was today, in the saddle, than upon the occasion of racing away from Campoblanco. He lifted a hand, like an Indian.

'Hi!' he yelled. 'If you haven't got Gerónimo back, Dolores, fumigated by smoke, Newark's not in New Jersey.'

'Reckon we can go down to the house,' Lance said to the girl. 'I—wouldn't be surprised if there's some mopping up to do around the place.'

He went up to saddle Gray Eagle and her bay. Tommy came up the slope and sat watching. At last, he met Lance's eyes—and for the first time in their acquaintance Lance saw the boy serious. He waited.

'Fine told me a thing or two,' Tommy said hesitantly. 'After you and Jerky—and

214

Dolores—had left Pepita. About Mesquite. About—a girl over there. You can always tell me to go to hell, of course, but I'd like to know how you feel about Miss Lucy Kane of the C Bar. Because for the first time in my long and crowded life—crowding twenty-three years— I've fallen in love. Head over heels. The way you fall when you don't get up but just lie there. And I know that if you're in the contest, I play second fiddle and play squeaky. Which is natural, but—'

'Ease your mind, my son!' Lance checked him, grinning. 'I am in no manner a candidate. I'm glad you feel that way about her. My advice to you is—stick around the place. Turn yourself into a cowman. She's very fond of you. Now! I've told you all I possibly can. That's because I like you. I felt toward you from the beginning as if you were—not my son, exactly ... No'—he grinned more widely and dropped the stirrup on Dolores's saddle— 'more as if you were my grandson! Here!'

He handed over Dolores's reins and Tommy rode down the slope leading the big bay. Xavier came up and got his mule. Lance and Fine found themselves together on the flat. Dolores and Estrella were talking—almost cordially. A beef was to be killed for the men of Pepita and the others. Winters and a grizzled Pepita rider were arranging for nephews and distant cousins of the Mexican to ride for Gerónimo.

215

Then over a distant ridge two men came. Estrella looked mechanically that way and as automatically said:

'It is Juancito Garcia—Abran Garcia's third son. But who rides with him I do not know. A Mexican, but—'

She shrugged indifferently, turning back to Dolores. The riders came nearer. Lance, watching, suddenly leaned a little, frowning incredulously. Dolores watched him.

'What is it?' she asked him. 'Who is it?'

'Fine! Look!' Lance said sharply. 'That's Arminio Salazar, from the C Bar. Now—what would he be doing over here?'

'You told him we was heading for Campoblanco,' Fine answered calmly, but staring hard. 'If he wanted you, he certainly knew part of the road to ride to find you! He—'

But Lance spurred Gray Eagle into a gallop and came up to the pair approaching. Young Arminio's thin, brown face split in flashing grin. He jumped his stocky sorrel forward past the slim youth of Pepita.

'*Patron! Patron!*' he cried. 'I have hunted you—In Campoblanco they talked of you—but it was hard to find you, and when I came here today there was so much shooting—'

'Yes, yes!' Lance stopped him impatiently. 'But why did you come, Arminio? Is it—something about Mesquite? About the C Bar? Tell!'

'It is a letter! That, and what I may tell you.

216

A letter from Judge Oakes. A warning. *Patron!* Have you seen, in Campoblanco or elsewhere, two men, *Anglos*, who call themselves Bill Ranier and Joe Yale? Ranier is much like you in size, in the yellowness of his hair, the blueness of his eyes; of much your age, too. He smiles much—and kills as he smiles. The man Yale is much older—perhaps he has fifty years. He is small and very dark and very quick. He strikes like the rattler. They came from Mesquite, hunting you.'

'I have not seen these men. Why are they hunting me?'

'They were chosen by the sheriff, by that coyote, Ull Varner, to find you! They have been ordered to kill Fine Upham or any other who may ride with you, then bring *you* back to Mesquite for hanging. Five thousand dollars, we hear, is the price the sheriff will pay.'

'What?' Lance grunted. He turned to Fine, who had thudded up a moment before. 'Five— thousand—dollars! Do you mean that the reward for me is of that size? In so poor a county as Mesquite! For killing Oscar Nall!'

'No, no! Here is the notice of the reward!'

He leaned to fumble in an *alforja* and fish out a folded dodger. Lance took it and opened it. Fine crowded up to see. They read quickly, then looked at Arminio.

'But this is for seven hundred fifty dollars— and that for my delivery to the sheriff in Mesquite. Arminio! Do you *know* these things you say, or do you but talk?'

'I was told them by the judge. He gave me a letter and I have sewed it in the skirt of my saddle. But because that letter might be lost, he told me some of what he had written. Told me to warn you of these men; of the pay they were to get and which would make them most anxious to take you; and to say—be most careful because'—Arminio scowled—'because "while Frank Larkman is no Oscar Nall, as husband of Lucy the C Bar would be put in the hand of Ull Varner by him." *That* is how he made me learn it.'

'Give me the letter,' Lance said slowly. Then, when Arminio swung down and began to open a corner of his saddle-skirt. 'Who *is* the man Frank Larkman, who is not so bad as Oscar Nall, but one to put the C Bar into Ull Varner's hand, when he has married *la patrona*?'

'He is the nephew of the sheriff. First he worked for old York Insall in the office of the freight corral. Then in the bank. Then at buying stock and trading for Ull Varner. At the last he was here and there, for Oscar Nall. We saw much of him on the C Bar, *patron. La patrona*—it seemed to some of us that she liked Frank Larkman as much as she liked Oscar Nall. And those of us who watched—we liked neither!'

He handed over the smudged envelope and waited. Lance unfolded the sheet of paper that came from that envelope and skimmed the even lines of precise, vertical writing. He laughed grimly at the judge's phraseology, and looked at Fine.

'Judge says this comes by the same hand that brought him "a package"—and that the "package" has accomplished or is accomplishing its planned purpose. Foxy old bird! That's one way of saying that the money you got back from Oscar Nall has paid off the mortgage and is restocking the place. And—'

He read the final paragraphs again and straightened, to stare at the waiting riders on the flat, who looked their way but courteously did not intrude.

'Ranier and Yale and a man named Eddy hit Mesquite and apparently knew Ull Varner. He offered Ranier this five thousand to snake me back across the line. But Eddy got cold feet and hit the bottle. Ran into old York Insall and spilled enough of the tale to send Insall—he's an old friend of the C Bar—to the judge. Then he must have got even more scared, for he hightailed.'

He shrugged, still looking almost blindly straight ahead.

'I don't know how the judge knows all he knows, but I'll trust him! Ull Varner has taken over the county where Oscar was knocked loose from it. Lucy was always fond of Frank Larkman. They're going to play on that. Larkman's to step in, now that Oscar's dead. He's to marry Lucy after I'm out of the way.

That will give Ull Varner the C Bar. Simple!'

'And you're heading for Mesquite,' Fine said wearily. 'What'll these hairpins—Ranier and Yale—do when they find we've slipped around 'em and got back over?'

'What do you mean—*we*?' Lance demanded. 'You don't think for a minute I'd hold in Eagle so's your billy-goat could keep in sight of him—when I'd be in a hurry?'

'Billygoat? Why—you forsaken, ignorant pilgrim! You wouldn't know a horse from a burro! That 'Chacho of mine'll kick dust in your crowbait's face every kick for fifty mile! Why—ah, hell! *You* don't think for a minute I'd trust you over there with rough people around, unless I could be in saving distance of you?'

Arminio looked from face to face, grinning delightedly.

'Ah, well,' Fine sighed, 'say no more about it, son. I'll side you if it gets me killed. My fond payrents always did say to me, if I never mended my ways, something awful'd catch up with me—like getting killed or married or such-like.'

Lance turned Gray Eagle. Winters and Warren were going off, now. Dolores faced him, Tommy beside her. Estrella Morro and her men were a little to the side.

'What's it all about? The conference?' Dolores called.

'A message from Texas,' Lance answered

slowly. 'Fine and I'll be pulling out, tomorrow.'

'But—I thought it wasn't safe for you—and—'

'Of course it's safe,' Lance scoffed. 'All I've got to do is stay out of sight of certain ones who know me. And—anyway—I've got to go back. There's trouble over there.'

'You can have every man on Gerónimo—and me!' she said impulsively. 'If it's a fight, Lance—'

'I think there will be men enough—thanks just the same. Arminio, did the men come, sent by Socrates Morrill?'

Arminio shrugged expressively.

'They came, yes. But—*la patrona* would have none of them when they said you had hired them. So they rode away. And she began to hire a man here, a man there—'

'I'll go with you,' Tommy Downes said a shade hesitantly.

'So'll I,' Jerky Xavier grunted. 'I was a fool ever to cross into Mexico. Looks like I never will take a picture, or pull a tooth, or sell a pair of spec's. All I been doing is climb off and on that blame' mule of mine.'

'You trail with us, Jerky,' Lance decided. 'I'd like to have you side us, Tommy, if it was a business of fighting. But, right now, it looks more like scheming! And I'm blessed if I know even what kind.'

They rode slowly in the dust of Winters and

Warren. Lance talked most casually to Dolores, of the things she needed to do. She nodded and answered shortly, absently, watching him.

'It's—about that girl,' she charged, abruptly.

'It's about my half of the C Bar outfit! I'm in danger of losing my neck and my money. Now, you can get old Quintus Lee down from Tecolote's—'

Estrella and her Pepita men surged past them and were scattered about the huge house of the *hacienda* when the six of them rode leisurely past the corrals and drew rein.

'You certainly did have a fight here,' Lance told Fine, surveying the bullet-pocked walls of house and hands' quarters, the sprawling bodies—at which Dolores tried not to look. 'You—Who were the two yonder at the corner? They're *Anglos!*'

'Do'no',' Fine said scowlingly, staring. 'Estrella's gang was over here. We started chasing when they bust out—'

Arminio followed when Fine trotted toward the fallen cowboys. And almost instantly the boy whirled and yelled:

'*Patron!* Oh, *Don Lancito*! Ranier! And Yale!'

CHAPTER TWENTY-TWO

'TIME TO BE HIGHTAILING!'

Five days later, Lance, with Fine and Jerky and Arminio, sprawled comfortably in camp some twenty miles above Mesquite. They had come to this hilltop by roundabout ways, after leaving Gerónimo. Now, in the dust of the gray *caliche* soil, using a greasewood twig for stylus, Lance drew lines. Fine and Jerky watched.

'We're here, the point of a triangle,' he said, squinting against the up-wreathing smoke of his cigarette. 'Down here is Mesquite, where the noble Mr Varner does sheriffing and odd jobs such as cutting throats from behind, robbing sick Mexicans—if small enough!— and stealing C Bars. Down here is Lanak, a right salty town, my pious friends and drunken companions! Yes, sir! Right—salty!'

He looked at the young *vaquero* and Arminio waited, expectant grin widening.

'Back to the C Bar for you,' Lance said— and repeated it in Spanish. 'By way of Mesquite, certainly. You will say to the good judge that your errand is finished. The letter has been delivered and—even if Frank Larkman is no Oscar Nall, I cannot find it in my heart to love anyone of Ull Varner's blood. When that anyone wishes to own my half of the

C Bar, I love him even less. And when I do not love this anyone—'

'Oh—*zapatazos*!' Fine groaned. 'If only you could get Larkman and Varner into earshot, you could talk 'em to death! Speak your piece and let the boy go. He's staggering, right now. He'll fall off his horse, trying to pack that load to Mesquite!'

'And when I do not love this anyone, he repeated,' Lance said with dignity, 'I take steps—long steps, in his direction. You will say to Judge Oakes that I am taking steps. He will hear from me. He may even hear of me!'

'I will go,' Arminio told him unwillingly. 'But, *patron*, I should like to ride with you, instead. And would it not be a good thing for you to have a man of the C Bar at your side?'

'You will watch on the C Bar, and when I come there you will tell me what has been done, what you have seen. Fine, if you and Jerky'll explore around Mesquite, I'll take Lanak. I don't know what Varner's up to—except for sending those two would-be hard cases across to Campoblanco. But there's bound to be a way to spoke his wheel, and that's what I'm after.'

'And you figure you can ram your nose into this Lanak—or any other place in Mesquite County—without having somebody know you? Lance, I swear—'

'I think so. In Lanak, anyway. I'll amble down and come in after dark. Not many saw

224

me, in Mesquite. And then only for a little while. And I'd been away seven years. Jerky, is it all right with you to head for Mesquite with Fine?'

'Sounds quiet,' the fat man said. 'And that suits me. I ain't a fighter, no more. I'm a tintyper and a spec's expert or I'll pull your teeth. All I want's to make an honest living— safe! Where'll we meet you next?'

'On the road from Mesquite to Lanak there's a bunch of arroyos below a three-jag hill. You and Fine wait there, tomorrow or next day. I'll be along. You can't miss the hill. A spring's up in the main arroyo, running a trickle of water.'

Jerky nodded and rolled to put out a thick arm and unbuckle the top of a saddlebag. He fumbled in the *alforja's* depths and brought out a flat brown bottle.

'Liniment,' he said gravely. 'For centipede bites. Ahhh!'

Fine rolled, in his turn, and snatched at the bottle.

'I swear!' he said marvelingly. 'I bet there ain't a bit of bottom to your *alforjas*. If a man was to ask you for a rabbit—not a white rabbit or a black rabbit, but one with a pink cross on his off hip—I bet you'd dig it out for him!'

'Well,' Jerky drawled, eyes twinkling as he watched Fine drink, 'that'd depend on if there was something worthwhile in the proposition. One time in Portugal I got a duck out of that saddlebag there, for the *Jefe* of a li'l' town. It was his duck, but what you don't know don't hurt you.'

Lance finished the pint, Arminio waving it away. Then Fine, Jerky, and Arminio saddled. Lance lazed on his blanket, watching them. He was in no hurry to ride for Lanak. The sun was just clearing the eastern hills and it was only fifteen miles or so to the little town. He saw them off and continued to sprawl and smoke and look down from the hill.

As far as eye could reach the flats stretched away, a wilderness of greasewood and mesquite and grass, studded with cactus and the crooked staves of ocatillo. A Mexican eagle made a dusky blob in air, where it circled hunting rabbits.

'And Ull Varner wants me—or wants the C Bar—five thousand dollars' worth,' Lance said slowly, viciously, aloud. 'If he can make a murder charge stick and send me to Huntsville or swing me on his rope, it won't be any speckled calf and sorebacked horse *he* sets up in the cow-business with. And Lucy—she was friendly with this Larkman before Oscar made his play. All he has to do is slide back into place...'

He flipped away the butt of his cigarette.

'Why the devil did I have to pick her? If I hadn't, I could tell her to take the C Bar and do anything she wanted with it. Dolores—I would give Tommy Downes all the fight his young

226

stomach could stand, in that direction.'

He pictured the girl as he had last seen her, before the corrals at Gerónimo, the dark hair, the olive-tinted oval of her face, the grave, dark eyes. He liked her. She liked him. But Lucy's face slid in between, blotted out Dolores's. He went over to Gray Eagle and freed the end of his lariat.

'Let's amble toward the Lanak, horse,' he said grimly.

He saddled and rode down into the flat and turned into one of the winding stock-trails that cut this section of the 99 range. He kept the ugly gray at a running walk and made a long nooning. He saw nobody until late in the afternoon and the cowboy he met was a stranger, a 99 rider coming out from Lanak on an errand for old Elbert Gore, his boss. He was heading for the house, he said, when he and Lance halted to talk for a few minutes.

It was good dark when Lance put Gray Eagle in Lanak livery barn and walked up the long, cottonwood-shaded main street of the place. He stopped before the Grizzly Bear Saloon and looked in. There was a long line of drinkers and the ceiling was canopied with smoke from cigars, cigarettes, and pipes. The noise of the Grizzly Bear drifted out to the street and Lance thought it must remind a passer-by of Sunday-School lessons.

'Not,' he told himself with grim humor, 'because of anything religious about the racket, but because it ought to make a person think of the Tower of Babel.'

He had a pistol in his waistband under the shirt. Now, he shifted it slightly and went slouching into the saloon to push between two tall men at the bar. They were talking to each other, and he listened to accounts of range conditions and thought how familiar it all sounded to a man who had been brought up in Mesquite County.

He looked up and down the bar with veiled sharpness, at these men who smelled of horse, and he was as alert as any lobo of the hills about. Then as he huddled over his drink he saw Tad Taylor, who for longer than Lance could remember had been the deputy of Lanak, serving under various sheriffs of Mesquite County. His pulses jumped with a pleasant thrill. Here was a test. If Tad, the Law in this end of the county, did not recognize him, he was safe almost anywhere.

He finished the drink and looked at the bartender. Some dozen years before, as a seventeen-year-old, Lance had seen 'Hair Oil' kill a tough customer with the bar shotgun. He came down the bar in answer to Lance's raised fingers, and this time he stared straight into the customer's face. There was no sign of recognition in the broad, pink face as he poured whisky into Lance's glass.

'There y' are,' Hair Oil said sourly. 'And if y' knowed as much as I know about the damn' stuff y' wouldn't never touch it none. Y' would—'

'I was in a place called the Astor House, once,' Lance interrupted dreamily. 'That's in a place called Shanghai in a place called China. And I recall a drink peddler there in the Astor Bar much like you in looks. But—the next time I went in he wasn't behind the bar. A new man told me this other one—the one that looked like you—had got killed. Yeh. For handing out too much of good advice...'

'Is *that* so!' Hair Oil snarled. 'Well, le' me tell y' something, young pilgrim, before y' git much older in Lanak: No cow-chaser I ever seen makes back-talk to me! No—'

Lance yawned elaborately. But he saw Tad Taylor coming along the bar and mentally he cursed the impulse to speak of China. There was nothing wrong with Tad's hearing or his head. Now, he had stopped to regard Lance's reflection in the bar-mirror. He was as tall as the younger man, but not so wide of shoulder; and he began to carry fat around his waist. Lance found him as dark and grim as the very butt of his Colt.

Lance picked up his drink. Hair Oil moved away, mumbling. Tad halted directly behind Lance, who kept dirty, stubbled face blank.

'A walking sight draft for seven hundred and fifty dollars,' Lance thought. 'That's what I am. Good thing it's only Ull Varner's special pets who can get more, or there'd be a real hue and cry. Better, that the commissioners are paying for my arrest, not saying "dead or alive."'

'Stranger, ain't you?' Tad asked after seconds of staring. He had a low voice and drawling, but that made his tone none the more pleasant. 'Don't recall seeing you around.'

Lance turned clear around as if noticing the deputy for the first time. He nodded yellow head and stared Tad fixedly in the eyes.

'Mister,' he said courteously, relapsing into the thickest of drawls, 'I reckon I was *bawn* to be a stranger. Sometimes I think I'm like that old steer you maybe heard about, over in the Glass Mountains. Used to be, every cowboy in Presidio or Brewster Counties couldn't build him a fire in a branding pen till he'd dabbed a loop on Old Coaly and slapped another iron on the critter.'

'Yeh, I heard about Old Coaly,' Tad admitted evenly. 'But *he* was a outlaw steer...'

'He had long horns, too! You wouldn't expect me to match up with him every way!'

'Ah, folks hit Lanak often, toting long horns. And git 'em knocked off. Where you from? What you aiming to do? I take it you can see my badge.'

'Uh-huh,' Lance said carelessly. 'I see it. Who's sheriff of your county?'

'Ull Varner. But he's over at Mesquite, the county seat. In Lanak you deal with me, Tad Taylor. You're dealing with me right now. I
230

asked you a couple questions.'

'Fair questions, too! I reckon I hail from the Tres Rios country—above Tularosa in New Mexico,' Lance said mendaciously. 'Do'no' yet what I aim to do. Might even take up punching cows. If I'm offered a job, I'll likely take it.'

He was thinking fast. If Taylor decided to make this inquisition official—though Lance could see no reason for Tad showing that much interest—and haul him over to Mesquite for examination, what would be best to do? And where? Should he pull a gun and smash out of the Grizzly Bear? Would it be better to wait, playing the harmless cowboy for Tad's benefit?

He showed his calculation by no smallest movement of a muscle, but continued to stare hard into Tad's eyes. And Tad himself settled the problem, for the time being.

'Be seeing you,' he grunted, moving off.

One of the cowmen who had been listening and watching now sighed gustily and leaned a little to the 'stranger.' He was a red little man, with flaming hair beginning to be salted with gray, and he had a loose, garrulous, good-humored mouth.

'Watch y' step!' he counseled hardly above a whisper. 'He maybe don't look it, but that-there Tad Taylor's hell on redstripedy wheels. Lots worse'n his boss, the sheriff.'

'I never mistook him none,' Lance assured

231

him in like low voice. 'But what's he so touchy about? Up and down and over Texas—and in Arizona and New Mexico and some other states—there's hundreds of roving cowboys that've got no more home than ary old cow. Ain't none hit Lanak, before?'

'We had plenty trouble around here,' the cowman said, looking at his silent companion. 'Yeh. Between four men: John Craig and Orval Kane was two old-timers and they owned 'em a fine ranch, the C Bar. A slick boy name' Oscar Nall kind of took charge of the county and put Ull Varner in for sheriff. Nobody exactly knows the straight of it, but Craig and Kane got killed on the range and—'

His watery blue eyes roved cautiously up and down.

'We don't talk a lot about this, unless we know blame' well who we're talking to and where we're setting. But I watched y' making up y' mind about pulling on Taylor ... A few weeks back all that was left of the C Bar was a big mortgage that Nall held. Just a boy and a gal owned the frazzled tassel-end of the C Bar: Craig's boy, Lance; Kane's gal, Lucy. Lance come back from some foreign parts unexpected and there was plenty powder burned and Nall got killed. Then somebody walked in with money to pay off the mortgage—Judge Oakes, a fine lawyer in Mesquite, I heard—and restock the C Bar.'

'Sounds like this Lance Craig and Lucy

Kane are setting all right, then. Way you tell it, somebody must have suspicioned this Nall was a scoun'el of sorts.'

'Somebody done just that. But Nall's killing, they're calling it a murder. Lance Craig killed him and no matter how he done it, there's a warrant out for him—murder. He split the breeze. Now, Ull Varner and his nephew, a big, good-looking, trifling boy name' Frank Larkman, they're starting the old trouble over ag'in. And the same stealing that put a mortgage on the C Bar, *that* has started ag'in! Looks like the outfit'll go bust' the second time. This Larkman boy's aiming to marry Lucy Kane after his uncle catches Lance Craig and hangs him and—'

He stopped short, for cowboys were coming in and toward where they stood. The other man, a tall and thin-mouthed cowman, shook his head disapprovingly.

'There's places where a man'd git hisself killed, for saying half what *he* just told you. In fact, some men riding out to thei'selves on lonesome range, they have got killed! Now, my notion is'—he looked at the cowboys and leaned to Lance's ear—'Ull Varner expects this Lance Craig to slide back over from Mexico and start shooting. If he can catch the boy, he can certainly convict him of murder, with the kind of jury he can pack in at Mesquite.'

With that, he moved away from the bar and away from Lance. A time or two that night, when Lance saw him, the gray cowman avoided his company. Which, Lance thought, was evidence enough of the condition of Mesquite County.

He slept in the livery corral and was up early. Lanak had nothing more to show him, he decided at noon. He had learned no more than he had known in the beginning, but it interested him to find that Ull Varner's plans for the C Bar were so well published. He had a last drink in the Grizzly Bear and again Tad Taylor came up behind him.

'Still job-hunting, huh?' Tad grunted. 'Say! You been in Lanak before? Something about you—'

'Uh-uh,' Lance lied calmly. 'Drink?'

Tad shook his head and went out. Presently Lance followed, careful to slouch along, confident that dirt and beard and shabbiness of overalls and ancient hat and worn boots made him a figure indistinguishable among cowboys.

'Time to be hightailing!' he thought. 'Tad's beginning to wonder and if he wonders enough—even without recognizing me—he'll have me in Varner's office. And I won't fool Ull!'

Going toward the big livery barn and Gray Eagle, he had to pass the room which Tad Taylor used for office. He looked in but saw nothing of the deputy.

He came up to the livery barn very quietly and, instead of approaching the wide front

234

door, he went a little way down the 'dobe wall to where a square, open window permitted a cautious man to inspect the dusky interior of the place.

Almost the first thing he saw was a broad, familiar back, not six feet from the window. Fine Upham stood very still, with something strained about his moveless pose. Staring past him, Lance saw the stall which held Gray Eagle—and in the door of it, leaning upon a bar, Tad Taylor lounged. The pistol in his hand was plain.

'Too many strangers, hitting Lanak all of a sudden,' Tad was saying. 'Specially nosey strangers that look like they're interested in other strangers' hawses.'

'But you can't ever go around, killing off strangers just because they're strangers!' Fine objected. 'Why—'

'Don't you be too sure about what I can do—or what I won't do, neither,' Tad halted him. 'Think it'll be a good notion for you to take a *pasear* over to Mesquite. Along with the fella owning this hawse. And along with me, too...'

'Just come in from Mesquite,' Fine said without alarm. 'Nothing to be going back for. Better pull in your horns.'

Lance moved from the window and ducked below its sill. There was another door almost at the corner and he slipped through it. From the line of stalls the voices of Fine and Tad carried to him. He had to go slowly, because his feet rustled on straw. But before the two had changed positions he had worked up behind the deputy sheriff. He lifted his gun and struck Tad deftly with the barrel...

CHAPTER TWENTY-THREE

'C BAR LINE!'

Fine moved as Tad fell forward. He looked down, then up, and shook his dark head.

'If you ain't just about the suddenest hairpin! And *he* ought to be glad. Because it saved his life when you cracked him on the knot. I was wondering what to do; auguring with myself about it.'

He lifted a hand to show the .41 derringer that had been resting in his palm during the talk with Tad. He sighed and shoved the wicked little Remington back into an overalls pocket.

'Reckon we better be fogging it,' he suggested easily. 'The hostler ought to be coming back from the Grizzly Bear any minute. He left me to look at things while he went after four fingers of red-eye. Jerky's out on the road at that three-jag hill you told us about.'

Lance whistled, nodding and staring at Tad.

At last he grinned. He bent over the unconscious figure and took Tad's pistols, his handcuffs, and his badge. For final touch he yanked the boots from the deputy's feet. Tad moved slightly, groaning. Fine came forward and stooped. He took one of Tad's pistols and rapped him across the temple lightly. Tad slumped again and Fine looked inquiringly at his companion.

'You get the *caballos*,' Lance drawled. 'I am going to show Lanak something the old town never saw before.'

Fine crossed to the stall and led Gray Eagle out. As he saddled the gray he kept an eye on that door through which the hostler might come. Lance got another horse into the open and borrowed a rope from the nearest hanging saddle.

'Lend us a hand with him, now!' he called to Fine. 'Up with him. We'll rope him to this bronc'—'

When they were done and their own horses waited at that corner door through which Lance had entered, Tad presented a figure which—as Lance had promised—Lanak had never seen. He sprawled along the little black's spine, bare feet tied beneath its belly, wrists handcuffed together under its neck. Around his neck was the double-holstered shell belt, pistols sagging down his back.

Lance led the black to the front door and slapped it on the haunch. It walked out onto the street and turned as by direction toward the Grizzly Bear. Fine shook his head:

'And I waste time traveling with a nitwit that plays child tricks like that!' he complained. 'Ah, me! First I decided to be a cowboy. That proved I ought to have my head examined. Then I turned over a new leaf and began to stick up banks and trains. But my noble soul couldn't stand dishonesty. And so I took up cowpunching again and had to fall in with you—Ah! They see him! We had better split the breeze.'

A group of men had gathered about the black, now. Tad moved upon it. Suddenly, the little horse shoved down its head and bucked through the scattering men. It pitched across the street and back. Then a cowboy rode up beside it and dropped a loop over its head.

Lance and Fine crossed the barn at a run and Fine's subdued whoops belied his reproval of an instant before. They mounted and rode out of Lanak into greasewood and mesquite. Lance led the way over this familiar country until a deep arroyo sheltered them.

'From things I heard around,' he said grimly, 'there won't be a lot of playing for us. Mesquite County does seem to get worse day by day.'

'From what I picked up in Mesquite, the county's a lot worse'n you think it is!' Fine assured him grimly. 'I swapped lead with Sheriff Ull Varner and a couple others, last

238

night. Jerky and me rolled up dust leaving that town.'

'Let's have that tale!' Lance commanded. 'I swear! Sometimes you do get under my hide even worse than other times. And that's amazing! You didn't say a word, back there, about any shooting scrape—'

'I know, I know,' Fine said meekly. 'I ought've stopped you while you was sneaking up behind that star-strutter, to tell you all the history. *He* would have been glad to wait, of course. What're we in Mesquite County for, anyhow? To stop Ull Varner and his precious nephew, Larkman, from taking over the C Bar—your half as well as Lucy Kane's—ain't we? That's what I figured I went to Mesquite for, to find out what's happened and how we can spoke that wheel. And *where* would I find out more about everything than around the sheriff's office?'

'You mean you went to Ull Varner, after all we said about keeping out of sight?'

'Well, not exactly,' Fine said, grinning. 'I didn't go up to Varner and give him my love and right name and ask him to tell me what he was scheming. I sort of hung around the edges and, when Varner and Larkman and a hard case I didn't get a name for, *they* went into the back of the sheriff's office, to begin talking, I slid under a window. I heard enough of the powwow to make a fine witness out of me: C Bar horses going to a place called Lone Cabin.

239

Then some soft-walking gunie stepped on my back and I hit him and he hit me and the others come piling outside. I hid up in the *bosque* outside town and Jerky rambled out to side me. Where's Lone Cabin?'

'I'll show you,' Lance promised. 'It's on the edge of C Bar range, between that and Wilbur Logan's tough Spear L outfit. The C Bar never used Lone Cabin much—any more than we had much to do with Spear L men.'

He turned north when they had looked over a high release with the glasses and found nothing of interest anywhere on the horizon. They rode during the remainder of the afternoon, stopping at the meeting place to pick up Xavier, then going on, talking little.

'C Bar line!' Lance announced as darkness came. 'Yes, sir! We're on the C Bar.'

'Love,' Fine said to Jerky, 'it's certainly a funny thing—when it ain't peculiar. Now, me, I never was bothered a bit by the feeling. I even swore time and time again I never'd ride with a hairpin worried by it. But, now, here I am! Yes, sir! Risking my valuable carcass just to help out a gunie that's been hit by one of them valentine things!'

'What d' you mean?' Jerky demanded with innocent face. 'Who's this-here hairpin Cupid's dabbed a loop on?'

'Yeh! Who is he?' Lance put in. 'Seems to me that, after that exhibition in Pepita, and our trouble getting you out of Estrella Morro's clutches at Gerónimo, you're the candidate!'

'Ah, me! And deceitful, too!' Fine sighed. 'And that's one of the worst signs when it ain't the plumb worst. Fella falls heels-over-tin-kettle in love, but he won't admit it. Well—she is a looker! Give me and Jerky jobs when you start running the C Bar again?'

'Who's a looker? The cousin, here, or Dolores?' Jerky asked. 'I never laid eyes, yet, on your cousin, Lance. But Dolores—and she's got a fine outfit, too...'

'Of all the one-idea'd cluckers!' Lance groaned.

'It's a hard, hard trail the boy rides,' Fine said solemnly to Jerky. 'Two lovely women... Now, there's some that holds with bigamizing, but I can say honest I never did. I always figured that a man that got married even once—'

He jumped Muchacho to the side and held up his hands.

'Now, now! Don't hurt me! I'm a only child and my skin's that tender—Ah, you wouldn't believe. Yes, sir! I'm delicate, kind of like a flower, a blue flower. But—'

He looked grimly straight ahead and tapped the stock of his carbine with two fingers.

'But, you have got plenty on your hands, young cowboy! Plenty! This is not Mexico. You can't just kill off Ull Varner and settle things. That'd be easy enough. But so long's they have got the law behind 'em, they can keep us on the run. If they need to—if we step on their toes too hard—they can call in a company of Rangers and run us out or wipe us out. And that is as sure as death and taxes; sure as li'l' green apples have specks—'

'Ah, don't say "specks"!' Jerky begged plaintively. 'Reminds me, I got six dozen pairs of assorted spec's riding the hull with me—and nary chance to sell a pair.'

They found a line camp, a little cabin of stone and 'dobe bricks. It was empty, but there was food inside and a bed roll. So the C Bar had become a working outfit again, Lance thought. And he had given Lucy Kane the money with which to clear it, set it going. He thought a good deal of Lucy, as the three of them sat eating C Bar bacon and beans and drinking the Arbuckle's. A pretty girl, lovelier now than he had expected her to be; lovely and—stubborn beyond belief when opposed...

A freckled and cheerful young cowboy rode up to the cabin as they finished eating. He finished the supper they had cooked, when he had accepted a drink from Jerky's bottle. Afterward, he settled himself to smoke and talk. Very apparently, he considered them the trio of saddle-tramps they proclaimed themselves. Like the other hands of the C Bar today—and he did not know how many hands might be on the place—he was new to the country. He liked the range better than the

Panhandle from which he had come.

'Looks like we're going to do all right,' he answered Lance's question. 'But they tell me it was plumb hell for a while, on this outfit. The boss—that's a fella name' Lance Craig—he got hisself into a jam. Ten different stories about how-come. Anyway, he's on the dodge for murder. In Mexico, some say. Canada or the Argentine, others think.'

'Not losing any stock these days?' Lance drawled.

'Not that I know of. But I'm just about learning the range. I don't think with them that says the Spear L fence is a bad place. I met this Logan and some of his hands on the range. Looked like good men to me. Say, Logan might give you men jobs. Or Miss Lucy—or her foreman, Parks—might. She is at the house, now, I think.'

Lance studied that guileless young face and decided not to ask more questions. He could hardly mention Lone Cabin or C Bar horses without rousing suspicion even in this boy. So he inquired the direction of the *casa grande* and refused for them all the hospital invitation to shelter and breakfast at the camp.

'All new hands—except for *vaqueros* like Montes and Anza and Arminio. If they're still on the place,' Lance said thoughtfully to Fine and Jerky. They were a long mile from the line camp. 'And Lucy's got a foreman; and she's on the place, now. I—wonder!'

Lone Cabin would have been hard to find, for any but a native of that broken range. It was like other ruinous places scattered the width and length of that vast Rio Grande country, an old house the history of which had been forgotten for years, a ruin sometimes glimpsed by stray-riders or chance travelers.

Mesquite and greasewood grew thick about it, even into the ragged doorway. A lonely place—and for that reason and, because it lay strategically near the line of C Bar and Spear L ranges, a good place for holding stock someone would not wish seen.

They studied it for a long time before going closer. At last, Fine shook his head.

'From what I caught of the talk in Varner's office, ought to be around fifty head of the C Bar's best and newest-bought horses around here. But—where are they?'

They explored the thickets all around, but of the expected horses there was no sign.

'No more'n if they had *flown* the miles to here from the pasture,' Fine suggested scowlingly.

'And that pasture would be Saddle Rock,' Lance decided. 'So we'll just ramble over and take a look at Saddle Rock.'

He took the lead again and they rode toward a high roll in the range. Twilight was near. All was very quiet as they sagged easily in the saddles and the horses foxtrotted drowsily ahead. Then three jets of orange flame seemed flipped toward them, from the crest of that ridge they approached. After that, the drum of the firing made a continuous rolling.

Lead tore the ground around them, whined in air about them, as they whirled their mounts and spurred furiously toward the shelter of rocks at the left of the ridge.

They were chased by bullets for a hundred yards and, as they made the cover of those boulders, the hammer of rifle fire died abruptly, to be replaced by the hollow pounding of hoofs.

Lance looked behind him, but the boulders were between. He wondered if they had come upon new and nervous riders of the C Bar. Or if Ull Varner, made suspicious perhaps by discovery of Fine beneath his office window, had laid a trap.

Either theory was quite plausible. And no matter who the riflemen might be, he and Fine and Jerky could not stop to investigate. So they sent the horses and mule deeper into the huge rocks, through to level country, then at the racing gallop toward Saddle Rock—which was merely highest, most conspicuous hill of a low, long range.

They had a long start of the pursuers, now— and owned the additional advantage of knowing every inch of this country as neither new riders of the C Bar nor men of Ull Varner could know it. Too, they were being forced straight toward the big house of the C Bar where, if necessary, Lance thought he might find help. And darkness was near.

They lost the sound of hoofbeats after a while and went on more slowly. Fine groaned:

'The man that sides you, he's certainly going to do his sleeping in the wintertime. If he ever does any. You happen to know where we can find some ni-ice, soft rocks? They will be allasame featherbed, to Jerky and me.'

Lance laughed.

'Well, I could take you and Jerky right up to the C Bar house. Let you sleep on a shuck mattress, anyway. But you accidentally might not wake up, tomorrow. I reckon it's going to be rocks for all of us, *Young Wild West*. This night, anyhow. Some rocks overlooking the house.'

They made their final stop on a hill above the fortlike 'dobe house of the Craigs. Fine made himself comfortable and looked down at the twinkle of lights. While Jerky snored he and Lance smoked and saw the lights vanish, one by one, until only in what Lance knew to be Lucy's room was there sign of wakefulness.

'It's a great old outfit,' Lance said slowly, at last. 'Worth risking something to save. If only they didn't have me crosswise with the law, I wouldn't worry. We could handle anything else. We—well, tomorrow's another day.'

CHAPTER TWENTY-FOUR

'HORSES DO DRIFT!'

Lance was first awake. It was the gray hour before dawn and he could see no sign of life about corrals or house below them. He went to where the animals had been staked in a motte of cottonwoods, saddled Gray Eagle, and rode off at the trot to make a long circuit of the house.

He had no expectation of meeting anyone at this hour. He hardly knew why he went—except that he did want to see how the place looked before he left it again. And, from what he saw through glasses, or at close range, Lucy was getting the C Bar into its ancient condition.

He turned back, after an hour, keeping to arroyos as much as possible. He was in grim mood. Everything that was familiar about the range—and everything he saw *was* familiar—made him realize the more keenly his outlawry. There were things to do, all about him, but he, the owner, must skulk over his own property—

Gray Eagle twisted about a flood-rolled boulder in an arroyo, turned a curve of the steep bank, and stopped short before Lucy Kane and Nancy Oakes, holding in their horses there. Lucy frowned at him blankly for a second or two, before her eyes widened and she shrank back in the saddle.

'You!' she breathed. 'You—what are you doing here?'

'Looking the place over,' he told her—and was surprised that his voice was even, almost casual. 'Seeing what's to do and what's been done. I didn't expect you out so early. One of the boys told me you were living out here.'

From head to foot he studied her—from narrowed hazel eyes to little alligator-hide boots.

'Lovely, lovely, lovely!' he thought. 'And still scared of me, hating me—same as Nancy. They're both scared stiff—as if I were a rattler in the trail—'

'You see,' he went on stiffly, 'I can be on the dodge and still own an interest in the place. Still entertain notions about—Ull Varner and Frank Larkman and—things.'

'Varner? Frank?'

The surprise in her tone and in her face was genuine, he decided. For it pushed out the tenseness as she stared, the strained fear that had stiffened both their faces with recognition of him.

'What—what *are* you talking about?' Lucy demanded. 'Ull Varner—what connection could he have with the C Bar? He or Frank, either one? Do you mean that some crazy idea about them induced you to come back here? With a warrant out for you and a

248

reward offered?'

'A warrant and a reward,' he said slowly, one corner of his mouth lifting as he fumbled for tobacco and papers without taking eyes from her face. 'A warrant for murder—when I gave Oscar the chance to kill me that he never gave your father or mine—a chance to make it a duel instead of the hanging he had coming to him—a chance he didn't have nerve enough to take. A warrant that you and Nancy and Homer Ripps are responsible for...'

His tone had grown harder and harder, and he stared at her so contemptuously that she flushed and her eyes wavered for a moment.

'I was late coming home. I admit that. But also I say I had no particular reason to come home, not being a mind-reader. Everything was well enough on the C Bar when I left—when I was invited to leave. But I did come back—and found the place gone to pieces. And *I* had eyes to see—more than you had. I could see, the same as Judge Oakes has seen all along, that it was Oscar Nall and his hired thieves and murderers who had ruined the place. Be still!'

She had leaned angrily with lifting hand. But she stopped short with the furious snarl.

'Oscar Nall! Ull Varner! Oscar, the smooth, sneaking swindler and assassin. Varner, his slinking sheriff. Not only did Oscar murder your father and mine, but he hoodled *you* into believing that it was a bandit from over the line; that you only had one friend in the world,

Oscar Nall. And I came back and I'm the only one who's done a thing for our side. By me and through me the C Bar's clear of debt and starting uphill again. Oscar, I killed—when he snatched for a gun and tried to shoot. I could have killed him without giving him a chance, but I didn't. I—ah, what's the use of talk? You can't see your hand before your face. You won't believe Judge Oakes. You—'

He snapped flame from a match and lighted his cigarette. Lucy was red, but she seemed unable to find the words she wanted. It was Nancy who spoke.

'Where did you get the money you sent father? Lucy didn't want to accept it, but he told her that she couldn't help herself; that you had a perfect right to pay off the mortgage and protect your interest. She—'

'Where did you get that money?' Lucy interrupted. 'The proceeds of a train-robbery or something like that?'

'That happens to be no affair of yours. If you had taken it without one of your usual fits of silly stubbornness, I might tell you. But there's no reason for me to tell you anything. Except this: Murder charge or no murder charge, I am looking after the C Bar. I—'

'You can't stay on this side! The minute word got to town that you were here, a posse would be out. You'd simply be killed. Why—don't you realize that for seven hundred and fifty dollars there are men who would follow

250

you across Texas? As for the C Bar—'

'Ull Varner will pay, not seven-fifty, but five thousand, for me,' he told her calmly. 'But you wouldn't know that. You are so busy telling the world how much you know that you never have a chance to listen. But Judge Oakes knows it. He knows that Ull Varner is so anxious to get me out of the way—now that he's stepped up into Oscar's boots and is going to make a fortune out of the county—that he hired two prize killers to cross into Mexico looking for me.'

'You—killed two men in Mexico?' she asked. Her face was white. 'Two more? Because you thought—'

'They were killed by Mexicans. And I didn't *think* anything!' he said harshly.

'Father didn't say anything to us about that,' Nancy told him quickly—almost as if she justified herself. 'Lucy! If Ull Varner did that— Why would he do that, Lance? If father knows all this, believes this—Lance, we didn't have anything to do with that warrant! It was Homer Ripps. Nobody even asked us to testify. Varner got Ripps's statement and a warrant was sworn. The grand jury indicted you—'

'But the warrant exists,' Lucy said tonelessly. He could not understand her quiet under his snarling contempt. 'You can't stay on this side without being killed or captured. I have hired a foreman, an old-timer from New

251

Mexico. Joe Parks. We're going to do well with the place. No matter where you got that money, it's cleared off the debt and we're restocking. I'll give Judge Oakes your half of all profits—'

Lance lifted wolfishly in the stirrups to look uneasily around. This arroyo was too easily approached to suit him.

'Varner been out, lately? Or Frank Larkman?' he asked Lucy. 'Do they come out, often?'

'No, to all questions. Why? Why are you so interested in them, in connection with the C Bar?'

'For one reason, because I'm likely to be around the place a good deal, popping up here and there.'

'But you can't! You'll be recognized and—'

'We'll start by having breakfast—Fine Upham and a tintyper friend of mine named Xavier,' he said calmly. 'All I want to know is, are you going to run to Ull Varner with word that I'm back? Or tell the bunkhouse gang you've got that I'm worth five thousand to Varner—*Por dios!* It would be dead or alive! Varner won't care whether I'm tried or not, so long as I'm out of the way!'

'I won't tell! Of course I'm not going to tell! But it's absolute insanity. And there's no reason for you to be watching the C Bar, as you put it. We're all right, now. We're going to make money. I put three thousand, almost,

252

into horses. A good stallion. A bunch of mares. A *remuda* for our own use—'

'A stallion and a harem ... I suppose they're in Saddle Rock Pasture ... That's pretty big, you know; pretty easy to get out of. Strange *mañadas* have a way of drifting. Yes—horses do drift!'

'There's a good boy with them. They are hardly left alone when they represent two thousand dollars. This Bill Foster is good with horses. Almost as good'—she hesitated, then went on defiantly—'as you used to be. Now, regardless of everything else; regardless of all you've said about Oscar and me and Varner and—and everything; you can't stay here without being killed or caught. You—'

Lance hardly heard her. So a man was supposed to be keeping an eye on the valuable stallion and mares around Saddle Rock. And—everything was well with the C Bar. It was restocked; it had a new, efficient foreman—

'Lucy,' he said grimly, 'I know some things that I'm not going to take time to discuss, right now. But this is flat: I am watching the C Bar. I'm going to do more: I'm going to just about run the C Bar from behind these whiskers and a rock. I will tell you certain things, likely, to tell this Joe Parks. And I want you to do exactly and precisely what I tell you, in each case. I haven't time for arguing, now. I'm going to see the C Bar clear of trouble. Then I'll leave. But you'll have to do as I say—'

'I'll do no such thing! I'm not going to have you here, not knowing when a posse's trying to catch you, or when you are being shot at—Go back to Mexico! It's all you can do!'

She roweled her chestnut past him. Nancy followed quickly frowning uncertainly from one to the other. Lance hesitated, then shrugged and gathered up his reins. He sent Gray Eagle along the arroyo and came by roundabout ways to where Fine and Jerky waited on the ridge.

'Well!' Fine cried with sight of Lance. 'You must have been riding around the ranch with your partner! And did she say anything about breakfast for a couple orphans like Jerky and me?'

'I was doing just—about—that!' Lance assured him grimly. 'Breakfast? Yeh! It's waiting for us down yonder. The mule-headed little—Come on! There's a thing or six I want to know, about a foreman who hasn't found out as much as we knew in Mexico, or as much as two outsiders could tell me in Lanak. Maybe what I want to know is loose in the bunk-house down there. You know, we *might* even hit up this Joe Parks for jobs. Maybe not. It all depends. If we do, Mr Black, my name is Mr White. We're all the way from Powder River. But a long time on the road.'

'And me, I don't want a job,' Jerky said calmly. 'Too fat to work. I'll move on toward

254

Mesquite and see how's business—if it's that or punching dogies around.'

Fine was studying Lance curiously. He shook his head.

'You know, you *sound* like you'd talked to her,' he said slowly. 'Is she—still calling you Nall's murderer? Still bound to see you stretch rope for that?'

'I'—Lance hesitated—'I swear, I don't know what she thinks or what she intends to do. She didn't testify about it. And that's about all I know. But I'm taking a chance on this range—a chance that she won't yell for Ull Varner.'

CHAPTER TWENTY-FIVE

'.45–70 CALIBER, TOO!'

The Big House seemed deserted as they rode across the open toward the corrals. There was no finer ranch in all this section. The Spear L, the 99, the Flying W—none could equal C Bar in range or house. Lance looked briefly at the great, fortlike 'dobe built by his grandfather.

'Worth fighting for—risking your neck for,' he decided mentally. Then, aloud: 'I wonder if anybody's home!'

'Cook's around—if that li'l' house yonder's the kitchen,' Fine answered, pointing to the smoke lifting above the detached kitchen's flat roof.

A one-armed man came to the kitchen door and looked at them. Instantly, a second man appeared. They crossed the yard to where these two waited and swung down.

'Boss around?' Lance asked generally. He thought that *he* would never have hired either the one-armed cook or the narrow-eyed, pointy-faced cowboy. 'We're hunting jobs...'

'No, he jist ain't,' the cook answered. He had a high, plaintive voice, almost a whine. 'Nobody around but me and "Dinky," here. Dinky, though, he's a kind of *caudillo*—assistant foreman—for Parks. Ain't you, Dinky?'

'Where y' from?' Dinky asked, narrow eyes roving from one face to the other, from their horses to Jerky's mule.

'Powder River, one time—long time ago,' Lance said in the flat voice he had used in the beginning. 'All over, these last few years. North Texas, mostly. We're hands.'

For what seemed much longer than the decision required, the *caudillo* continued to study them. Then he shook his reddish head.

'Full up. Try the 99 or Flying W.'

'Where're they?'

'Ride on to town; to Mesquite. Ask anybody there.'

He stepped back into the kitchen. The cook lifted an enormous hand to the back of his neck, squinted at them, then shrugged and let his hand fall. But not before Lance had seen what the gesture had shown briefly—a pistol butt above his waistband, under the flour sack that was his apron.

'Might's well eat,' the cook said. 'Come on in.'

The lean Dinky sat in a corner when they stopped beside a long and scarred table one side of the big kitchen. He smoked without talking and the cook seemed to be infected by Dinky's manner. For he fed them leathery steaks and soda-streaked biscuit and bad coffee without doing more than grunt in answer to Lance's occasional questions.

Lance found the atmosphere peculiar. But, if anything were going on, here on the C Bar, suspicion of drifting strangers would be natural. He wished that Foreman Parks had been here, instead of his silent assistant.

'This Parks,' he said suddenly, looking straight at Dinky, 'is he an Arizona man?'

'Uh-uh,' Dinky answered, looking straight at him.

And he said nothing else. Lance turned to Jerky, then, grinning cheerfully:

'How about digging that quart of red-eye out of your *alforjas*? Maybe—that is, *maybe*—a few jolts of that snake-poison'd help these fellas out—get 'em to where they wouldn't be scared to talk.'

Dinky was leaning back against the wall,

257

now, but hidden from elbows down by the cook's small work table. His hands were in his lap. He stared at Lance.

'And what affair is it of yours, if we don't talk?' he inquired metallically. 'Keep your red-eye. And—the road to Mesquite leads off that way.'

His left hand appeared, to indicate the direction with jerking thumb, then dropped out of sight again.

'Fine! If that's how you feel, why, you must feel like that,' Lance told him easily. 'Thanks for the breakfast, Doctor.'

He rose, keeping his hands relaxed at his sides. Fine and Jerky followed silently to the door. Fine turned there to face the *caudillo*:

'Uh—one question I *would* like to ask,' he drawled. 'Them other outfits you mentioned— the 99 and Flying W—they wouldn't be cut off *this* coil, now?'

No answer came from the kitchen. Fine laughed and trailed Lance and Jerky to the horses. Jerky was fishing in an *alforja*. He produced the quart of which Lance had spoken. The cook was not in sight, but it seemed that he could see Jerky lift the bottle and pass it to Fine. For he made a husky noise, somehow very yearning, very plaintive. Lance had a drink and Jerky put back the lessened quart. Then they mounted and, as they jogged off on the Mesquite road, Fine lifted husky baritone in *Windy Bill*:

'Windy Bill was a Texas man—
And he could rope, you bet!
He swore the snake he couldn't tie—
Well, he hadn't seen him yet!
But the boys they knowed an old black
        steer,
A kind of a damn' outlaw,
That run down in the malpais
At the foot of a rocky draw—

This old black snake he'd stood his ground
With punchers from everywhere.
So the boys bet Windy two-to-one
That he couldn't quite get there.
Then Bill brought out his old gray hawse.
Its withers and back was raw,
And fixed to tackle that big black brute
That used around the draw—

'Certainly a friendly place you-all run,
Mister Craig! That C Bar. Maybe that's the
female-ing touch I've heard about so often?
Miss Lucy Kane's tender hand on the rein,
a-steering the C Bar into softer ways?'

'Don't be in a hurry about turning off,'
Lance warned the pair. They had covered a
hundred yards and more and were breasting a
rise. 'Happen to see a twinkle in the kitchen
window when you looked back, a minute ago?
I did! I noticed a good pair of glasses hanging
on that wall, too. That's a hair-trigger gunie,
that Dinky. If he sees anything suspicious

about us, we'll meet something trying to pass us—from behind ... 45–70 caliber, too!'

'And just where do we head for, now?' Jerky asked. 'I'd be worried more about that grub-destroyer! If I had to eat his cooking much. If he's a cook—You didn't miss the self-cocker under the *Four X* brand on that flour sack, I hope?'

'I saw it. Same time you did. *We* are going to Saddle Rock again. For a look at Saddle Rock Pasture. That lovely 'steenth cousin of mine tells me that the C Bar has got a stallion and some mares up there—about twenty-five hundred dollars' worth. I—hope she's correct in that notion!'

When he was sure that Dinky could not see—even through glasses—their change of direction, he led the way by short-cuts, going fast toward the hill from which they had been chased the night before.

But they approached the hills from the opposite side, this time. This was better range, crowned with mottes of cottonwoods and dotted with scrubby 'islands' of mesquite. It was Fine who pulled in his horse with a grunt to point at the ground between two such islands.

'Horses and—some more horses ... *Drove* horses, too ...'

Lance looked at the trail of the band, then up again.

'We've got to split. One of us has got to

follow these horses,' he said slowly. 'Lucy said a boy named Foster was keeping an eye on the *mañada* in Saddle Rock Pasture. Fine, do you and Jerky mind heading for that gunsight pass in the hills, yonder, and snaking over it to explore that pasture? There used to be a dugout just the other side. If this Foster boy camped anywhere, I think it would be there. I'll go on after these—it may be part of that *mañada*, or it may not. They may be drifting or—'

'Or you may get the damn' seat shot right out of those already patched overalls!' Fine snarled. 'Suppose that's the whole harem, being drove off? What'll you do? Tell the hairpins it's again' the law?'

'I'll find out where they're going—and I know every foot of that country ahead—and on across to Tula County. You two can check the pasture just as well as I can. But you *can't* trail these horses as well as I can. Because you don't know the lie of the land. Now, if I see trouble ahead, I'll come back for you. And I certainly won't tangle ropes with a bunch. You see what you can see in Saddle Rock Pasture, then trail me.'

'All right! All right!' Fine gave in, sulkily. 'But you ain't got brains enough to be left alone. We'll probably ride up on the trail and find you splattered over about six of these mesquite bushes!'

He turned his horse; Jerky wheeled his mule.

261

They were fifty yards away when Lance checked them with a yell and waved. They came at the pounding gallop, looking at Lance, looking at the ground.

'You took the quart,' Lance said. 'Gi' me a drink before you hightail.'

'Well, *por amor dedios*! Of all the short-eared jacks—'

They finished the quart and tossed away the bottle, then separated again and went on at the long, hard, mile-eating trot. Lance had spoken truth when he said that, by knowing the land's lie he could easily trail—

'Funny!' he said suddenly. 'Funny! I am certain that I'm trailing men. Certain that if young Bill Foster's not ahead of me, along with the horses, Fine's going to discover him completely dead, in Saddle Rock Pasture...'

But he knew the country so well that he could ride off to the side of release and divide, without showing himself to anyone watching the back-trail.

Throughout the morning and part of the afternoon he rode, and long before noon he knew that his feeling had been correct; he was following men who followed horses—C Bar horses. For in softer ground he saw, first one, then another, set of shod prints, the hoofmarks of *ridden* horses.

He went more carefully as the trail seemed fresher; carbine across his arm; glasses ready. At last he saw a thin column of dust on a flat below him.

'They've headed so you can't say if they're going to push right into Tula main street or make for that little *malpais*,' he said aloud, scowling. 'And that's only two-three horses down there...'

He turned to the side to avoid showing himself on the flat, then rode hellbent to a little hill from which he had another view. Still there was only the dust of two or three animals in sight. He worked closer, off to the side, until he was up abreast of those riders. And when he made them out through the lenses, he stiffened. For Lucy's chestnut went ahead of two other horses—and Lucy rode the chestnut.

He considered flashingly and decided that these men were well behind those actually driving the stolen *mañada*. There was time— there would be time—to cut in between them and the rest. He sent Gray Eagle around a hill and into a shallow arroyo. He found the precise position he wanted behind a boulder and settled himself to wait. Hoofbeats came closer; he lifted his Winchester.

Lucy appeared in the open, riding ahead as when he had seen her last. Her shoulders were drooping; she came with hands on the saddle horn, reins sagging.

Lance came to his feet with a savage grin. Two men—strangers, so far as one glance showed—jogged behind her chestnut as casually as if the three of them were the best of friends. One thing only told another story—the length of lariat that coupled the girl's slim ankles together beneath the chestnut's belly.

Lance shot past the girl—shot three times. He was past shooting at horses, now! He drove a slug into the black-bearded little man on the right, missed a shot, then knocked down the lanky second man.

Lucy had straightened in her saddle to gape incredulously toward the boulder sheltering Lance. He yelled at her—to ride back; to ride off to the side. But she only sat as if frozen by the shock of lead singing past her.

The black-bearded man was motionless on the ground and his horse—scratched, perhaps, by a rowel—trotted away. But the other man was crawling toward a mesquite bush. Lance shot twice more and saw dust jump from his clothing. Still the lanky one crawled on, if more slowly.

Lance whirled back to Gray Eagle. He fairly threw himself into the saddle and found the stirrups after the roman-nosed gray was running. He charged back past the boulder— and heard Lucy scream and, like heavy echo to that thin sound, the roar of a Colt. Gray Eagle jumped and spoiled Lance's shot. The lanky man fired again and, for all his three wounds, his shooting was dangerously accurate. That second bullet burned Lance's hip.

He was in the open and could do nothing but drop down over Gray Eagle's neck and charge that mesquite bush. He saw the smoke and heard the bellow of other shots. But if any came near he did not know it. He came up to the bush, had a blurred vision of the man turning on his elbow, then jammed the muzzle of his carbine down and squeezed the trigger. Gray Eagle went past and turned about with scattering of gravel under his trim hoofs.

But the warrior behind the mesquite was dead. One look showed that. So Lance, panting as if he had run for fifty yards instead of riding went on to where Lucy sat the chestnut with arm up across her face.

'Come on!' he told her thickly. 'Back-trail for us—and fast! Come on, girl!'

'I—I thought he had killed you...' she whispered shakily, still with arm covering her eyes. 'I—I couldn't see how he could miss. He—he looked so deadly—so steady!'

'But he didn't,' Lance said in more natural tone. 'He just nipped Gray Eagle and put his brand on my hip. Come on! No time for talk, now. The others may have heard the shots.'

She was so childlike that sudden pity rose in him. But he sensed that show of pity would shake her more. He dropped his hand quickly.

'Now,' he commanded sharply, 'turn that horse around! We've *got* to go—or all this will be worth exactly nothing.'

At that she nodded and made a gasping sound. He pushed Gray Eagle closer to the chestnut and the big horse turned instinctively.

Lucy gathered the reins and Lance reached over to slap the tall gelding on the haunch. She straightened, and they trotted past the moveless figures of her guards.

'Now—gallop!' Lance ordered.

For a half-mile they pounded and the motion seemed to rouse her. She looked sidelong at his grim face and called to him. He could not distinguish the words. He shook his head impatiently and looked under his arm. No sign of anyone back there, yet; only two straying horses...

They slowed to a long trot and made the crest of a rise. From it, when he had reloaded his carbine, Lance studied the land's lie through the glasses.

'No sign of 'em yet,' he grunted. 'So—'

'You were right—about the horses in Saddle Rock Pasture,' she told him almost eagerly. 'I didn't think you were right—that you could be right. So I sent Nancy back to the house and rode straight over there and—'

She drew a long breath and when she faced him again her mouth was hard and tight, her dark eyes brilliant.

'That poor kid—Bill Foster! He was just—fairly shot to pieces! But not quite dead when I first saw him ... So—'

CHAPTER TWENTY-SIX

'I'LL TRAIL FINE'

Lance nodded almost absently. He was lifting the glasses again. He said:

'Of course.'

'You—you mean you *knew* that?'

'I knew he'd be one of three things—fogging it for headquarters, riding with the thieves or—dead. Who were the men who grabbed you?'

'I don't know. All I know is that while I was on the ground beside Bill, trying to do something for him, they rode up on me. One held me while the other rode away. I tried to fight, but it was no use. The man just sat in the saddle and laughed—that was the tall one who shot at you. He held me by one arm until the little black-bearded one came back. He said:

'"Boss says he don't want her; she'll be a damn' nuisance. But he says to bring her along—after while." So they smoked and talked—it was awful, with that poor boy dying on the ground almost under our feet. I begged them to do something, but they didn't even answer me. Then we heard a pistol-shot quite a way off. The black-bearded man said:

'"Well, that's our powder." So they put me on Gold and tied my feet and we followed the horses. I never saw anyone but those two.

Then—then you jumped up from behind that boulder and—I couldn't believe my eyes!'

He nodded. But the softening in her tone he hardly noted. Considering what lay ahead of him, he resented bitterly the loss of time involved in escorting her back to safety. If he had not needed to consider her—and those men who would pretty surely be riding on their trail in a little while—he could have turned to the side. Night would be soon. And they would never find him. Instead, *he* would find *them*!

The corners of his mouth lifted snarlingly as he thought of what he could do to that band of killing horse-thieves, hanging to their flanks and harrying them with bursts of shots from the darkness, or from points high above them in daylight. Mexico had taught him that!

'We'll just back-track,' he said curtly. 'Fine Upham and Jerky Xavier will have found Bill Foster—and the place where the horses were. They'll be riding hellbent this way on my trail. We'll meet 'em and take you into Mesquite—'

'Mesquite? Why not to the house? We can gather the boys and come after the thieves— And Nancy's there—Oh! Who *are* the thieves, Lance? You talked this morning as if you knew.'

He shook his head. He did not dare tell her of his suspicions about Joe Parks and the pointy-faced Dinky. She would give away those suspicions before he was ready. Neither could he let her go back to the C Bar, where she

268

would be at the mercy of Parks and his crew.

'Tell you tonight,' he evaded her. 'We have got riding to do; plenty of it. I don't know who that bunch is.'

They rode as he had promised; rode fast and without knowing if they were followed. Twilight came, filling the arroyos on the hills with shadows that were like solid, inky floods rolling down the slopes. Lucy sided him and, if she felt weariness under the hard, steady pace he set, she said nothing. With good dark Lance drew off to a hilltop from which the trail could be seen—if moonlight came through a cloudy sky.

He loosened the *cinchas* on both horses and sat down beside the girl, to pass over Durham and papers.

'Make us a couple,' he said wearily. 'I haven't been so blame' tired in a month of Sundays.'

He took the cigarette she handed him and lighted both slim cylinders, drew in smoke, and exhaled explosively.

'Gather round me, children,' he said bitterly. 'For words of wisdom and just a *handful* of instructions are going to issue out of Grandpa Craig's whiskers . . . I'll try to make the sermon as short as possible, but I do want to say some few things. First—'

He looked at her tense face, lighted by the coal of her cigarette as she drew in smoke.

'Lord, but she *is* pretty!' he thought.

269

'Dolores can nearly match her—beat her in some ways—but—'

He smoked for thirty seconds, then:

'Lucy, my grandfather established the C Bar. Since his day it has grown to be a sizable outfit. Your father was my father's fourth cousin. He made a wad in Montana, came back to Texas, and went in with John Craig. They got along fine. They were getting along when I fell out with Dad seven years ago and hightailed to see the world from the ships. I came home expecting—well, maybe not a fatted calf, but anyway not to be butchered in the slick-ear's place...

'What I'm getting at—if by way of *Billy the Kid's Corral*, that was a territory wide—is that I own a bigger stake in the C Bar than you do. Not in money, but in—oh, call it pride, if you want to! So long as I can smoke a Colt, nobody's going to take the C Bar away from us, or lift a horse, or beef a steer wearing our iron. Not without paying! Today, we're up against the beginning of what can break us. And it's my war!'

'But—' she began slowly. 'Who is responsible? We haven't lost stock, since you left. Joe Parks and Dinky are both good men. Hard men, possibly. But we need that kind: hard and honest men. The hands are off the same coil. Joe Parks told me he handpicked every mother's son for double qualifications. Every man is a hand and every man can and

270

will fight. So—'

'There are things going on here that don't meet the eye. I don't want to tell this Parks or Dinky anything. Now, all I'm asking of you is—if you won't help, don't hinder. You ought to see by this time that you don't know as much about the range as I do. So when I say that I'm going to watch over the place—over our interests—you ought to understand that I've got reasons.'

'But, why do you want me in Mesquite?'

'Because you know a little and not enough. I'd forgot Nancy! You'll have to go back to the house and pick her up. But while you're there—are you going to help, or hinder? Can you keep clear out of C Bar affairs and let me handle all this for the time being?'

'I'll do what you say,' she assured him quietly.

'All right! You and Nancy decide to go back to town. A whim. You're tired of the ranch. If you have to talk to Parks or Dinky, you don't know a thing about horses stolen. You just want to go to town. It's your place. You can say that and nobody has a right to question you. When you're in town, stay there!'

'I'll do that. I—don't understand all this, but I'll do it. Lance, about—everything—'

'You've had a hard day. Let's don't do any more talking. Lie down for a while. I'll watch for Fine and Jerky.'

He stripped off his overalls jumper and

271

rolled it into a pillow. She put her head obediently down upon it and was quiet. But as he sat smoking, carbine close to his hand, listening mechanically and watching the sky for signs of moonrise, she moved slightly, coming closer to him. He looked down at the vague shape of her and shook his head.

She was young, very young, and she had come that day for the first time against men who were moved only by their own wills or needs and who could be stopped only by their own grim kind. He was sure that she had never before suffered the hands of such men as 'Lanky' and 'Blackbeard' upon her; had never faced men who laughed at her furious protests—or merely ignored them. Small wonder that she was shaken!

The moon came from under clouds, but disappeared almost as quickly. An hour passed and what Lance guessed to be another. Still there was no sound of hoofbeats from either direction. He could understand the thieves giving up pursuit quickly, thinking it more important to move the horses to cover than to chase the killer of Lanky and Blackbeard. But Fine—

'Nothing could have happened to him in the Pasture,' Lance reassured himself uneasily. 'But how he could have missed us I just don't see. It was certainly a plain trail.'

He waked Lucy after a time and tightened the *cinchas* on their saddles. They rode, now in darkness, for brief periods in moonlight, until they came to that dugout of which Lance had told Fine. It held only Bill Foster's bedroll and scanty cooking equipment.

'Nothing to do before daylight,' Lance decided. 'Let's move out from here, up the creek, and catch some sleep.'

At dawn he was awake before Lucy had moved, where she lay in the dead wrangler's blanket. He saddled her chestnut in preference to Gray Eagle, who began to show signs of the hard riding and scant food of days past. He rode out, then, to look for Fine's trail, and for Bill Foster.

Both the familiar tracks of Fine's black and the cairn of rocks above the dead men were easily seen—and together. Fine had piled those rocks over Bill Foster. Then—

'Right back up to the dugout,' Lance said aloud. 'And on—We'll have to see about that...'

He rode back to find Lucy washing the dust from face and hands in the little creek that watered Saddle Rock Pasture. He told her of what he had seen.

'We'll have something to eat, then you'll head for the house. I'll trail Fine,' he said. 'Oh! I'm going to take Gold for a while. Gray Eagle is pretty well frazzled. Besides, the C Bar on Gold will be a trademark, if I need it. It'll show that I'm riding on C Bar business. I'll change that hair brand on Eagle a li'l' bit, though, before you ride him off.'

CHAPTER TWENTY-SEVEN

'SMITH OF THE SCAR'

Beyond the *malpais*, somewhat off to the side of the Mesquite–Tula road, a big 'dobe store-saloon stood all by itself. Lance had stopped there, once, eight or nine years before. He recalled that a pockmarked Mexican had owned the place in those days and that it had the worst of reputations.

But he had lost Fine's trail and that of the stolen horses in the *malpais*. It had occurred to him that the store—if still on its lonely hill—would be a natural place to find some trace of the *mañada*.

He rode up to it in late afternoon. Three horses drowsed under a cottonwood, 'tied to the ground' by their reins. Under the brush roof of the shed behind the store was another, unsaddled. Lance let Gold's reins trail beneath the cottonwood and went with apparent casualness up to the deep veranda that ran across the whole front of the store.

In the doorway he stopped to look about the big, cluttered room. Five men were there, and one woman. She was hardly more than a girl and she was perched on the long counter that

274

served as bar, with a big man beside her, his elbows on the counter, talking to that pock Mexican whom Lance recalled from other years.

'Yeh. Going to Tula. See the others,' this big man was saying when Lance came in. 'I reckon this one's going to be—'

Then he stopped short, as if the storekeeper had spoken a warning—or he had merely heard the clink of Lance's spur rowels in the door.

Once he had been a handsome man, Lance thought, while the man's eyes—strangely light in dark-tanned face—met his. For he had a square face, well shaped, and a mouth that showed reckless humor in its faint grin. But now a long, white scar ran from left eyebrow diagonally across the dark skin to the right jaw-angle, nicking the strong, arched nose.

Only for seconds did the scarred man stare at Lance, then turned back to poke the girl's cheek with a forefinger. So Lance looked at the others drinking, two nondescript cowboys who might have been found on any Texas ranch, and two equally average Mexican riders in short cotton jackets and tight-fitting leather *chivarrias* over cotton trousers. They turned to glance at him, but without any appearance of interest that was unusual.

He came on in and found a wide, vacant place at the bar. The Mexican storekeeper came down and nodded slightly. He nodded again when Lance asked for whisky and reached behind him for a quart bottle and a tin cup.

Lance poured his drink, then made a cigarette. The two cowboys talked little, but drank steadily, like two men who had ridden together so long that neither had anything to say to the other. The Mexicans were discussing a girl in Tula and a *baile* of some days before the fight ending the dance. Lance placed them mechanically as two acquaintances, met here by chance. For only one of the horses under the cottonwood had worn a big-horned Mexican saddle; the other pair had been rigged with worn Texas saddles—the property, doubtless, of the two cowboys.

The tall, scarred man was talking lightly to the girl and she giggled and protested. The storekeeper went back to stand beside these two and stare vacantly across the big room as if tallying the strings of peppers and onions, the bolts of cloth, behind the other counter.

Then the big man slapped the girl's shoulder lightly and turned. He passed Lance without seeming to notice him and disappeared into the darkness of the rear. He was gone perhaps five minutes and in that time the *vaqueros* left by the front door, still talking.

'How's things around here?' Lance asked the cowboy nearest him. 'Much stuff moving?'

'Not much,' the cowboy answered. 'Nothing to hold a fella in this whole damn' country.

Think we'll hit for Arizona. Which way you figure to head?'

'Do'no',' Lance shrugged—and grinned inwardly with thought of how true that statement was. 'Kind of rambling.'

'Well, ramble somewhere besides this Tula country, if you want to hear yo' pockets jingle,' the other cowboy said with a grin. 'Come on, Bud. Let's drag it.'

They went out and presently there was the soft thud of their horses' hoofs trotting away. The tall, scarred man came back and resumed his former position at the bar. Now, he spoke softly to the girl. It was only one word, in Spanish, his tone so low that Lance could not be sure he heard it. But it sounded like '*Go!*' and he wondered.

The girl jumped down from the bar and came toward Lance. He looked at her without interest at first, then sight of her tense face— the liquid dark eyes widened, the heavy red mouth sagging—as she stared at him made him stiffen inwardly.

He looked at the big man. The storekeeper was still expressionless of features but he was no longer leaning on the bar with vacant stare. He had straightened, and as Lance looked that way he came slowly, almost silently, down the bar. The big man stared fixedly at Lance. His mouth stretched in a grin that held nothing of good humor; his light eyes shone like silver coins. He held left hand out of sight beneath

277

the rough gray coat he wore.

'Well, C Bar,' he said explosively, 'that's a damn' nice hawse y' riding. Would y' mind a man straddling him?'

Lance had turned only his head. There was no doubt, now, what he had found in this shabby store! This scarred man had been suspicious of him from the beginning; he had gone out the back door to round the store and look at Gold. Only sight of the brand on the tall chestnut had sent him back in here. So, he had some connection with the gang which had run off the C Bar *mañada*. Now, he intended to kill a C Bar rider. The killer-light flamed in those pale eyes. Lance had seen it all too often to be mistaken.

'Do'no',' he drawled, as if nothing about the big man was unusual. 'Ain't a C Bar horse, exactly. Mine. Want to buy him? Or trade for him? Less horse'd do me, for riding chuck-line.'

For an instant the scarred one stared. Then his hand began to come deliberately from beneath his coat.

'Nah,' he said slowly. 'Don't want to buy—or trade. Want to show y' something...'

Lance twisted and thrust his hand beneath jumper and shirt all in a motion. He was facing the scarred man with short .44 leveling before the other's gun came in sight. He let the hammer fall and flipped it back again, walking toward the big figure steadily. His every shot whipped dust, from the gray coat. He sent three slugs, a fourth, into the scarred man—and *he* had not got his pistol up!

Lance only leaned, when within a yard of the man. Instead of shooting again, he smashed the other's gun-arm with his Colt barrel and sent the pearl-handled double-action to the floor. Then he stepped back.

'I—I—*ahhh!*' the scarred man said gaspingly. 'I—'

He crumpled as if his legs were suddenly turned to paper, squatted, fell sideways. Lance watched grimly, brown face murderously hard, blue eyes steel-bright.

A scream from behind him jerked him back to thought of something other than this would-be assassin. He began to turn, saw the shotgun coming over the bar and above it the snarling pocked face of the storekeeper. He simply sat down and above him the shotgun roared—so close that he felt the waves of shocked air upon his face. Tinware jangled across the store. A rack of slickers fell with a dry rustling.

The dead man's gun was at his hand. He scooped it up as the storekeeper lunged farther over the bar, trying to bring the shotgun to bear. He leaned a little—Lance—and began to press the trigger with left forefinger. The Mexican fell backward. There was another bellowing shotgun report and a section of a sapling-and-mud roof came raining down in

279

dust and chunks of wood and 'dobe.

Lance twisted and came to his feet. But he ran toward the front door stooping, to keep below the level of the bar. A man's voice came from the rear; a girl's voice joined it:

'He is dead! Do not fear; he is dead—*gracias ádios!*'

Lance glared uncertainly that way, holding the pistols at waist-level. That girl who had sat upon the bar came forward, beside her a slender Mexican.

'He is dead—her uncle and my employer,' the man said calmly. 'So is *he*, that other. You know him? Smith of the Scar. Two scarred men, both'—he stopped beside Smith and poked him with a toe as if punching a sack— 'both devils. It is very good that both should die in the same hour. *Señor!* We thank you. This Fierro was one feared by us both. He made of Dolores, here, the girl of his bar, that cowboys and thieves might come here. He was a wolf; I could never find the way to kill him.'

'And I had to kill him—kill them both,' Lance said irritably. 'So that, now, I must either ride fast for the Bravo or prove to the sheriff at Tula that I was forced to kill...'

'There is—some reason for your wish not to speak with this sheriff?' the man asked shrewdly. 'If so—what is simpler than to arrange them as if they had killed, each the other. Sheriff Brush does not like either Fierro or Smith. I mean, of course, that he did not like

280

them. He thought them the thieves they were. So he will not ask too many questions.'

'I do not wish even to talk to this Sheriff Brush,' Lance explained. 'And as for arranging them, how would you do that? Smith was killed with a pistol. Fierro, also. But Fierro fired a shotgun. How explain to Sheriff Brush that odd thing?'

The man's face—thin and lighter of color than the usual Mexican's; intelligent, also—showed amusement. His thin-lipped mouth lifted at the corners in a smile that was faintly sinister. He looked from Lance to Smith.

'Ride where you will, *amigo*,' he said softly. 'There was none other here when these two quarreled. *You*, a man I did not know and cannot describe, had gone an hour when the quarrel began about stolen horses. Leave to me and Dolores the arrangement. Even the simple matter of the shotgun fire which killed Smith of the Scar...'

'Oh!' Lance grunted, nodding. 'I—see. I will ride, then. And if you thank me, so do I also thank you. For there *is* reason for my wish to avoid the sheriff.'

'Of course! You are a man of the C Bar which is in Mesquite County. You have lost—cattle? Horses? It is horses, I think, that you hunt. Because he, Smith of the Scar, rode here upon a fine black *bestia* which he was to sell to someone of this neighborhood. The brand on this mare is Box O, but I have seen too much of

281

hair-branding not to guess that it may once have been C Bar. She wears also the Spanish brand of some Mexican *rancho*.'

'Keep her for me!' Lance said grimly. 'Keep her for—one week. If then I have not come for her or sent for her, the *bestia* is yours!'

When he rode away from the store he shook his head angrily. It was a *slow* trail, he thought, if a *red* trail, this far. And apparently it led him no closer to the two men he had come back to kill—Sheriff Ull Varner of Mesquite County and his nephew, Frank Larkman. They were the planners, he was fairly certain, of every blow against the C Bar.

'It's a simple scheme,' Lance told himself. 'They hire our stuff stolen and either hold it or sell it and pocket the money. The C Bar goes broke again—and stays broke!—because of their raids. Larkman marries Lucy, the mortgage is lifted and—they've got a fine ranch practically for nothing! Paid for by itself, you might say. I'm the stumbling-block, so Ull Varner wants me—along with the reward he got the county to put up.'

Behind him sounded the dull roar of a shot, then another. He turned in the saddle, frowning. Then he shrugged.

'A tough young man!' he complimented the Mexican he had left in the store. 'If Sheriff Brush can *prove* that Smith was killed by a pistol, it won't be that boy's fault, now.'

He rode steadily toward Tula. For that

chance-heard remark of Smith's, about going to Tula, had made him believe that in the county seat he might find trace of those he hunted—even cut the trail of Fine and Jerky.

Dark found him still riding. It was ten o'clock when the lights of the county seat shone like a yellow necklace on the flat below the last hill.

He stabled Gold on the edge of the lengthy, narrow town and went clumping down a board sidewalk to the restaurant of a Chinaman. He saw other late eaters at the far end, but only when he had come too far inside to turn back without notice did he see that old Nathan Wingo of the Flying W was having his supper here.

'And if he can't see through these whiskers and this collection of dust, nobody ever will!' Lance thought disgustedly.

For the Flying W adjoined the C Bar. Old Wingo had been the best friend of Lance Craig's father.

But he saw nothing to do but brazen it out. He shambled to a vacant stool and slumped there. When the Chinaman came to him he ordered ham and eggs and coffee, and smoked. Nathan Wingo turned, craned long neck, and stared at him.

CHAPTER TWENTY-EIGHT

'YOU GOT PLENTY RECORD'

Lance continued to slouch on his stool, elbows on the counter, hat rim low. He blew smoke toward the shelf that held catsup and pepper sauce and vinegar. But out of an eye-corner he could see old Wingo staring. Then the Flying W owner seemed to shake off speculations and settle again upon his stool. But he spoke to a cowboy beside him.

This cowboy turned full about to stare at Lance. Then he turned back and grunted something to Wingo. They went on eating. Time passed without event. Then a tall puncher, very recently barbered, very neat, came in. He walked back to Wingo and sat down. The Flying W owner growled at him.

'Now, now!' the newcomer reproved him. 'I tell you, it was a ni-ice poker game. What's on the mee-new a young fella with all his teeth can eat? What you having—soup?'

'Yah!' Wingo snarled. 'Come on, Whitey!'

He and the cowboy got up and went out. The tall puncher grinned at Lance and ordered his meal. But he had only begun to eat when three men walked into the place and came as if they were looking for him straight to his elbow.

'You was short twenty, Grimm,' a tow-haired little man said without preface. 'Hand it over! You Mesquite County buckaroos ain't helling around here none. Shell out; quick!'

The tall man turned on his stool. He seemed more amused than alarmed. His dark eyes twinkled.

'You ever have fits, too, as well as my-rages?' he inquired drawlingly. 'When I throwed in that last bunch of trash you dealt, I cashed in. I was clean with you.'

'Like hell! You kick out that twenty—'

'I'm a peaceful man,' the tall Grimm said. 'But there ain't a bit of use putting off what has got to be. So—'

Then Lance saw how the other two were crowding closer to Grimm's back. He caught the furtive movement of one man's hand, bringing a dagger out from under his coat. This man was closest to Grimm.

Instinctively, he put out a hand to the catsup bottle before him. He threw it at the man with the dagger as Grimm smashed the towhead. It hurtled across ten feet of intervening space, a glinting comet with scarlet tail of catsup, to crash end-on against the knifeman's temple. He staggered and dropped the dagger.

The third man hit Grimm viciously in the neck and he fell sideway from the stool. The knifeman recovered and kicked at Grimm. Then Lance charged into the fight swinging furiously. He struck the man who had hit Grimm, slipped on spilled catsup, recovered,

285

took a blow in the body. From the front door someone yelled encouragement:

'Yaaaiiiah, Lance! Give 'em hell! We'll clean 'em up!'

He had no time to turn. Grimm was on the floor, snatching at the knifeman's ankle. Lance knocked the third man backward and followed, hammering him. Grimm got his man down and pounded his head against the floor. Lance drove a long left and a longer right to his man's face and saw him drop. He turned back—and Tommy Downes, with a stocky Mexican at his elbow, grinned at him.

But in the street door bulked a short, tremendously wide man, a silver-plated Colt in each hand, a gold badge shining on his buttonless vest. Authoritatively he began to bellow.

'It's nothing. Nothing at all, Brush,' Grimm told him pantingly. 'Just a bunch of polecats. Collecting grief. Made a set at me and—couldn't get there.'

Lance began to move backward slowly, to get behind Grimm. The Sheriff came in and looked at the men on the floor. Men crowded in from the street. Nathan Wingo and the cowboy with whom he had eaten were among these. Wingo shouldered through until he stopped before Grimm.

'Now, what you been helling into?' he demanded.

'I reckon they're settled,' Grimm was telling

Sheriff Brush. 'Do what you're a mind to with 'em. Nothing to me.'

Lance moved still farther back while Brush looked uncertainly around. Grimm explained that an argument had risen over a poker game. That was all. The men got up and stood weakly. Brush snarled at them, herded them out. Lance looked curiously at Tommy Downes. The boy grinned and shrugged:

'I'm not the only one here,' he whispered. 'Dolores—Estrella—Pedro, here. Dolores couldn't help thinking you'd be wanting help—that she'd let you come over alone after you'd done so much for her—So, she insisted on coming over. Estrella insisted on coming along. Wants to see that Fine hasn't got hurt, I do believe! We've chased you-all back and forth. They're outside town, now. Pedro and I came in—'

Grimm turned to Lance, now. He was rubbing the red welt on his neck. He grinned at Lance.

'Thanks, cowboy!' he said. 'I'm Grimm. Foreman of the Flying W. This old white-headed fella, he's my boss. Wingo. Hadn't been for you, reckon I'd have got that knife in a soft place. Thanks a lot.'

The curious ones were going out, now. So Wingo, Grimm, the other Flying W cowboy, Lance, and Tommy stood alone.

'Who're you?' Wingo grunted. 'Besides the hairpin that saved the bacon for this wild-eyed nitwit. Seems to me I've seen you before—'

Grimm stiffened suddenly, looking at Tommy, then at Lance. He turned to Wingo and caught his arm.

'Let's get outside,' he said quietly. 'Ne' mind all the wa-waing. Outside. We can talk better out there.'

He led the way and Wingo looking curiously from face to face, trailed him. Lance and Tommy and the silent Pedro followed with the Flying W cowboy. In the darkness beyond the eating house Grimm halted.

'You're all right with us,' he told Lance. 'I happened to think, back there, how this man called you—"Lance" ... I'm not surprised about the kind of battle you put up. You got plenty record. Wingo, you ought to know this man better'n I do. You've been talking about him—and his pa—enough! This is Lance Craig.'

'Huh!' Wingo grunted, whirling. 'Lance—Son! I'm certainly glad to see you. I never got a chance to talk to you in Mesquite. Then you took it on the run—What you doing in Tula? Ne' mind, that don't matter! What I want to tell you is, ary thing on the Flying W you need you can have. John Craig and me, we seen plenty hell in our day. John Craig's boy—'

'Thanks!' Lance said gratefully. 'But, right now, I've got some things to do. Some friends of mine are outside town and I've got to see 'em. And I'm trailing some thieves—'

'And that's what we're doing!' Grimm drawled. 'What we come into Tula about. What caused that li'l' fracas in the restaurant. This place is nothing but a damn' thieves' nest. Flying W has been losing stuff—same's the C Bar. We've suspicioned everybody but never pinned a thing onto anybody. We decided to drift over here for a *mira.* Harry Brush couldn't help us.'

'Yeh,' Wingo thrust in. 'I did think I'd stumbled onto something, today, but I never. Stallion and a bunch of mightily fine mares is being shipped to Tyroe tomorrow, from the pens here. Going on account of Eldred—and if *he* ain't the slickest, crookedest buyer in Texas, he'll do till somebody else puts in bigger proofs. He—'

'Stallion and mares!' Lance cried. 'What's the brand?'

'Box O. I never paid much attention when I see they wasn't mine, but I did see the Box O. Why?'

Lance drew a great, slow breath—of sheer triumph.

'Why? Because—crowd around close and listen to the tale of the C Bar—and a new stallion and harem—and Box O horses being shipped! With a word or two about Oscar Nall and Ull Varner and Frank Larkman—'

They edged up about him and as he talked curtly, Wingo swore again and again. At the end, the Flying W owner smacked hard palm

289

against his thigh.

'Oscar Nall, huh? And Varner and that trifling Larkman and maybe Logan and the Spear L ... We'll side you, Lance, come daylight, me and Grimm and Bert Gillis, here!'

'Thanks! Tommy Downes and Pedro and I will meet you—there's a motte of cottonwoods down yonder at the end of the street, just outside town. How's that? Just before daylight. Fine! Now, I've got to meet some friends—'

He and Tommy watched the three Flying W men go down the street toward the lighted front of the big Travelers' Bar. Tommy laughed. He said:

'I *hoped* you weren't forgetting Estrella and Pedro and Dolores and me, when these plans were running through your mind. It does seem that you've got about as tough a little war on your hands, over here in law-abiding Texas, as Dolores had on the other shore. If you practiced over here, no wonder you were so valuable on Gerónimo!'

'It's really worse, over here. For the best I can do is win a battle—never the war. Killing Ull Varner and Frank Larkman and other thieves may help the C Bar but, as I told you on Gerónimo, it won't clear me of that murder charge. I will have to hit and run. I wish Dolores hadn't come across—'

When he and Tommy had mounted and ridden out of Tula, to the arroyo where the others waited, he swung down and held both

290

the hands Dolores held out to him. And he said the same thing to her that he had said to Tommy.

'Well,' she told him defiantly, 'if I can't repay a favor, I'd like to know why I can't! There are plenty on Gerónimo to handle everything. And if you're in trouble over here—Where's Fine? And Jerky?'

He told them—Estrella Morro crowding up to listen necessitated English and Spanish versions of the report—of the vanished horses and the trail followed by Fine and Jerky.

'We'll be with you at the loading pens tomorrow,' Dolores promised. 'With those Flying W men, we ought to make a party big enough to eat your thieves!'

'You will stay out of that fight!' he told her flatly. 'I'll take Tommy and Estrella and Pedro, gladly. But you're not going to risk stopping a slug, young lady! Your fighting days are over.'

She protested bitterly, but he shook his head grimly and in the end she surrendered sulkily. Later, as they sprawled and smoked and talked idly, she moved closer to him.

'And what are you going to do, when you've settled your sheriff and the rest of his gang? That doesn't open up Texas for you, Lance. Will you—come back to Gerónimo? Bring Fine back. Dodging Estrella will give him all the excitement he needs. And—'

'And dodging Tommy ought to keep me interested,' he said quickly. 'I don't know,

Dolores. I just don't know.'

'You've seen—Never mind! I'm just an idiot, like most other girls. I—oh, let's get some sleep!'

'Yeh, let's do,' Lance agreed. Then he reached impulsively to pat the slim shoulder. 'And—thanks a lot, my dear. Thanks just a lot.'

CHAPTER TWENTY-NINE

'CROOKED AND CAREFUL'

The sky was gray over the loading pens on the railroad spur, a half-mile north of Tula. But in the dimness there was the noise of horses moving and men's voices lifting. Lance rode quietly along the slatted pen and pulled in at a corner. Somewhere out of sight to the west were Wingo, Grimm, and Bert Gillis. Tommy Downes, Estrella Morro, and Pedro were on the east side. A man rounded the corner and all but collided with Gold. He jerked back his horse with a grunt. It was the lean and wolfish Eldred, who, as Lance had known for years, perfectly filled Wingo's description of 'the slickest, crookedest buyer in Texas.' Apparently, Eldred was nervous today, and from his knowledge of the buyer, Lance was perfectly sure that under the brown duck jumper was a gun—with Eldred's accustomed hand upon the butt.

'What you doing?' Eldred snarled. 'You ain't one of mine.'

'No,' Lance admitted, keeping his hands conspicuously in sight. 'I'm not. But—could you use a top hand, Mister?'

'I couldn't! I got enough eating their dumb heads off, now, without taking on more. So—hightail it! We got business to do and—'

Lance looked past the buyer. He could see three or four men, bringing up the mares. There was much of dust and confusion. He and Eldred sat apart from it all. None seemed to see them.

'Yes, sir,' Lance said meekly. 'I just thought—'

He turned Gold and began to move away. But Eldred's yell halted him. When he turned in the saddle it was with hand up at his jumper front.

'Hey, you!' Eldred cried shrilly. 'Ain't that a C Bar hawse you're riding?'

'Might be,' Lance answered. 'What's it to you?'

Now he could see Grimm and Bert Gillis riding in between Eldred and the moving mares. He wheeled Gold and rode back toward the buyer. The turn had covered his draw. Eldred sat scowling in the saddle, a pistol in his hand. Lance dropped his mask; grinned at him savagely.

'What do you care, Eldred?' he demanded. 'It's Box O that *you're* shipping. It—*couldn't* be that our C Bar mares have been rebranded . . .'

Then instantly he and Eldred were shooting at each other. Gold was not the fighting horse that Gray Eagle's experience had made the ugly gray. He reared with the whine of lead passing him. But Lance held him grimly and merely took three shots to knock Eldred from his black. He had a hole in his hat, another in his jumper, before that was accomplished.

Grimm and Bert Gillis had spurred off out of range. Now from the dust about the mares three men came at the gallop. Who they might be, Lance could not say. But their intention seemed proved by the guns they pointed. Grimm appeared to have no concern about their identity. His pistol roared and like echo to it was the sound of Bert's firing. The stocky Gillis fell over the saddle horn under the fire of Eldred's men. Grimm's horse began to buck. Then, from behind Lance, Tommy Downes yelled and other voices lifted savagely. Guns bellowed. At a corner of the pen a man appeared—the pointy-faced Dinky of the C Bar cookshack—with Colt lifted.

Gold reared again as his rider's guns threw staccato sound across the space between Lance and Dinky. Lance felt the burn of a slug on his shoulder-point. But he set himself grimly to line Dinky over the sight as Gold came to the ground again. Few men were his equal with a pistol—but he admitted without thinking of it with more than a part of his mind, now, that Dinky was an expert of experts...

Too, the narrow-eyed man had the advantage—he was on the ground and he had begun the shooting. He nipped Gold once before he had emptied his Colt and wheeled to find cover. Lance lowered his empty gun. Dinky was running along the pen, now, running toward some riderless horses up at the corner. A slug came from somewhere, and Dinky staggered, ran another step, then dropped on his face.

A high, wolfish yell—easily recognized as the war-cry of Wingo coming to the battle—carried through shots and yells, the squeals and stamping of frightened mares.

But there was no more fight when he charged up, Winchester in gnarled right hand, to glare around for an enemy. Lance rode over to stare at Dinky. He shook his head grimly. A man who knifed his own outfit in the back rode under the death penalty, anywhere on the range. Dinky had known it. There was no room for any regret, here. Lance swung down and turned the little man over. He was looking at him, going through his pockets, when Wingo and Grimm came up behind him.

'It's the one I was telling you about,' Lance told Wingo evenly. 'The *caudillo* from the C Bar—this Parks' side-partner. He's got quite a bit of money on him—around nine hundred. I

295

think I'll call it C Bar money. What about the rest of 'em?'

'Dead or hightailed,' Grimm said casually. 'I made out two-three fogging it off when it begun to look like we had 'em by the tail feathers. Bert Gillis is pretty bad shot—shoulder and leg. But Bert's tough. He'll make out. Eldred's dead—and this dirty thief; the two that bucked Bert and me and your friends. Too bad the boss's rheumatics kept him out of the war. Else we'd have some more. Ah, well! All of us have to git old, I reckon.'

'Old! Rheumatics?' Wingo yelled furiously. 'If you goddam nitwits had did what you promised me you'd do—But, nah! You come in to look things over. You was going to come back and say what we'd better do. And—and—'

'This has to be reported to Sheriff Brush,' Lance interrupted. 'How's this for a tale? You know a C Bar hair-branded to a Box O when you see it. You asked Eldred about it. He put up a war. Naturally, being neighborly to the C Bar, you resented that. And it all happened too fast to keep check on who was who.'

'Good enough!' Wingo told him explosively. 'Plenty good enough. I'll pour it onto Brush about Eldred shipping stolen mares right under his nose, I will! I—'

He grunted warningly. For a man was coming toward them at the pounding gallop. He had just rounded the loading corrals. Lance

296

looked at the sheriff of Tula and moved a diplomatic step into the background. He had time only to grunt:

'We all work for you! Remember it!'

Then Brush sat his palomino down upon its tail and glared fiercely to left and right—and at the dead Dinky.

'*What* the hell—?' he began in his enormous voice.

'Yeh? What'd you mean?' Wingo stopped him, matching that bellow. 'A bunch of Mesquite County mares—C Bar mares—being shipped by this—*that*—damn' thief, Eldred! And if it hadn't been for Grimm and me and the boys coming along in time to see the brands, they'd have got out of your pocket, clear to Tyroe. Listen—'

Glibly, he told the tale that Lance had invented. Brush nodded, scowling, beating huge hand upon his leg.

'You got to have some proof of this,' he said almost quietly, at the end. 'I don't doubt it's like you say, Wingo. But—we run a decent county. We got ways of doing things. Legal ways—'

'Proof?' Wingo whooped at him. 'Look at them brands! And I bet Eldred's got on him, right now, a bill of sale that'll show the kind of skulldugging he was up to.'

'Who killed 'em?' Brush asked, with jerk of head here and there. 'We got to have all this plumb straight.'

'Why,' Grimm said gravely, 'I reckon *he* done it—the boss! Which I don't know that I ever seen his match. He come around the corrals like a—a—mountain lion! A old lion—with rheumatism—yes, sir! And he started smoking it. Just in time to save us. We was shooting, of course—seems like everybody was shooting—and all of Eldred's thieves shooting at us. But *we* was missing. Then the boss—'

Wingo glared at him. But Grimm's brown face—with a red weal on it, now—was only admiring as he faced his employer. The sheriff dismounted and looked at Dinky.

'Yeh, I know him,' he said. 'Goes by Ames, Poker Ames. Seen him around Tula with some hard-looking strangers. Well—if them mares show a hair-brand, I'll believe you, Wingo. And if Eldred's got ary paper on him to show what you're saying is so—'

'He'll have it,' Wingo prophesied with conviction. 'Listen, Harry Brush! I have knowed that son more'n thirty year. *Crooked and careful*—that was his motto.'

Brush moved unhappily toward the fallen Eldred. Lance and Wingo looked at each other. Lance clapped his hands soundlessly and nodded to the Flying W man. Then from somewhere behind the corral—or out of it—Fine Upham and Jerky Xavier appeared. They had the careless air of strolling spectators of some thrilling play. Fine looked at Lance, at Wingo and Grimm, then toward Brush, who

298

was hunkered beside the buyer's body.

'Not bad,' he drawled in a voice that did not carry to the sheriff. 'In fact, not bad a-tall. Speaking as a kind of expert-er on things like this-here, I would say for *amateurs* you all done right tol'able. We watched from in between the slats. No use mixing into it if you boys could handle her by yourself. Good practice for you. But—anybody says *he* downed Dinky is either a liar, or, if he wants to fight, badly mistook. Dinky was about to stitch buttonholes around you, son. So Jerky and me, we *bopped* him from the c'ral.'

'You killed him?' Lance grunted. 'And here I was, thinking Grimm was a fair liar—'

Brush was rising, with something white in his hand. Lance looked quickly at Wingo. He jerked his head toward Fine.

'This hairpin,' he told the Flying W owner, 'happens to be a friend of mine. His name's "Black"—and mine's "White"—and—both of us are hands of yours. Jerky—I reckon *you* just drifted up to see the war—'

'All right!' Brush called to them. 'He had her. A bill of sale for Box O mares, bought off Poker Ames.'

'It'd be just neighborly,' Wingo said thoughtfully, 'if we was to drive them mares back to the C Bar range. You wouldn't mind us doing that, Harry Brush?'

'I do'no',' the sheriff began, frowningly. 'You see—'

'I see this!' Wingo snarled. 'We wiped out a crooked buyer and some crooked folks that was selling to him. That's all to the good of the honest folks in Tula. If your county attorney can't see it, something's wrong with him. You know the Flying W. You can send over for us, if ary thing comes of this. So—what's to hinder us driving them C Bar mares home? You want us maybe to set in a damn' court and talk law?'

'Take 'em!' Brush surrendered. 'But if something comes up, Wingo, gi' me your word you'll come back to see about it.'

He was better than that; he helped round up the scattered mares and the stallion. He stopped his palomino when the *mañada* was strung out on the homeward road and lifted a hand to them.

'I'll take care of Bert Gillis,' he promised.

Lance looked at the stallion and mares ahead and at the eight of them who rode in a loose group. He spurred across to Tommy and asked about Dolores.

'I'd better go after her,' the boy said. 'We can catch up with you, don't you think?'

Lance nodded absently, turning in the saddle, thinking.

'I think so. Go get her.'

And when Tommy had raced away on his tall black, he went on for a half-dozen miles after the *mañada*, answering curtly such questions and remarks as his companions made. Then he pulled in short and faced old Wingo.

'Do something for me!' he grunted. 'You and Grimm are on your way home and it won't be off the road much to go by Saddle Rock Pasture. Well, ride along with the *soldada*, there, and her man—I'll make it right with them—and with Downes and the girl he'll bring out. I want to take Fine and Jerky and go back to Tula. I'm not satisfied with what we did at the pens. I want to see if I can cut the trail of that bunch Dinky had working with him—the ones who cut stick from the fight. If they *should* happen to be some of Logan's Spear L crowd—'

'They might've gone back to Tula, all right,' Wingo admitted, with wolfish look at the back-trail. 'But, Lance, if you need Grimm and me, the Flying W is your spread!'

'Three of us will be just plenty. Thanks. Tell Downes and Dolores Donovan to hang around the line camp at Saddle Rock. We'll be along after while.'

He went over to talk with Estrella. She refused point-blank to leave them. Where he and Fine rode, she and Pedro would ride.

'But you cannot,' he told her patiently. 'We go into a town and that quietly. If you go with us, we cannot do the spying it is in my mind to do. We will come to this pasture on my *rancho*, Fine and I. If you are the friend of Fine, do this for friendship.'

'You will surely come, *querido*?' she asked

301

Fine. 'I know that you two must ride back to Mexico. So—ride with the *Jefe* of Pepita. When the killing is done, you will surely come to this *potrero* where we wait?'

'Certainly!' Fine assured her nervously. 'Oh, yes. After we have done this killing—if killing we do.'

She nodded unwillingly and grunted to Pedro. Fine, Jerky and Lance sat their horses, watching the others ride on toward the C Bar. Then they turned back to Tula.

CHAPTER THIRTY

'I OWE YOU ONE!'

They had covered perhaps half of the distance between the drag of the *mañada* and Tula Spur when a rider appeared on the skyline. Fine reached for his glasses and trained them on the jogging horseman, grunted, and handed the binoculars to Lance.

'Well!' Lance grunted, after an instant of staring. 'We were talking about the Spear L. And here comes a Spear L man, now. Old Manny Todd. Manny's topped the rough string for the Spear L, it's many a year, now. We used to be good friends.'

They rode on down the slope, and as they foxtrotted toward Manny Todd, Fine and

Jerky talked.

'Reckon we passed you in the dark, after we left Saddle Rock Pasture,' Fine said. 'We went plenty quiet after we got away from that dead kid. And we missed Tula—plumb missed it. But a cowboy told us last night about some mares being shipped out of the pens at Tula Spur and we come up. They was still talking about the fight in the eating house when we hit town. Kind of sounded like the C Bar Craigs, that. We couldn't find you—'

Manny Todd had seen them. Now, he pulled in with hand on his Winchester. But something about them seemed to reassure him and he came on again. So they met on the flat.

'Hi!' Manny greeted Lance, looking hard at the others. 'Tula-bound? They kind of had some hell at the Spur. You happen to meet Wingo?'

'Was Wingo battling the Spear L?' Lance asked in artfully curious tone. 'Well he never was fond of Logan. You ought to go over to the Flying W, Manny. You're the best hand with stallions this country ever saw—'

'I been aiming to do exactly that. I quit the Spear L right after you—lit a shuck. Logan and me never did hit it off too good, but lately—'

He stopped short, and his faded blue eyes met Lance's squarely and steadily.

'No reason I can't talk straight to you, now, Lance,' he said quietly. 'Things happened and I

303

wasn't sure. But I don't ride for no sticky loop outfit if I know it. And I do believe the Spear L has got to be that kind of outfit. Wingo wasn't fighting the Spear L, far's I know. They was fighting—'

'I know. We happened to be there. I always did take you for a friend of mine, Manny. I take you that way now. We know all about the business at the pens. But a couple or three of the thieves got away—'

'If you're hunting 'em in Tula, it's no good. Ull Varner and Wilbur Logan and Frank Larkman and two new Spear L men have gone to Mesquite. Logan and Varner and Larkman come in right after the fight. The Spear L hands was already around. They seen Eldred and Poker Ames and them hands of Eldred's. Somehow, it made 'em all mad as hell! Varner and Logan, they told Harry Brush a few and he told 'em a lot more'n that. So they rode for Mesquite. The short trail.'

'And what, do you reckon, was their business in Tula?' Lance said softly, his tone very much at odds with the grim tightening of his mouth. 'What would Varner and Logan have to do with shipping a bunch of Box O mares—that happened to be C Bar before a job of hair-branding was done?'

'Oh, goodness!' Manny cried, hooking a knee around his saddle horn while he rolled a cigarette. 'You wouldn't never expect a pore bronc' buster to understand all them long words! I wouldn't even set up to guess a riddle like that. All I know is, Varner and Logan come to Tula on some kind of business; and they was awful worked up about Poker Ames and Eldred being killed and the Flying W being let off to ride scot-clean. And they went back to Mesquite.'

'To Mesquite!' Lance drawled. 'You hear that, Fine? To Mesquite. It's been a long, long time since I looked around our fair county seat. It just mustn't be any longer.'

'Now that I think about it,' Fine said thoughtfully, 'I promised myself to speak to Sheriff Varner about how he run me out from under his window the other night.'

'Oh, Lord!' Jerky groaned. 'If ever I was to sell a spec' or pull a tooth or take a tintype— Mesquite she is.'

'You know, I think Mesquite suits me,' Manny told Lance. 'I just remembered a couple things I forgot to tell Logan when I was quitting him. Some more reasons why I don't like the man and never did. I'll side you-all.'

They nodded, one to the other, and Lance turned Gold off to the left. For he knew that short-cut Varner and Logan and the others had taken. It was rough, but it cut miles from the regular Tula-Mesquite road. It would get them to Mesquite well before dark.

They rode steadily, watching the country ahead against any stop by the sheriff and his companions. But Varner and the men with him were evidently riding as steadily; it was drawing toward sunset when Manny Todd, leading, pulled in his horse on a mesa rim and looked over with a grunt.

'Logan, anyhow, stopped for a drink,' he said, pointing. 'I know that black. I'd know it a mile off.'

From the mesa the store-saloon of Sime Choteau was plain on the flat of Cow Creek. The four studied it from the rim, Lance counting the horses in sight behind the oblong block of the stone building. He did not need glasses.

'The tally seems right,' he said very softly. 'Five horses. Ull Varner, Frank Larkman, Wilbur Logan, and the two Spear L riders who may not have been in our fight at the pen, *but* were in or around Tula when Logan came in with Varner. Well?'

'Well?' Fine repeated suspiciously. 'Well—what?'

'Am I rodding this young army?'

'Depends! If you have got one of your regular crazy notions up the sleeve, buck her off.'

'Yeh, what is the notion?' Jerky echoed Fine.

'This: I'm going to slide in first. Take their minds off things. The rest of you'll slide up sock-footed. All I want is four-five minutes. No more. You'll cover me.'

He went into details, drawn from ancient knowledge of Choteau's premises. At the last,

Fine nodded grudgingly.

'A' right! Even if I do still think you're twin brother to the jack that wouldn't go into the Ark.'

So they separated and Lance, hitching his belt a little against the tug of the six-shooter in his waistband, very conscious of the second pistol under his arm, rode across the flat and pulled in Gold before the store.

They were all at the counter when he stepped inside the door to look around. He saw the huge, still-faced Choteau leaning great arms upon the planks by a jug. And a sixth man, a dapper youngster and a stranger, was farthest down the counter.

Lance nodded to them all, then came to the counter and halted opposite Choteau. He leaned slightly and got a dollar from his overalls. Choteau pushed a cup his way and tilted the jug deftly over it. As the whisky ran into his cup, Lance wondered if dirt and stubble and shabbiness would be mask enough; if Varner and Logan would recognize him. The two Spear L Cowboys and the smooth-faced youngster and Frank Larkman he had never seen, so it was unlikely that they had ever seen him.

Varner shifted his lank length and stared. Then he came erect and walked swaggeringly the three paces down to Lance.

'Who're you?' he demanded arrogantly. 'I'm the sheriff in this county. Talk up!'

In spite of the determination with which he had come into Choteau's, to control his temper, to act like a machine, Lance knew that utter fury was rising in him with sight of Varner. He could not help recalling that this was the man who had been Oscar Nall's tool and, on his own account, the thief who had robbed the C Bar and intended to take it altogether.

He looked past Varner at the others. Logan, narrow-faced and dark, only stared. His cowboys were grinning as in anticipation. The heavy, rather handsome face of Larkman seemed puzzled. He could not see the small stranger. From outside he heard no sound. But the others must be close, he thought.

'I'm a man that hates to be bothered,' he told Varner thickly. *'Get that hand out in sight!'*

Someone yelled, from down the counter. It sounded like a warning, but whether to him or to Varner, Lance could not say. The sheriff's hand was behind him. Something like a ripple went along the men at the counter as each began to move, to straighten. Lance snapped right hand into the front of his shirt and it came out with the back-lash of that smooth movement, bringing his tested Colt.

Varner was bringing a pistol from behind him when Lance leaned toward him and let drop the hammer of his gun. Past Varner he saw that small cowboy come from the end of the counter, strike at a Spear L puncher with left hand, and snatch the puncher's gun from holster with his left. Logan was drawing from low-swung scabbard, drawing left-handed. Varner dropped his Colt and swayed. The smooth-faced youngster was out in the middle of the floor, with the gun he had grabbed roaring. Logan whirled and fired at Lance. Then out of doors front and back came shots.

Smoke stung Lance's nose and throat and eyes. His ears rocked with the roar of the firing. He sagged back against the counter. The whisky jug burst almost against his shoulder. He felt a hammer blow in his body, an agonizing rap on the knuckles of his gunhand, then it seemed that a fiery claw raked his head. But that pain, all pain, was gone instantly.

He tasted whisky before he saw or heard anything, afterward. And it seemed to him that his whole body ached and burned, so that he could not say where the pain was, exactly. A buzz of voices was over him in darkness. Then a light flared and came down closer to his face.

'Now, pick him up,' Fine said sharply. 'Easy. We'll have to drive slow. That damn' wagon—'

'What wagon?' Lance heard himself say thickly. 'Le' me up! I'm not hurt I—'

'Nah! Not a bit!' Fine grunted scornfully. 'Except you're a kind of fringe holding a bunch of holes together, ain't a thing wrong with you. Pick him up, Jerky. Lieutenant, hold that candle so's we can see to walk.'

He was raised and carried a little way, set gently down at full length. The light came close to his face again. Someone grunted and the neck of a bottle was put to his mouth. He drank and now he could see a smooth face that seemed to float above him.

'All right, Craig?' the man inquired. 'I'm Lieutenant Collins, Ranger. Adjutant General's staff. I owe you one. I was up Salt Creek when you walked into Choteau's. Varner and his fellow-scoundrels, Logan and Larkman and the others, had uncovered me. They had my gun. I heard the pearly gates flapping. Then you came in—'

'Ranger,' Lance said dully. 'Then—I guess *I'm*—up Salt Creek—with a hole in the boat!'

'You're on top of the world! I've been investigating for a month, around here. I know the whole story, now. That's why they were going to rub me out. Craig! Are you listening? Can you hear me? That indictment will be quashed as soon as I say ten words to your crooked county attorney in Mesquite. You're clear, man; clear to ride the C Bar—'

'Uh-huh,' Lance said drowsily. 'Sure-ly—'

Vaguely, he knew that the wagon creaked on and on; that after an endless time he was lifted out again, carried somewhere, set down. Hands pulled at him, and he cursed without much force or conviction until he was left alone again.

Light shone in his face, a long time after that.

He blinked weakly.

'He's all right, now,' a man said. 'Reminds me of the time I patched up his father and old Nathan Wingo, after they had a little meeting with some rustlers at Dog Cañon. But I think Lance is one hole ahead of his father. I'll leave him with you.'

A hand came down to his cheek, smooth, cool, restful.

'Who's it?' he asked. 'Doc' Wallace?'

'He's gone,' Lucy Kane said. 'How do you feel?'

'Do'no'. I've been—pretty sick? I know I've had wild dreams—a Ranger lieutenant was sitting on the foot of the bed—and Fine and Jerky—'

'Lieutenant Collins is gone. He left three days ago. Rather to the relief of certain Mesquite County people. He told you about—the indictment?'

'Then—that wasn't one of my nightmares?'

'Nightmare! He went to Hale Baggley and—I don't know what he said; Judge Oakes probably does, he was with him. Anyway, Hale isn't going to run for county attorney again *and* that indictment against you is quashed. You're all clear, Lance.'

'All clear...'

He lay thinking of that for a long time. It seemed unreal; he had lived like a hunted wolf, killed like that same wolf. All clear ... He turned his head to look up at the clear, somewhat pale, face above him.

'Then it is so!' he thought. 'She wouldn't be here if it weren't so.'

Then memory began to come back, fully.

'Where's Dolores? And Tommy Downes? And Estrella?' he asked abruptly. 'Lord! They're not still at Saddle Rock?'

'Gone back to Mexico. Two days ago. Estrella'—she laughed—'was hard to deal with. Jerky had to prove to her—and I don't yet know how he did it—that Fine had just got on a boat bound for China. Dolores—'

'What about Dolores?' he demanded, when she was silent for a full minute. 'She and Tommy went back?'

'Yes ... You see, Dolores and I talked a good deal. Quite frankly. I'm afraid I talked you out of a large Mexican ranch. Well, your loss will be Tommy's gain.'

'What are you talking about? I didn't want any Mexican ranch. All I've wanted was a chance to run the C Bar and—never mind!'

'That's what I thought,' she said calmly. 'Dolores agreed with me. I told her about my foolishness and how one thing and another showed me the truth about Oscar and various other matters and she went back to Gerónimo. To avoid scandal, she married Tommy before she went.'

'Fine!' Lance said heartily. 'Just—fine!'

'I've been thinking ... I gave her that advice—about getting married to avoid the

312

scandal; they couldn't stay on the ranch together, she and Tommy, loving each other, without being married. I don't think anyone should give advice she isn't willing to follow herself. Now, when you're up again and running the C Bar, we'll be out there together. Would *you* marry *me*—to prevent scandal?'

'I would not!' he said promptly. 'I'd marry you because that's what I've wanted to do for—years, I guess!'